Come Alive

THE CITYSCAPE SERIES: BOOK TWO

JESSICA HAWKINS

"Beauty is unbearable, drives us to despair, offering us for a minute

the glimpse of an eternity that we should like to stretch out over the whole of time."

– Albert Camus

CHAPTER 1

I BLINKED MY EYES OPEN and quickly squeezed them shut again. Knowing I'd been caught, I fluttered my eyelids as though I hadn't been about to feign sleep. My husband stood over me, watching, but I focused on the nightstand to avoid his stare.

"It's nine," he said gently. "Better get a move on."

I rolled over and faced the wall with a small sigh, unable to handle his soft expression. "I'm not going."

"Liv," he started.

"I have to work today."

"Work?"

"Things are crazy at the office."

"It's the weekend, and I told you about this birthday party last week. Can't it wait 'til Monday?"

"No. I'm under deadline."

"I'm sure you could spare a Saturday afternoon," he said wryly.

"Call Serena if you don't believe me."

"Of course I believe you," he said, taken aback. "But you're working too much. You need to take some time off, babe. It's been over three months of this."

I gulped. Had it only been three months?

When he continued, his tone was tentative, hedging. "I know it's been hard, but this isn't what Davena would've wanted. She would want you to move on."

I almost laughed out loud, but I didn't. I never did. The mattress dipped when he sat. Hesitant fingertips touched my shoulder, and my skin pebbled. I couldn't remember when he'd last touched me. When he'd stopped even trying. His caress was strange; unexpected but not unwanted. It triggered a wave of guilt that left my heart pounding. Because of what I knew. Because of what I'd done. Because, after three months, I still burned with desire. But it wasn't for him.

I braced myself as David's image appeared. I wished I wouldn't think of him every morning and dream of him at night. I wished his memory would fade, the way he had from my life. *Three months.* Three months since I had stormed from his apartment, since *that night.* My insides flurried as I remembered, the details still fresh in my mind despite the time that had passed. Despite the fact that every time they surfaced, I dashed them away immediately.

"Well, I have to go to the party." Bill's voice cut into my thoughts. "You know how my sister can hold a grudge."

"Of course you do, sweetie." The endearment was forced, unnatural, but Bill wouldn't notice. "I wrapped Jimmy's video game last night; it's on the kitchen counter."

"Thanks. I'll bring you back a piece of birthday cake." When I didn't respond, he stood and left the room. Soon after, I heard the front door shut. I exhaled a long breath.

Hours were slow; stretched and elongated like a rubber band that never snapped. On the better days, I woke up numb. *Today is not one of those days*, I thought as I dragged myself from the bed.

Dressed in an outfit much too crisp and binding for the weekend, I meticulously applied my makeup. Every strand of my golden brown hair was combed into obedience. Inside, I had cracks, but I wouldn't let them break the surface.

I was on the train within the hour. I found comfort in the way everything blurred together through the windows. A child's squeal had me blinking from my trance. Across from me, a young man wrangled two toddlers as his wife cradled a baby on her lap. It was chaotic and messy, but she watched her husband with obvious love. The woman smiled goofily as he dodged apple juice spray. I looked away, fiddling with the clasp of my purse.

The morning after my night with David, I'd cried my eyes raw against the brick wall by his apartment. I hadn't known up from down, left from right, love from despair. But I'd locked it up so tightly I could still feel the chains digging into me with every movement. When Bill returned from his trip that day, I mustered the biggest, most convincing welcome I could manage. But I couldn't look him in the eye. And I couldn't pretend to want his hands on me. And though Bill was never one to pick up on my subtle cues, I had made it impossible for him not to.

Somehow, the week passed. After a late night at work, I walked into an apartment filled with twenty of our closest friends and family. I gritted my teeth and let them wish me a happy twenty-eighth birthday, barely making it through the night. Not even Lucy or Gretchen, my closest friends in the world, could scratch the surface. I could only put my energy into acting normal. I'd scoffed to myself overhearing Gretchen and Bill in the kitchen toward the end of the party.

"How's she doing?"

"I can't tell, Gretchen, and it freaks me out. She won't talk about Davena at all. She keeps to herself and pretends nothing is wrong."

"Well, Davena was like a second mother to her," Gretchen said. *"There are times in her life when she was closer to her than to her actual mom."*

"I think that's why she's taking Davena's death especially hard. She and her mom haven't been getting along."

"She doesn't look well."

"I haven't seen her eat in days. I'd feel better if she at least cried, but she does nothing except smile and laugh in the weirdest way."

"She was like this when her parents divorced. I tried to tell you. She's hurting. She doesn't deal well with loss."

"I don't know what to do."

"Have you tried talking to her?" Gretchen asked.

There was a pause. "She leaves the room when I do."

"It's still fresh. Just give her time, Bill."

After the last guest had left, we fought. I had made some empty promise to come home early from work, but I'd unknowingly missed half of the surprise party. I asked him how he could have possibly thought a party was a good idea.

I started leaving for work early and coming home late every day. With my recent promotion, it wasn't hard to find projects at the magazine. Days turned into weeks, weeks into months. And not a day went by that I wasn't reminded of him. Of that night. And of the irreversible thing I'd done.

As the train barreled along, I tried not to remember. After all, the separation from David had been longer than the time I'd known him. Surely that was enough time to move on?

But it was impossible to forget. I fought myself as I always did when the memory threatened, but in that moment, alone on the crowded train, I wasn't strong enough to stop it. I remembered the pain in his hard brown eyes when he'd demanded that I speak up. That I tell him I wanted nothing more to do with him. I rewound through our final conversation, when he'd said he wanted me in his life. He wanted us to be together. I remembered how he felt pressed against me and how I'd wished he would take me again.

His hands on my hips had held me steady as he'd mercilessly driven me to orgasm . . . twice. It was unforgettable. Haunting. Relentless. Under his affection, under his touch, I'd come alive. And since then, I was slowly drowning; hounded by the memory I tried to repel and weighed down by the guilt.

~

I was alone in the *Chicago Metropolitan Magazine* office. Maybe it wasn't necessary for me to work on a Saturday, but the thought of sitting through a child's birthday party with Bill's family was daunting. I weaved through the empty cubicles until reaching the door to my office. *Olivia Germaine*, it read. *Senior Editor.*

I flopped into my big chair and rubbed my eyes tensely. On the days I wasn't numb, everything seemed sharper, more excruciating; shame, grief, desire. It was a constant battle to swallow the emotions that rose up my throat one after the other.

My fingers flew over the keyboard, but my mind was occupied with other things. I owed Bill more than I gave him. He'd been patient, and I knew he was becoming concerned. Whenever things turned intimate between us, I pulled away without an explanation. He attributed my distance to Davena's death, but that was only a small part of it.

When my cell buzzed, I glanced at the screen and ignored the call. Within moments, my office phone began to ring. I sighed with defeat, knowing Gretchen wouldn't give up.

"What's wrong?" I asked when I picked up the receiver.

"Good afternoon to you too, Liv."

"Seriously, Gretchen. Is everything okay?"

"Yes," she said with feigned irritation. "I'm downstairs."

"What? Why?"

"Bill texted me that you were coming in today, so I thought I'd surprise you for lunch."

"You should have called first. I'm in the middle of something."

"So take a break and pick it up later."

"Later I have other things to do."

"How? You work nonstop, and it's *Saturday* for God's sake. What could be so important? I haven't talked to you in weeks."

"My schedule has been full with this promotion. Beman has me under impossible deadlines. They need me."

"I know they do, but I need you too. We need you. Come on – lunch is on me."

"Fine," I said, exhaling forcefully.

There was a brief pause on the line as I saved the document on my computer. "Fine?" she repeated after a moment. "What the fuck is wrong with you? I made a special trip over here to take you to lunch."

"I didn't ask you to do that."

"No shit. I miss you," she said, her voice softening.

"Look, I said I'd come. Just give me a minute." I hung up before she could respond and locked up the office.

Downstairs, I felt mildly better after a deep breath of fresh air. She was waiting in a sleeveless tank top and denim cut-offs. Despite her casual outfit, her bright blonde hair was curled into perfect ringlets as usual. I tucked some hair behind my ear as I approached her.

"Aren't you hot?" she asked.

I pulled my sweater closer. "I only have an hour."

She rolled those big blue eyes of hers, pulled on my arm and started walking. "Then you'd better get talking."

"Talking?"

"Yes. It's time to have a conversation, and that's why I'm buying you lunch."

"What's the topic of this conversation? And don't say Davena, because that's all anyone ever wants to talk about."

"Because you won't," she whined. "You won't talk to Bill about it, you won't talk to us and you refuse to see a shrink. Forget about poor Mack." She waved her hand. "He's beside himself, and you can't even pick up the phone."

My heart stopped along with my feet. "Who told you that?"

"Bill."

"Wow," I said. She continued walking, so I ran to catch up to her. "No wonder you sound exactly like him. Do you guys get together and talk about me? Have little powwows about how to get me to spill my guts? Well here's a tip: get a new hobby, because there's nothing to spill. I loved Davena, but I've made my peace with her passing. Life goes on, Gretchen."

She muttered something under her breath.

"What?" I challenged.

She sighed. "Liv, you can talk to me," she said in an atypically delicate voice.

I glanced down at the pavement as we walked, willing myself to stay calm. "Everything is fine. You don't need to worry."

"I do, though. You never talk about her, and you haven't seen Mack since the funeral. It's not healthy and . . . it shows." I pursed my lips and rewrapped the sweater as I crossed my arms. "Lucy needs you," she continued. "With the wedding next weekend, she has to know she can count on us."

"Of course she can," I said defensively. "I've been there every step of the way – did I not host the wedding shower, and have I not done everything she's asked?"

"Yes, you have, it's just obvious that your heart isn't in it. And it hurts her feelings."

"She said that?"

"She doesn't have to."

I swallowed. "Okay, I get it."

"Good. So let's start with how you felt when you heard the news. Maybe you can explain why you hid it from us that night. It's no wonder you got wasted and went home early. Nobody can keep something like that inside, not even you."

"No – what I meant was that I get it. I'll change. I'm not up for this random therapy session."

"You can't change without talking about it."

"Again, there is nothing to talk about," I intoned. "People grieve in different ways, so please just drop it. As far as the wedding, I get what you're saying. I will try harder. For Lucy."

Gretchen heaved a deep sigh and looked away as she bit her thumbnail. "You're a stubborn bitch," she muttered.

An unwilling smile found my face. "Where are you taking me anyway, Milwaukee?"

"Nope, we're going to a place with the largest, juiciest burgers around. You need some nourishment," she said, tugging at the hem of my sweater. I almost gagged at the thought of a hamburger, but I figured this was what choosing one's battles meant. My heart dropped, however, when we rounded the corner. I was standing in front of the restaurant where David had taken me to lunch months before.

"Hello?" she urged, holding the door open.

I fumbled for an excuse. It was Saturday, though, and David wouldn't be working nearby, so I followed her inside. I recognized the red-lipped hostess, despite the fact that she wasn't nearly as cheery as she had been when I was with David. I wondered if she was trying to place me, since she gave me a curious, narrow-eyed look. I scanned the restaurant furtively as she led us to an open, conspicuous table.

I ordered a burger, or rather, Gretchen ordered one for me, but I found it hard to stomach. After making a show of the first two bites, I nibbled on the side salad while Gretchen caught me up on the goings-on at her public relations office.

"You've got to come with me next time," she was saying. "California in the summertime is the shit. I even took a couple surf lessons."

"Doesn't sound like work," I muttered.

"It's all about schmoozing, Liv, and – "

I froze. *Was that . . . ? No.* It came again from behind me, and I stiffened instinctively.

"David, my man!" the voice boomed.

My heart whipped into a violent pounding, filling my ears as blood rushed to my head. Gretchen looked at me with her head cocked. Her mouth moved, but I heard nothing.

With slow precision, I turned my head over my left shoulder and glanced back. Two men I'd never seen before were pumping hands emphatically. Through my decelerating heartbeat, I heard one call the other 'David.' I shook my head quickly and returned my attention to Gretchen. She was still talking about California, though now she was looking at my plate. To preempt another argument, I forced myself to take another bite. I chewed the patty methodically until it was mush in my mouth and swallowed because I thought she might notice if I spit it out.

"Well, that's an extra hour on the treadmill," she groaned to her empty plate and covered her tummy with her hand.

CHAPTER 2

DAVENA'S FUNERAL HAD BEEN like every funeral
before it. I'd sat in the pew, staring forward as Bill clasped my
hand in his. At some point I had looked over to find him in
tears, but my hands were lifeless in my lap, and I didn't have
the words, so I returned my eyes forward. My only moment of
reality was when her husband, Mack, had hugged me. He'd
squeezed the breath from my lungs, holding me too tightly.
And when he'd let go, I felt nothing again.

She was predictably lovely in her open casket, with
heavy makeup and untamed, sheared blonde hair. Cancer had
not tainted her in life or in death. I wondered how she didn't
even look vulnerable from that position; I wouldn't have been
surprised if her eyes had popped open, and she'd invited me
out for a cocktail at Sunda.

But she didn't. And eventually they eased the coffin
closed and took her away. Back at their place, Mack did his
best to turn the reception into a celebration of her life, but the
pain in his eyes was searing. It was unavoidable, even when I
looked away. We left early.

Although my belief in the afterlife was dubious, I
sometimes prayed to Davena for relief. In my head, I
confessed everything; that I was a sinner, an adulterer and a
liar. That I only felt remorse for deceiving Bill, not for the
crime itself. Sometimes I believed maybe she heard me.
Sometimes I imagined she would make everything right.

"Did you look at the article yet?" Lisa, also known as my toxic co-worker, glared at me from the doorway of my office, arms crossed, lips drawn.

Her words rattled in my head a moment as I shifted back into reality. "Which one?"

She exhaled her annoyance. "The guide to Logan Square."

"It's on your desk already."

"Oh." She pivoted and stalked away, revealing Serena behind her.

"She's always super grouchy on Friday morning," Serena said with a warm smile. "And Monday. And Tuesday. Wednesday, too . . . . You get the idea."

"Where did your hair go?" I asked.

"I'm taking a cue from Hollywood and embracing the pixie cut. What do you think?"

"Cute," I remarked, turning back to my computer.

"So, boss lady, are you excited for this weekend?"

I blinked my attention back to her. Serena had taken to calling me 'boss' since her recent promotion from intern to assistant editor.

"The wedding?" she prompted uncertainly.

"Yes. Lucy has been planning her wedding for as long as I've known her, so it should be impressive."

"I love weddings, I mean they are just, so romantic, and everyone is just like, so happy to be there. And it's supposed to be a gorgeous weekend, I mean – "

"Serena, I'm really swamped here."

"Oh. Sorry. Actually, I have an idea I want to run by you."

"Shoot," I said while tapping out a quick e-mail.

"It's about the *Chicago's Most Eligible Bachelors and Bachelorettes* issue – "

"What?" I froze mid-keystroke.

"Well, um – I think we should do a follow-up piece on the website. I'm sure the people we featured like, went on dates and stuff. Maybe some even found relationships because of the article. We could even do, like, a teeny-tiny article in the mag next month."

I shook my head rapidly. "No, that won't work. Let's try and come up with some new concepts, not beat the crap out of old ones."

"Oh, okay, cool. I like that too."

She lingered a second longer and then scurried away. I hadn't meant to shut her down, but I couldn't risk a run-in with David Dylan: Bachelor Number Three. I didn't want him anywhere near me.

I had gotten lucky at the launch party for the *Most Eligible* issue two months earlier. Every bachelor and bachelorette had shown up to the event, the best in the magazine's history. Except for David Dylan. I'd overheard Lisa say that he accepted a job in New York and absolutely could not attend, even though she'd begged him. Knowing he was out of town was no more painful than knowing he wasn't right next to me. He was gone forever, and the physical distance wouldn't change that.

I couldn't ignore his presence at the party, though. Despite his non-attendance, his smiling photo, which far outshone the other attendees' pictures, was everywhere. Lisa had gleefully taken over David's segment for me, and the way she'd styled the photo shoot, it could have been an ad for any top menswear designer. He was all teeth and hard muscles in the three-piece suit Lucy had sold him. Clutching his jacket casually at his side, he was the definition of roguish businessman.

I'd given my boss the issue for final approval without ever proofing David's spread. The wounds were too fresh. Even now, I still hadn't had the heart, or the guts, to read about David Dylan: wealthy, charming and handsome Chicago bachelor. Every girl's dream catch.

I got up and locked my office door, allowing myself a minute to lie down on the couch. I was thankful for my weighty sweater to block the blasting A/C unit above.

I'd told David I was black inside, but I was wrong. I hadn't known it, but I was empty. And for one stolen moment, he had filled me with himself, physically and emotionally. *Now* I was black. Now I was poisoned. I was so reprehensible, that instead of the constant regret I should have felt, it only came in fleeting waves.

I recalled his hands in my hair, his breath on my skin, his mouth between my breasts . . . . *Just fucking stop,* I pleaded with myself. *I have to forget, please, I can't do this anymore.*

The reason I didn't feel was because I didn't want to, not because I couldn't. The scorching memory of our one night would destroy me if I let it. The guilt was already a steady drip into my system, seeping into the cracks of my interior.

The ringing of my office phone shredded through my thoughts. I pinched the bridge of my nose and sat upright. Work was the one thing in my life that never let me down, never judged or condemned me. I returned to my desk and hit the speakerphone button.

"What time is the bachelorette party tonight?" Bill's voice filled the office.

"Seven o'clock," I said, wiggling my mouse to wake up the computer. "When is Andrew's?"

"Same. Think you can get off a little early? I have a surprise for you."

"A surprise?" I repeated cautiously.

"Yeah, can you?"

"I don't know. I'm sort of backed up here." I rubbed my eyes and refocused on the screen.

"Please? I'm really excited."

"All right," I relented. "I can work through lunch."

"I'll pick you up downstairs at four, k? Love you."

~

I waited downstairs for Bill on a street-facing concrete bench, wondering what the surprise could possibly be. When the car arrived at the curb, I could hear Bon Jovi on full volume: that was a good sign.

"Hey," he said when I climbed in. "Ready for your surprise?"

"Yes." Because I had promised myself to try harder, I took his hand.

He squeezed it. "It's a bit of a drive, so sit back and relax."

As we discussed our impending parties, it became evident that we were leaving the city altogether. I recognized the point when we were entering Oak Park, but I still had no idea what his intentions were. It was when we turned onto a familiar street that I recognized my surroundings.

"Don't get any grand ideas," he warned.

Our search for the perfect home had been put on pause after Davena's death. Now we were on the block of the last house we'd seen over three months before. I recalled the afternoon with our realtor Jeanine; the awkwardness at her suggestion of a nursery and the ensuing argument where he'd tried to convince me that we were ready for children. That house had sold though, he'd told me bitterly back in June. Unless it had fallen through, and . . . *Oh, no. Don't let the surprise be a house. Would he go that far?*

He pulled up to the same spot we had parked with Jeanine months before.

"Bill – "

"No, no," he stopped me. "Just wait." We both climbed out of the car, and he turned around. "I've been working on this with Jeanine for a while." He wasn't looking at the house we'd visited last time, though. I followed his gaze to the eyesore of a house across the street from it.

It was still as ugly and unkempt as before. Ferns drooped heavily, blocking the front door. Grey stone crumbled in some spots. Paint under the windows peeled. But it had that same draw. The same endearing character that had appealed to me the first time I'd seen it.

"The owners are big shots in Hollywood," Bill explained, "who don't even care about the property. They told her they'd be willing to sell it for a good price because of the poor shape. Since they rarely get to Chicago, they granted her access to show it to us."

I looked from Bill to the house. He had remembered my comments that day. To my surprise, I smiled. "Wow. Honey, this is so thoughtful."

"It would be a lot of effort, and we'd probably have to stay in the apartment another year or so, but . . . I just can't stand to see you this way anymore. I want you to be happy, and if this is what it takes, then we'll do it." His voice was laced with sadness. I'd been punishing both of us for my crime, but it was the first time I realized just how much he was hurting.

I loved what he'd done for me, so I took his hand. "Let's go see the inside."

The interior was almost empty with the exception of some covered pieces of furniture and an antique grandfather clock as tall as Bill. The main room's greatest feature was a toss-up between the expansive, central fireplace and a ribbon of windows that made up the back wall separating the backyard.

The sprawling wood floor creaked with each step, and it was cold inside, but I could tell it must have been very warm once. Dust caked the surfaces and dead insects were scattered on the floor. I stepped into a decent-sized backyard that was overrun with weeds and in dire need of some attention. But it was large enough for outdoor entertaining, and I envisioned strung Chinese paper lanterns, a concrete and rock bar, rose bushes, a trickling fountain . . . .

When I reentered the house, Bill was standing with his hands in his pockets. I watched as he inspected the stairway railing and kicked at a loose floorboard. The corners of his mouth tugged, suggesting a frown. I scanned the room around him. Honey-colored flooring would complement the warm light that flooded from antique lamps. Heavy, earthy furniture made of oak and aged leather would fill the open floor plan.

And, yet . . . something felt off, though I wasn't sure what. The house had potential, and I was already wondering what it looked like in the early morning when the light was just starting to filter in. Still, I struggled to complete the picture.

"What do you think?" he asked.

I froze, and seconds passed; I could hear the soft ticking of the grandfather clock. Maybe it was my imagination. Maybe once we'd overhauled it and made it into the beautiful place I knew it could be, things would be different. They had to be. Bill had been right all along. It wasn't going to be perfect right away or maybe ever. It would take time for it to feel like home. I took a step backward and pointed to the second floor. "Upstairs?"

I followed as he carefully climbed the noisy steps. The master bedroom, located at one end of the hall, was spacious – bigger than any others we had seen, which I knew would appeal to Bill. It had a large, unobstructed view of the backyard and a corner window on the opposite wall that faced the street.

He reported that there were two more rooms down the hall. I nodded, taking his words in but still studying him. "Can we afford it, really?"

"No," he said honestly. "The house, yes. But I have no idea about the remodel. It's outside our budget, I'm sure. It would mean cutting back on some things for a while."

"Is this what you want?"

He squinted his eyes while his tongue ran over his front teeth. "I don't know how I feel about taking on a project like this when we're both so busy. But I really want to get out of the city, and I want you to love your new home."

It was undoubtedly the nicest thing he'd ever done for me. I shifted, and a floorboard groaned beneath me. The bedroom was growing dark, and I blinked at his disappearing silhouette. "Okay," I said. "Yes. Let's do it." I crossed the room and hugged him close for an overdue moment of intimacy. We walked to the stairs arm in arm before separating to descend.

~

"Open mine next."

Lucy squealed with delight as she accepted the overstuffed party bag from Bethany, who had a playful gleam in her eye.

"Oh, my," she groaned as she pulled out a pink, feathered tiara with the word 'Bachelorette' branded across the front. We were ten girls at a noisy restaurant downtown, egging Lucy on as she unwrapped gifts between sips of her pink Cosmo.

"You're wearing that now, and you're wearing this too," Dani said, placing a necklace with mini phallic-shaped candies around Lucy's neck.

"Dani! It's definitely inappropriate for my little sister to be draping me in penises."

"It is perfectly appropriate," Dani retorted, clearing a mass of brown, glossy ringlets from her shoulder.

I picked up a green gummy penis and popped it in my mouth before scrunching up my nose. "Sour apple," I lamented. "Yuck."

"Oh, no you don't, Olivia Germaine. You will swallow that penis," Gretchen scolded, waving a finger at me.

I laughed and gulped the candy down exaggeratedly before chasing it with my Cosmo.

I sat between Lucy and Gretchen as Dani, maid of honor and official party planner, stood to raise her glass. "There will be no toast tonight because between the rehearsal dinner and the wedding, I'm running out of material. Lucy is too good, and there aren't enough naughty stories to go around. There's only one decent one from high school, involving her bedroom window and a football jock named Jack, but I'm saving that for the big night."

"Dani, no! You wouldn't!" Lucy cried, her face a veritable bright red.

"I'm teasing, sis. That one isn't nearly good enough for a wedding toast. Anyway, please raise your glasses for my non-toast, and let's get this party underway."

"I can't believe you're getting married in two days," Gretchen said to Lucy, leaning into my lap.

"Me neither. I never thought I'd say this, but I'll be glad when it's over. It's been so much work."

"Yes, it has, but you've done an amazing job," I reassured her. "Sunday is going to be beautiful."

"It had better be," she said. "What are you doing about a date, Gretch? You RSVP'd plus one, so you must bring a plus one."

"Actually, I'm just going to bring John. Is that cool?"

"Of course! I love your brother."

"Why don't you have a date?" I asked skeptically.

"No reason," she responded with a shrug.

"Hey, whatever happened with Brian?" I was embarrassed that I'd never asked about the date they'd gone on months ago.

"Who?"

"Brian Ayers. I introduced you at the magazine's Meet & Greet."

"Oh, that guy, no, yuck."

"Yuck? He's hot. He's like freakin' Hemsworth hot, if you're into blonds, which you are."

"Agreed, but he's a pretentious prick."

"Oh," I said with surprise. "I don't think so at all."

She shrugged. "Then you fuck him."

Her roommates, Ava and Bethany, giggled from across the table, but I gave Gretchen a reproachful look.

"Who are you bringing, Dani?" Ava asked.

"This guy I've just started seeing," she replied with a half-smile.

"He's coming from Milwaukee?" Bethany asked.

"He lives here," Lucy interjected. "You guys know him from my engagement party. David Dylan." For the first time, our end of the table was silent, and I was sure they could all hear my heart drop. "It's still new, which is why I didn't mention it."

Ava looked confused, but Bethany reminded her that he was 'that tall, gorgeous hunk from that one restaurant's soft opening' before declaring that she was supremely jealous.

I fielded a sidelong glance from Gretchen. She and I hadn't discussed David beyond the night I'd confessed my feelings to her. I hadn't let our conversations go that way again. She didn't know about what I'd done, but I hated that she knew anything at all.

"You . . . You lucky bitch," Gretchen joked awkwardly. "I've had my eye on him for a while. How did that happen?"

Dani's eyes brightened. "Well, I was in town last month for some wedding planning, and Lucy set us up. He took all of us on his sailboat, no big deal," she said with a giddy grin.

"Can you imagine having David Dylan as a brother-in-law?" Lucy asked. "I'd never stop staring!"

"Hands off," Dani kidded.

"I'm trying to convince Dani to move to Chicago, and this is part of my plan," Lucy said proudly.

Dani rolled her eyes. "She acts like Milwaukee is another country."

"You're here all the time anyway," Lucy pointed out.

I was spinning my wedding ring at the same pace that my mind was whirring. I glared at the girl across from me. She was Danielle officially, but insisted on being called Dani. She had Lucy's dark brown hair and green eyes like mine. I had always been worried about Gretchen catching David's attention with her blonde curls and Windex-colored eyes, but now David's words from a few months back rang through my head: '*I prefer brunettes with big, green eyes . . .*'

"I'll be honest, I thought David was something of a womanizer, but they've been out twice, and he hasn't made any moves," Lucy revealed.

"He's such a gentleman," Dani boasted.

Gentleman. My insides tightened at the term, and I gripped my thighs. He was no gentleman. He was rough and harsh and callous but tender and sweet and considerate. The adjectives flowed through me, and I bit my lip. He deserved someone like Dani, who was cute and spunky and most importantly – available.

"He's flying back just to take her," Lucy said, and everyone twittered.

"Where is he?" I asked hoarsely before I could stop myself.

"New York," Dani answered as though the information was nothing. "He's an architect, and he's working on a project there. Originally he said he couldn't make it because of work, which I thought was weird because it *is* Labor Day weekend, but he changed his mind all of a – "

"Excuse me," I said, standing.

"Do you want company?" Gretchen asked, moving to get up.

I sighed inwardly, wanting nothing more than to run away and cry, but my self-preservation instincts kicked in. "No. I'm fine." I gave them a big smile. "I'm going to call Bill and tell him I miss him."

The table cooed harmoniously. Lucy nearly melted in her chair.

"What can I say, all this wedding talk has me feeling romantic."

I made a show of retrieving my phone and went to stand outside in the warm night. Warm, yes, but I was cold. I was always cold to the bone lately. I didn't call Bill as I had said but took a moment to collect myself. *Dani. And David. Me. And Bill.* It made perfect sense. I wondered if he had even considered how it might hurt me to hear that. Surely, after all this time, he didn't consider my feelings anymore. Why should he?

And would it matter if he did? In the end, things were as they were supposed to be. Who was he to me? A mistake. A mark that could never be erased for the entirety of my marriage. Long after I will have forgotten him, he will remain a part of my past.

Long after I've forgotten him . . . . When will that be? How much longer until I forget?

It felt like a lifetime had passed already since that night. But though I worked hard not to think of him, the way he'd made me feel persisted. When I was near him. When I watched him watch me. Kisses, whispers, sensations in the dark.

I looked up at the night sky for a long time. In moments like these, I longed to be back in the suburbs of Dallas, where I could lie in the backyard and blanket myself with millions of stars. Tonight there were few. *So this is how it goes.*

When a prick of light shot across the sky, leaving a faint silver streak in its path, I didn't bother making a wish. I just turned and went back inside.

CHAPTER 3

GRETCHEN'S FISTS SHOT in the air. "Feel the burn!" she screeched.

I quickly bit into a lime to abate my tingling jaw. My face scrunched, and I plucked the rind from between my teeth to drop it in the empty shot glass.

"Nice," she said. "Three in a row. I'm impressed."

I hiccupped and smiled. "I'll take another Cosmo," I told the bartender.

"You're going to make yourself sick, mixing liquors like that."

"I'm no rookie. Are you forgetting who taught you how to drink?"

"That's debatable. Still, tequila shots and Cosmos? Gross. And maybe even lethal."

I answered her with a shrill laugh that hurt even my own ears. I could almost feel the alcohol eating away at the pit in my stomach. It was just acidic enough to erase the toxicity of my shame for a night. It was relief, sweet and bitter. I took my drink and followed Gretchen back to our booth in the VIP section of the downtown club.

"Anyway," Bethany was saying, "that was it for them. After an affair, three years of counseling and two children, it was forgetting to replace the milk that finally did it."

Ava shook her head. "So sad. That happened to my colleague, too. One day she came home from work, and her husband said, 'I can't do this anymore.' Can you imagine?"

"Not everyone is as lucky as me and Andrew," Lucy said, shrugging as though she were helpless to the fact. "We have the kind of romance that most people can only hope for."

"It's true. You guys are soul mates," Ava said.

"I know. How sweet is that?"

I laughed into my Cosmo.

"What?" Lucy asked.

"Oh, nothing," I said after a sip.

"No, what? Why is that funny?"

"It's not funny, it's just . . . idealistic, I guess."

"How so?"

"I mean, Luce, really? You guys haven't even walked down the aisle yet. It's a little early to be so sure."

Her mouth parted. "Andrew and I aren't like those people. We have something unique and special. True romance."

"Honey, romance is fleeting," I said, waving a hand in the air. "When it fades away, you have to know that you and Andrew will still be able to stand each other."

"Call me naïve – "

"You said it!" I shrieked, giggling by myself.

"Um," Lucy continued, "okay, but I don't think that for us, the romance will ever 'fade away.'"

"I agree, Lucy," Ava cut in. "I think you and Andrew are meant to be. I envy you guys. I can't wait to meet my soul mate."

"There's no such thing as soul mates, Ava," I said. "That's just a bunch of fairytale bullshit. The sooner everyone realizes that, the better."

"Liv," Gretchen warned.

"What? It's true. Marriage is work. You'll see soon enough. That euphoric stage wears off pret-ty quick-ly. I'm not being cynical; it's science." When I noticed their frowns, I nodded. "Yep, science. Hormones, oxy- " I hiccupped, "tocin, and shit like that. Not very romantic, is it?"

"What about earlier when you went to call Bill?" Lucy countered. "Some might say that was a romantic gesture."

I glanced down at the table and took one of those painful breaths, the ones where you feel the simultaneous constricting of everything in your chest. I thought about confessing that I hadn't gone outside to call Bill but to remind myself of why things were better off as they were. It was only a brief moment though, and instead, I said, "That exactly proves my point. Being around all of you makes me want to call Bill and tell him that I love him."

"Which is romantic," someone said.

I nodded. "It is, but why should I have to be reminded of that? Because relationships aren't always that way. Sometimes you forget that you're madly in love." I hiccupped. "Happens to everyone."

"Olivia," Gretchen said again.

"Sorry, but I don't want Lucy to be disappointed."

"Are you disappointed?" Bethany asked.

"No, because I learned early on what marriage is about. It's work. Thinking that it will be easy because it's 'true love' is stupid. That's just another form of faith for those who can't deal with reality."

"That's enough," Dani said.

I shrugged at her. "Better to be prepared."

"I really don't think Andrew and I are that way," Lucy said. "We're – "

"Different?" I interjected.

"Yes."

I nodded. "I hope you are."

"I mean, I get what you're saying," Lucy continued. "I know you and Bill work at your marriage, but I'm excited to work together with Andrew. I love him. There's no one else I would have wanted to do this with."

"Not even Kyle Medley?" I asked, giggling to myself as I took another sip. "Come on, you said the same thing about him in college."

"I think you've had enough," Gretchen said, reaching for my drink.

I recoiled, sloshing pink liquid on my dress. "Damn," I muttered, swiping at the stain.

"I didn't know what love was until I met Andrew," Lucy said.

I blinked at her once and then burst into laughter. "Lucy, do you hear yourself? You're just saying that because to admit otherwise would mean you could be marrying anyone right now. Including Kyle Medley."

"You're not making any sense."

"I'm making perfect sense! If instead of dumping you, Kyle had proposed, you would have said yes. Hence, the eradication of the soul mates theory. At the time, you thought he was your soul mate. And if you and Andrew broke up and you met someone else, you'd say he was your soul mate."

"You're putting words in my mouth. I never thought Kyle Medley was 'the one.'"

My face scrunched under the weight of my skepticism. "Okay," I said, holding up my hands. "If that's your story."

Lucy's face etched with worry when she looked from her sister to Gretchen. "So are you saying that Bill isn't your soul mate?" she asked after a moment.

"I'm saying the whole ludicrous idea doesn't exist. And I know Bill would agree with me."

"So what do you suggest, that nobody ever get married?" Dani asked.

I felt my brows crease as I looked at her. "No," I said emphatically. "That's not what I'm saying at all. Just don't make it into something it's not. Obviously Bill and I love each other, and we're happy and we are building this life together – but to say that it's this fairytale romance where we make love on a bed of rose petals every night, I mean . . . that's what Lucy wants."

"No, I don't. But Andrew and I share something pure that neither of us could experience with someone else. Romance isn't exclusive to sex. And even as we get older or fight or have kids, we'll still have that passion for only each other."

I only raised my eyebrows and gripped the table when the room undulated suddenly.

"Don't listen to her," Dani said softly, but I heard her anyway.

"Oh, I'm sorry, Dani. How long have you been married?"

"Liv!"

"It's fine, Lucy," Dani said, pursing her lips at me. "She's right. I'm not married. None of us are, so maybe she has a point."

I gave the table a hard nod and pointed to Dani. "See? She knows what's up."

"I'm calling you a cab," Gretchen said, digging in her purse.

"Don't make me the bad guy, Gretchen," I pleaded, suddenly upset. "I'm just trying to be honest. It doesn't mean I love Bill any less or that I'm not happy. I am happy. I just want Lucy to be happy, too."

Lucy came to sit next to me. I was enfolded in a lavender cloud when she hugged me. "I know," she said, squeezing my shoulders. "Nobody thinks you're the bad guy. Everyone is happy."

"Good," I said. "You smell nice."

She threw her head back and laughed. "Thank you."

"Do you want me to call her a cab?" Gretchen asked.

I frowned. "I'm sitting right here."

"Actually, I think it might be time to call it a night," Lucy said. "I don't want to be puffy on Sunday."

Everyone agreed emphatically that they did not want to be puffy either, so Ava and Bethany went to hail cabs while

Lucy left for the restroom.

"You know, you really should keep your marital problems to yourself," Dani said to me as we settled the bill. "Lucy doesn't need to hear that a couple days before she walks down the aisle."

"I don't have marital problems," I declared.

"All the same, don't spoil this for her. She already worries about you too much when she should be focusing on herself right now."

I looked over at Gretchen for backup, but she only shrugged. "She's probably right, Liv. Remember what we talked about? This weekend is about Lucy."

My eyes drifted back to Dani and narrowed. I imagined David sitting next to her, touching her hair and rubbing her back. He would smile mildly at me, and that'd be the worst part. His eyes would regard me impassively, like an old friend. Maybe he still had that passion, but it would be for her or someone else. Not for me. He wouldn't look at me the same way anymore.

~

I stumbled into the apartment and shut the heavy door quietly behind me. I tossed my keys at the table but missed, so they landed on the floor with a clang. Stifling a laugh, I kicked off my heels. *Tiptoe, tiptoe, shh . . . .*

"Shit, fuck!" I hissed.

"Liv?"

"Sorry, babe, I hin my shit. Er, I hit my shin on the bed," I said, giggling.

The bed rustled with movement. "How was it?"

"Good," I responded, and I could see his teeth flash in the dark. "We drank *pink* Cosmos at dinner and then tequila and . . . other stuff, I don't remember."

"So you had fun?"

"Yup. You?"

"Yeah, we had a good time too. Andrew's brothers are a little immature, but whatever."

"Gretchen fell off a curb." I snickered and then broke into a fit of laughter, clutching my side.

"You seem better," he said cautiously when I'd recovered.

Am I? I didn't know how to respond, because I wasn't sure. Since my talk with Gretchen, I had tried to be more affable. I didn't feel back to normal, but I wasn't sure I ever would. How could I, knowing what I did? How could things ever go back to the way they were?

"Bill," I said softly. "Do you believe in soul mates?"

I heard the sheets rustle again and jumped when he touched me. He rotated me and unzipped my party dress so it fell to the ground. His figure rose from the bed, and he found my lips with a gentle kiss.

"Wait," I said when he pulled away. I wrapped my arms around his neck. It felt nice to be kissed and touched after months of loneliness. Maybe being with Bill again would remind me of our love. He could end all my inner battles.

He removed his boxers quickly as we kissed and then urged me backward onto the bed. He climbed atop me, and I held his face to mine. When he nudged between my legs, I whispered, "Slow down. Kiss me first."

I ran my hands over his long back and shut my eyes while he kissed me excitedly. I sought a connection with my hands and my tongue, but my head began to spin. I opened my eyes, but the room was spinning too. He pecked me on the lips before pulling away.

I blinked up, focusing on the ceiling. *What have I done? Something is lost, I've driven a wedge between us – does he feel it too?* He was back suddenly, his hands sliding down and spreading me open. "Wait," I groaned as dread and tequila flooded me. He started to push into me. "Wait, just – just slow

29

down! Jesus."

He jerked back and hovered over me. "What?" he asked, bewildered.

"You're . . . moving too fast, can't you feel that I'm not ready?"

"All right," he said sitting back on his calves. "What do you want me to do? You don't like foreplay."

I heaved a sigh. I had told him that once, because it was usually a tedious race to see if I could finish when I knew I wouldn't. After all these years with Bill, I'd gradually given up the chase for my orgasm.

"Never mind," I said, getting up and righting my underwear.

"Seriously? What do you want?"

"I want you to know what I want." My stomach knotted, and I swallowed.

"I thought I did."

"I'm sorry, I'm drunk." I backed away and stumbled over my dress. "It's my thing, it's not you. I'm really sorry."

"Babe, the sex . . . I know it's been a while . . . but you don't mean that, do you?"

I closed my eyes and rubbed them. "No. No, of course not." The world moved behind my lids, and my jaw tickled. "I'm sorry," I repeated and took off for the bathroom.

He called after me. I scrambled to my knees and leaned over the toilet seconds before throwing up.

"Oh, shit," I heard as Bill gathered my hair in his hand. "Did you eat anything at dinner?"

I shook my head into the toilet and released a stream of pink liquid. I sat back against the wall and whispered, "I'm sorry."

He crouched down beside me. "It's all right. You had too much to drink, huh?"

I nodded.

"I'll get you some water."

I let my head fall into my hands. I was awash with shame for spurning him and for letting the alcohol incite memories of David all night. *I just want it to end. I want to rid myself of David and of everything I've been holding inside. The guilt, the shame, the lust, the longing.* When I was hit with another wave of nausea, I gripped the toilet and vomited every last thing inside me.

~

I'm running, but I'm not moving. I'm being chased, but my legs are heavy. Impossible to lift. The leadenness rises up my arms and settles in my chest, strangling me from the inside out. And someone's hands are around my neck. My chest is collapsing, and I am gasping, rasping for air . . . .

I sucked air in suddenly, and my eyes flew open. When I couldn't move, panic filtered through me until I realized why. Bill was holding me. It had been a while since he had, so I fought the urge to break free and move to my side of the bed.

"Liv?" he murmured sleepily.

"It's all right, just another nightmare," I said.

"Hmm? Nightmare? Must be the alcohol." He pulled me closer, and I sighed, yielding to him.

CHAPTER 4

I PULLED THE ZIPPER UP over my ribs and wondered if I could get away with wearing a shawl. I was already cold in the revealing dress and up until now, I had been consciously disguising my weight loss. I remembered Lucy's serious expression as she had warned us about altering our bridesmaid dresses in any way, because she wanted the three of us looking identical as we stood next to her.

"Where's Liv?" I heard from the next room.

"In here," I called.

We were at Andrew's family's behemoth of a house in Winnetka, taking up a few rooms in the 'east wing,' as Andrew's mother had called it. I leaned into the mirror and gave my makeup a once-over. Because my face had become thinner, my eyes looked even larger than normal. The deep Bordeaux gown perfectly complemented their shade of green and the dark honey color of my hair.

Lucy had hired professionals to transform the four of us for her big day. She was the glowing princess while Gretchen, Dani and I were sultry triplets. We donned identical messy chignons and dramatic makeup, with wine-colored pouts to match our dresses.

I swiped a lipstick smudge from the corner of my mouth. In the day's chaos, it had been easy to avoid my thoughts. But now I braced myself against the vanity table. Tonight I would see David again, and I had no plan. I could see beads of sweat forming on my upper lip just thinking about it. *Good, then. Perhaps I won't need a shawl after all.*

Gretchen breezed in, still dressed in one of the red satin bridesmaid robes we'd all received. She halted when she saw me. "Liv," she said, passing her eyes over me. "You're really skinny."

"Stop," I said, crossing my arms into myself. "Don't look at me like that."

She walked over and pulled on the armhole of the dress. "This is big. I knew you'd lost weight, but this is too much. I can like, see your ribs." She ran a finger over my chest that left chills in its wake.

"You cannot," I countered, puffing up. "I just know I'm going to be cold, though. Do you think Lucy will let me wear something over my shoulders?"

"After this weekend, will you please go talk to someone? You're depressed."

I reeled back at the accusation. "I am not depressed. Yes, I've lost weight, but I have been working *a lot*." *And how can I eat when I feel so sick to my stomach all the time?*

"Don't make me call your father. I will, I swear."

I scowled and turned sideways in the mirror, which only made it worse.

"Otherwise you look beautiful," she commented in a softened tone. "Your skin is literally flawless."

"You're making me blush," I said. "Go get dressed."

Lucy's glossy brown locks were twisted up and away from her face, not a single strand astray. Her dress was simple, with delicate, beaded cap sleeves and a fitted bodice that emphasized her small waist. I was surprised and thankful when she didn't comment on my weight. Instead, she told us all that we looked perfect and that she was honored to have us in her bridal party. We met at the window and watched the gathering crowd from the second floor. The sprawling lawn was vibrantly green, and guests followed a walkway lined with candles to their seats.

"Are you ready?" Dani asked, touching Lucy's shoulder. "I think it's time."

Everyone filtered out of the room. "Lucy," I called.

She turned and linked her arm with mine.

"I'm sorry about what I said the other night."

"I know," she said, her smile genuine.

"I don't really think you'll be disappointed. You guys will be so happy. I'm not sure why I said what I did."

"It's no big deal. Andrew and I are meant for each other, and we know that. That's all that matters."

I nodded, but something about the confidence in her voice gave me a sinking feeling.

Downstairs we found the wedding planner that Lucy had finally broken down and hired. She led us to where our corresponding groomsmen were waiting. I'd gotten Bill into a tuxedo. The fabric hung nicely from his tall, slender frame because I'd insisted that he see a tailor. He extended his hand to me, and I slipped into place comfortably beside him.

"You look gorgeous," he whispered in my ear as we waited behind Gretchen, whose arm was linked with Andrew's brother.

"Thank you." I rose up on the balls of my feet and kissed his crooked nose. "Our turn," I whispered, stepping forward. I squeezed his hand with the intention of hanging on to it all night.

~

The ceremony was Lucy-style perfect, without any glitches or awkward pauses. We all clapped and grinned giddily when they kissed, Lucy more than anyone. After congratulations were dealt, we, as a bridal party unit, broke off from the crowd for pictures. Having kept my eyes glued forward, I hadn't seen David during the ceremony. I hoped he had changed his mind about showing up.

I became colder with the sun's descent. Bill was making humorless jokes with Andrew's brothers that grated on my nerves. Once again, his touch was unwelcome; I wished for a bottomless glass of wine and an oversized sweatshirt to hide under.

We entered an enormous white tent that glowed with soft light. The guests appeared to have become thoroughly buzzed while they'd waited for us.

As I caught up with Lucy's parents, Bill found me and handed me a glass of water even though I had only wanted wine. He put his arm around me, and I stiffened so noticeably that he removed it right away.

"Lucy tells us you're looking for a house," said Lucy's mom.

"Liv's been swamped with her promotion, so it was on the backburner," Bill explained, "but we've just started up again."

"It's a grueling process, isn't it?" she asked. "I would love for Lucy and Andrew to settle into somewhere more practical."

"Hey." Lucy's dad tugged on his wife's sleeve.

"What?" she asked. "I'm in the middle – "

"Look at Danielle," he said. She turned slightly, giving me a clear view across the tent. Dani's adoring gaze was fixed on David as he gestured to the group around them. Even in the outdoor tent, the room lit up around him, intensifying his dark, grave features. Recognizing him instantly, my heart vaulted from my chest, clawing against the ribcage that so cruelly separated it from where it wanted to be.

As if he felt my eyes on him, he looked up and met my stare. It was just us again in that moment; the crowd was merely a conductor of our crackling energy. It was like seeing him for the first time but with the knowledge that he had felt me in a way that no one else ever had.

His expression remained as passive as mine. My senses were stolen by his presence, and I didn't have the wherewithal to smile politely or acknowledge him in any form. I didn't look away as I had the first night we'd made eye contact but held his gaze instead. My body responded to the memory of his touch, craving him like a drug, instructing me to reach out and consume him. To take him into my bloodstream so he could once again kill the pain and warm me from the inside.

He flinched and blinked – once, twice – before looking away and leaving me cold. My breathing was labored and ice cubes rattled in my glass, but I could barely hear them over the heartbeat in my ears.

"Don't you agree, dear?" Lucy's mom asked with an expectant look.

I nodded and swallowed dryly, emitting a small noise.

Bill waved me off and said something else to her. My disobedient eyes gravitated back to David. He sported a perfectly-tailored tuxedo and looked the same as I remembered: relaxed, easy and painfully, bring-me-to-my-knees handsome. Not nearly as distraught or sleepless as I felt, which wasn't surprising since in bachelor time, our liaison was ages ago. His jet-black hair was styled with precision, and I could see from where I stood the smoothness of his square jaw. It was seeing his chestnut brown eyes and the sexy cleft of his chin again that almost did me in. His hands in his pockets strained against the fabric of his expensive suit. Dani tugged on his sleeve, but he stared distractedly at something beyond her.

My legs tensed with the urge to run away, but I was loath for him to know how he still affected me. When Dani giggled and looked at her feet in response to something he'd said, I seized Bill's hand, causing him to freeze mid-sentence. That was when I noticed David steal a furtive look in my direction. I'd almost missed it, but it had happened.

~

I wrung the paper in my hands and then immediately smoothed it out.

"Nervous?" Bill whispered.

"No." I hadn't been until my audience had fallen away, leaving only one person to hear my toast. If I'd been blind, I still would have seen David; he was a beacon in the sea of faces.

"You're up," Bill said, motioning that I should stand.

The room became silent, and I scrambled up to look out over the crowd. I touched my earlobe gently and took a deep breath.

"I'll keep it short and sweet, like our bride here," I started. I glanced down at the piece of paper and then back at the room. "How do you know when you've met 'the one'? Do both hearts suddenly change rhythm, syncing to form their own beautiful symphony? Do you see yourself," I paused, dropping my eyes to the champagne flute in my hand, "suddenly exquisite and irresistible through their eyes? Does love become something tangible, something that others can see but only the two of you can touch?"

I looked at Bill, who smiled encouragingly, and I set my hand on the back of his chair. "I don't think anyone can answer that because for everyone, it's different. Andrew and Lucy are meant to be. Period. There aren't two people more perfect for each other. When Lucy told me one night that she wanted to spend the rest of her life with Andrew, I said, 'Duh, tell me something I don't know.'" A light laugh rippled through the crowd, and I raised my glass. "I love you both, and I am so honored to be a part of tonight. Cheers."

I dropped into my chair and crumpled the paper in my hands. It wasn't the speech I had written, but the words weren't hard to find. They were within reach, right in front of me.

CHAPTER 5

A CURTSY FROM LUCY and a bow from Andrew signified the end of their first dance. I bolted to the house for a much-needed bathroom break. Alone for the first time, I breathed through my distress. David's presence had thrown me so far off-kilter that I almost felt alive again. With only one glance, he'd managed to stir up my emotions while simultaneously providing comfort. I felt somehow safer in his bubble, like everything was better when he was near.

I exited the bathroom and skidded to a halt as I almost ran into David's wall of a body.

"Shit, sorry," I muttered, swerving at the last second. He leaped into my path, and my eyes automatically darted around the empty foyer.

"What is this?" he asked angrily. Hard eyes scanned over my dress.

"What?"

"When was the last time you ate anything?"

"This afternoon," I said smugly. He shot my hand a glance, and I dropped it instantly. Though no one else had ever brought it to my attention, David never seemed to miss my nervous habit of tugging on my earlobe.

"Don't play coy with me, Olivia. Why are you so thin?"

"I've been busy," I said, straightening my posture.

"That's bullshit." He touched my arm with obvious restraint. I bit back a gasp, because his skin on mine was like liquid sun, radiating through my body. "What is going on with you?"

I sighed. I wanted to yank my arm from him, but he was slowly warming my bones again, and I was tired of being cold. No, my body had not forgotten the feel of David Dylan. "Don't worry about it. It's not your problem."

"The fuck it's not. Why are you doing this?"

"I'm not doing it on purpose," I said defensively. "I just can't . . ." I faltered and took a breath. "I can't eat; it makes me sick."

"I've been watching you. You're different." His tone softened into velvet, coating my skin. "Tell me what it is, and I'll fix it. I'll do anything."

Faint cologne filled the space between us, instantly transporting me back to moments when I'd been lost and drowning in him. I flickered back to reality. "No. It's not fixable. You can't just swoop in and fix everything all the time."

"What's the problem?" he insisted, his tone heavy with warning.

I drew my lips into a line and looked away.

"Olivia."

"You, David! You're the problem!" I snapped. "What happened between us is eating me from the inside; it's all I can think about. It haunts me day and night. It *consumes* me!" Brown, melancholy eyes searched mine until I pulled my arm from his grip. "I have to go, I can't do this," I said, dropping his gaze.

"I'm surprised you're still here," he countered.

"Don't." I raised my eyes to his again, and my heart wilted at the way his expression had hardened. "You have no idea what I've been through."

A burst of air left his mouth, and he scoffed. "That's where you're wrong. Don't forget that you walked out on me. You have no idea what *I* have been through. *Me*. Fuck, I shouldn't even be talking to you," he muttered. "I promised myself I wouldn't."

I blinked at him. "You promised . . . what?"

"I only came here tonight because . . . because I needed to see you. I promised to leave you alone, but I just needed to see that you're all right. Even from a distance."

"But it's been so long, and . . . I thought you'd be over –"

"Everything okay, Liv?" Gretchen's brother approached us, puffed up and obviously ruffled as he took in the scene.

"Yes, it's fine," I hastened to reassure him. "Thanks, John."

David looked warily at John and then back at me before stalking away.

"Where've you been, you handsome devil? You owe me a dance," I said before he could ask.

He looked after David for one short second before turning his attention to me. "I'm afraid I'll snap you in half," he joked.

"Oh, really? You think I'm that weak?" I asked, surprising him with a punch in the upper arm.

"Ow!" he wailed.

"Don't be a baby. Come on, John Harper. Escort me to the dance floor."

I stowed my conversation with David for later and followed John from the house. We were almost to the tent when we spotted Lucy and Gretchen flailing on the dance floor.

"They must be drunk."

"Aren't you?" he asked, tugging me along with him. We joined them for the rest of the song, dancing and laughing carelessly. Seeing Lucy so happy made me feel lighter.

"Remind me to tell you when you're sober what horrible dancers you are," I called out as the song ended. I squealed when Gretchen pinched me. Andrew's dad appeared at Lucy's side and held out his hand to her as the next song started.

"A dance?" John asked me. I agreed and let him draw me into his arms.

"Well, you're a shitty date," Gretchen muttered, and we laughed as she sulked off alone.

"So, little Liv, what's new with you? Gretchen says you're cranky."

I smiled a little and looked down between us. "Maybe."

"So what's up?"

"I'm just overloaded at work, and that's enough to make anyone a little testy."

He regarded me thoughtfully while we danced. "Okay. You'd tell me if something was wrong, wouldn't you?"

I looked up at him from under my lashes. "Yes."

"You know you're like a sister to me. An extremely hot sister, but a sister all the same. If I were here in Chicago, I'd volunteer as your bodyguard."

At that I laughed loudly. "Oh, John, I love you."

"Hey, Bill," he said suddenly. "Guess you want to cut in with your lady?"

"No, no," Bill said, giving John a wary glance before turning to me. "I just came to tell you that I'm running up to the house to have a cigar with Andrew and the guys."

"Okay," I said. "I'll save you a dance."

"Sounds good." He leaned over John's arm and pecked me on the cheek.

John whirled me around dramatically and dipped me so my hair almost touched the floor. "Hi," he said from above, grinning.

"John, damn it, let me up. Everyone can see down my dress."

"Oh, then I'm on the wrong side," he jested.

When he lifted me back up, my gaze locked with David's not two feet away. His smooth voice slathered over me. "May I cut in?"

"Get lost, dude," John said. "She's married."

My skin prickled at the thought of those big arms around me. David shifted his focus to John, and they stared at each other. When I noticed David's jaw set, I quickly cut in. "It's okay, John. He's a friend."

John stepped back and bowed. "As you wish," he said. "I'll be over there if you need me."

The first notes of panty-dropping, sex-infused "Wicked Game" came through the speakers. My legs quivered as David wrapped an arm around my waist and took my hand in his. I secretly thanked Lucy for picking a backless dress that allowed us the intimacy of skin-on-skin contact. A cologne and whiskey infusion washed over me, and I closed my eyes to remember the heady combination of him; I could taste the whiskey on my tongue now, I could feel the soft cashmere of his sweater warming me that night.

"I can't stop thinking about you," he whispered.

"Don't," I objected. He slipped the tip of one finger inside the loose dress and skimmed it lightly along my back.

"Look at me," he urged as he had once before. I could only feel that fingertip, possessing me with its feather touch. He pulled me closer, and I opened my eyes slowly for him. His eyes were blazing, and he was unmistakably hard against my silken thigh. My teeth bit into my bottom lip. He groaned softly in response and slid his finger down the length of the dress, repositioning his hand lower. "You never finished your sentence."

"Hmm?"

"Earlier. You said you thought I was over . . . what? Over you?"

I glanced around to find that each couple was engrossed in their own dance. It was as if Chris Isaak had cast a four-minute-long spell on the tent. I nodded fractionally.

"I'm not," he said softly. "I'm so under you, it's ridiculous."

I was near mad pressed against his erection, and I squeezed the hand that held mine. I drew a deep breath. I had no words, but even if I did, what could I say? I closed my eyes to take in the moment, to memorize its every detail.

"Stay," he breathed when the song began to fade.

When my eyes opened, I saw Gretchen staring at us from across the floor. She shook her head slowly so that nobody else would notice. With a great sigh, I pulled away from him.

"Not yet," he instructed, holding me in place.

"I can't. It's agonizing being this close to you. And everyone I know is here . . . . I have to go."

I didn't give him a chance to respond, but just walked toward Gretchen, who never took her eyes off of me. Warmth receded, as though I were in a comfortably hot shower that was quickly turning cold.

"We need to talk," she stated as I approached.

"I know. Not tonight though, k? Just not tonight."

~

"This's been the best night of my life," Lucy slurred, draping a heavy arm over me.

"Well, it's not over yet." I pulsed my brows and jabbed my elbow at Andrew. "Time to make it official."

"Oh, yes, official," she repeated. "I have to wait for everyone to leave though, don't I? I think I have to."

"You probably should," I agreed. We waited by the exit as the remaining guests filtered out. Bill's hands kneaded my shoulders while Lucy dealt overexcited good-byes.

"I don't know about you, but I'm ready to hit the sack," Bill said into my ear.

"So glad we don't have to drive home. I'm exhausted."

"Daaav-idddd," Lucy called, and every hair on my body bristled. I pinched myself in hopes of waking up from the ensuing nightmare.

"Thank you for inviting me, Lucy," David said as he approached.

"I'm so, so glad you could make it. Did you know he flew back early from work to attend?" she asked, swinging around and looking directly at Bill.

"I did not know that," Bill said. I didn't have to see him to know he was smiling at her. "Bill Wilson," he said, sticking his hand out over my shoulder. "And my wife, Olivia." My stomach dropped as David flashed me an uneasy look.

"They know each other, Bill," Lucy said with an exaggerated eye roll.

David's voice seemed to drop an octave when he said, "David Dylan." The handshake, so close to my face, was firm and lasted uncomfortably long. I watched as David studied him with drawn lips. Bill had heard David's name in conversation, but I doubted that he remembered. Still, his hand tightened on my shoulder. *Or is it my imagination?*

"Thanks again, Mrs. Greene," David said, causing Lucy to titter into her hand. "You are a vision, and the ceremony was beautiful. Well done."

"Oh." She waved him off but blushed.

"Are you driving back tonight?" My voice was thick, and I immediately regretted speaking when David looked directly at me.

Lucy gasped. "You're staying! We have room. Er, Dani has room."

I stilled under Bill's hand.

"No, thank you. I don't have anything with me."

"Who cares? You can borrow stuff. Dani, come here!" Lucy's hand flapped enthusiastically, and she almost fell over.

"Easy," I said.

Her eyes widened. "We can play board games. Dani, shouldn't David stay the night?"

"Yes," Dani agreed quickly. I looked at the ground when I felt my cheeks heat.

"I wouldn't feel comfortable – "

"Oh, David, you're such a gentleman," Lucy said, swatting his arm. "We'll give you your own room, I was just teasing. John was supposed to stay the night, but he's not. You can take his room."

Dani's mouth fell open, but David nodded his agreement before she could protest. "Great!" she said instead. "Come on." She walked toward the house and then looked over her shoulder. "David, come on. This way." He looked anxious, but took a step backward before pivoting to follow her.

I watched their retreating figures until Bill stepped around in front of me. "Did you have some cake?"

"Yes." I'd had a bite, so it wasn't a lie. My stomach was far too distressed for something so sweet, though.

"Good. Let's get the hell out of these clothes," he said, resting his hand on my upper back and leading me up the steps.

"I'll be right up," Lucy called loudly.

"Yeah, actually. I didn't think I would like it, but I had a good time."

When we entered the house, I searched furtively for David or Dani, but neither was in sight. I groaned inwardly. Was this really happening? Maybe tonight he would finally make his move. *She'd be thrilled about it*, I thought bitterly. But could I really blame her? *Just let it go. Let him be happy. Isn't that what I want ultimately? For everyone to just be happy, myself included?* I nodded.

CHAPTER 6

BILL'S HAND SLID DOWN my shoulder. With a quick kiss, he pulled softly on my dress strap until it fell. I stood watching him as he backed away and undressed.

"What?" he asked.

"Nothing." I pulled my dress off the rest of the way and tried to shake David's lingering touch from my back. I tugged Bill by the waistband of his boxers, and he stumbled to me.

His lips found mine with a deeper kiss. I grabbed his hand roughly and put it around me, trying to erase any hint of David. I recognized the softness of Bill's tongue and the smell of his soap, but the kiss was flat. My hair came free when I pulled on it, and he brushed it from my neck. Behind closed eyes, I remembered David's expansive hand sliding down to my lower back, his fingertips alone driving me wild. I moaned into Bill's mouth, and he became instantly hard.

I squeezed my eyes tighter. I needed to forget David and to remember what Bill felt like. I had done this to us, and now I had to make things right. Or had we always been this way? I dashed away the thought and fell back on the bed, splaying out my arms. "Come on, Bill," I said gruffly. I arched my back, offering my breasts. "Fuck me."

"What?"

"You heard me," I said. When he didn't move, I huffed and sat up to grab his arm. "Get over here."

He aligned himself with the edge of the bed, and I wrapped my legs around him. *Replace the memories, Bill. Now. Let's make it right. Now, now, now –*

"The other night you said – "

"I don't care what I said, just do it." I needed him to take me because he couldn't resist me another moment, because he was overcome with desire. I squirmed on the bed as I fought off the memory of David cornering me in the stairwell and proving that he couldn't, wouldn't, wait another second.

"Okay." Tentatively, he moved my thong aside and pulled down his boxers. He ran one hand over himself while licking the fingers of his other hand.

"Yes," I moaned loudly when he touched me.

He bent his knees and entered me slowly.

"Oh, yes, Bill, come on." I bucked my hips and used my heels to urge him deeper, trying to recapture the insatiable need that I'd felt with David. He grimaced. "What?" I asked.

His chest deflated with a loud exhale. "Nothing."

It wasn't nothing. He was still holding the base of his penis, but I felt him softening inside of me. "You can't . . . ?"

"I had a lot to drink," he snapped. "And you're . . . yelling at me," he said as his fist stroked back and forth.

"Do you need help?" I sat up and reached out, but he pulled back.

"Don't."

"Okay."

"And stop looking at me like that."

"Like what?"

"Like I can't get it up."

I searched for something else to look at, because I didn't think I could not look at him that way. After a few moments, I sighed. "It's fine, babe, let's go see what the others are doing. We can try again later."

"No, I can do it," he said, panting.

I slid off the bed and kissed his shoulder. "It's no big deal." I was secretly relieved. Seeing David again had freshened the memories. It was unfair that I'd be thinking about him instead of Bill.

I pulled on my striped pajama shorts and matching camisole before yanking a brush through my tangled hair.

Bill groaned behind me. "I can't fucking believe this," he uttered, squatting to rummage in his suitcase.

"Babe, it happens. Don't worry. Lucy said it happened to Andrew a few weeks ago."

"What?" he exclaimed. "I did not need to know that."

"Um, don't repeat that, seriously."

"What am I going to say, 'Hey, dude, heard you can't get it up either?'"

"You're fine. One time does not mean anything. Come on, get dressed." When my hair was in a presentable state, I wrapped myself in the red robe Lucy had given us.

Bill was close behind as I padded down the stairs. We found the group seated around the fire, surrounded by glasses of wine and bottles of beer.

"Where have you two been?" Dani asked, arching an eyebrow in our direction. David sat barefoot and cross-legged on the floor next to her in a pajama set that looked small. He resembled a Greek statue, beautiful and eerily still as he stared into the fire.

"Just changing," I said quickly, and Bill shot me a glance.

"Liar," Dani chimed. "We've been down here for twenty minutes already."

"I need a beer," I muttered, leaving to the kitchen.

"Bring a few," Andrew called after me. I loaded up my arms and returned to the room to distribute drinks. I had one extra, so I offered it to David, who accepted it without looking up.

"We were just telling Lucy that if she gets knocked up, she might have to move to the 'burbs," Gretchen said as I settled by Bill's feet against the base of the couch.

Lucy groaned and fell over onto Andrew's lap. "You won't make me do that, will you?"

Andrew just burped into his fist and shrugged. "Everyone's doing it."

"Truth," Bill said, patting my head. "Liv and I looked at a real fixer-upper in Oak Park on Friday."

David sputtered suddenly and coughed into his hand. Dani patted his back softly while he cleared his throat.

"What's it like?" Gretchen asked.

I closed my eyes and envisioned the house. "It's really . . . amazing."

"Well," Bill said through a chortle, "I'm not sure 'amazing' is the right word."

I opened my eyes, and the image evaporated. "It's not, you're right. It's a mess, but it has this really charming aura that sort of encompasses you when you're near it."

"That sounds nice," Lucy said sleepily.

"It's not bad," Bill said. "It needs a lot of work before it'll be on par with the rest of the neighborhood, though."

"Honey," I said quietly. "I don't want it to look like the rest of the neighborhood. Those homes are so generic."

"Okay, okay. It's a little early yet, babe."

"Anyway," I said to the group, "we aren't sure we can even afford to take on a project like that. That's what we're trying to figure out."

Andrew was looking off into the distance, stroking Lucy's hair when he perked up suddenly. "Have David look at it."

"What?" David and I asked in unison.

"Isn't this, like, your thing, dude?"

"Well, uh," he stammered.

"What do you do?" Bill asked him.

"Architect."

"But he flips houses too," Andrew offered.

"It's not even really for sale," I interjected. "The owners are just letting us see it."

"I remember now," Bill said thoughtfully. "Andrew mentioned that before. It would mean a lot if you could check it out, give me an idea of how much it would cost."

David cleared his throat again and looked down into his beer bottle.

"Honey, David's at the top of his field," I said. "He's probably really busy."

"Dave, what do you say?" Andrew asked. "Help out a friend? Bill's a lawyer. Maybe you can swap expertise."

"I have a lawyer," he replied sternly as he obviously avoided my pleading stare. When everyone remained quiet, he swallowed loudly. "But sure," he said. "Maybe."

"Cool." Bill nudged me with his foot. "There you go, babe. We're gettin' things done." I nodded downward and picked at the label on my bottle.

"Do you still want to play that board game, Luce?" Gretchen asked.

"Hmm?"

Andrew put his finger over his lips and rolled his eyes. He mouthed, *She's sleeping.*

"So much for wedding night sex," Dani said under her breath, and everyone laughed. I caught her lusty glance at David and inadvertently ripped the label from the bottle.

"I'm tired too," I said suddenly, getting up.

"Oh, okay." Bill went to stand.

"No, honey, it's fine. Have fun." I waved at him to stay seated, and he fell back on the couch. "Goodnight, everyone."

I rubbed the tip of my nose and sniffed as I ascended the stairs. *Shit.* If they were going to sleep together, I definitely didn't want it flaunted in my face. I had enough to deal with as it was.

When Bill returned to the room, I feigned sleep. I smelled cigar on his breath as he climbed in and kissed me on the cheek. I gripped my pillow and willed away my insomnia.

I wasn't sure how much time had passed when I finally

got out of bed and went to sit in the bay window. Drawing my knees to my bare chest, I looked over at Bill in the faint moonlight. He exhaled and flipped onto his back. I looked out the window at the backyard. It was quiet and peaceful, opposite from the bustling city I was used to. Even in that perfect stillness, I was having trouble sleeping.

Who was I kidding? It wouldn't have mattered where I was. David and Bill in the same house had my mind buzzing. David said he'd come to the wedding to see me. But why? Why make things harder than they already were? And he looked so handsome. He possessed every woman within proximity. Why did he have to be so damn irresistible? So exceptionally gorgeous in his urbane tuxedo?

I scanned the lawn below. And why did he hold a permanent place in my thoughts?

Bill coughed, and I looked back at him. "Come back to bed," he mumbled.

I nodded, but I didn't move. When his breathing evened again, I stood and fumbled for my robe in the dark. I slipped into the hallway and ran a hand through my hair before tiptoeing downstairs.

There was a soft, single light on in the kitchen. I hesitated. I looked back over my shoulder and then again at the doorway. My brain caught on quickly to what my heart already knew: in that kitchen I would find David.

CHAPTER 7

SOMETHING DARK FILLED the shallow glass in David's hand. He looked up at me with hooded eyes as he leaned casually against the counter.

I remained in the doorway as we stared at each other. "Water," I said finally.

He straightened and grabbed a glass from behind his head. I entered the kitchen and went to take it from him, but he turned and opened the refrigerator.

"Can't sleep?" I asked while he retrieved a pitcher.

"Not at all."

I glared at him while he filled my glass. When he'd finished, he handed it to me and set the pitcher on the island behind me. "What?" he asked.

"Because of Dani?"

"Oh . . . No. I just have a lot on my mind." He resumed his stance against the counter opposite me.

"So you didn't . . . with her?"

"I have my own room."

"Hm." I sipped my water.

"What about you?"

"I can't sleep either."

"Why not?"

I set the glass down and looked away. "I guess I have a lot on my mind." I sighed. "I'm not really used to the peace and quiet."

"I know what you mean. I sleep better in the city."

I nodded and looked back at him. "That was nice of you to fly back early for the wedding. I'm sure it made Dani happy."

"Like I told you earlier – I didn't do it for her."

I crossed my arms and played with the tie of my robe until the silence became awkward. "It's been a while since we were, like, alone together," I said softly. "I guess."

"Fifteen weeks." He shrugged. "But who's counting?"

He looked too good for three in the morning, reclined against the counter. His dark hair was soft, no longer perfect, as though he'd showered since the ceremony. My fingers tingled with the urge to touch it. His t-shirt was tight over his broad shoulders, and he wore drawstring navy and green tartan pants. I struggled for something to say, not trusting my disobedient thoughts. "So you took a job out of town, I heard."

He nodded. "I'm here half the week to finish up the hotel and in New York through the weekends. I needed the distraction."

"From?"

He hesitated. "Life."

I waited for him to continue. When he didn't, I said, "Sounds like you've been busy."

"You as well. Congratulations on your promotion."

"How'd you know?"

"I just know."

"I see."

"What I didn't know is how much weight you've lost. It's upsetting. It concerns me."

"Does it?"

"Yes, of course. Your well-being is – I mean, it's your health, Olivia."

I looked out the window over the sink. "Have you heard anything from Cooper about Mark Alvarez?" I asked.

"The piece of shit knows he's guilty for attacking you, so he took a plea bargain."

53

I widened my eyes. "Oh. Nobody told me."

During waking hours, I actively avoided thinking about the encounter, but as I slept, my mind refused to let it go. The memory that haunted my nightmares flashed before my eyes: Mark chasing me into an empty alley, laughing as he pinned my front against a wall. He hissed in my ear that Bill would pay for what he'd done: prosecuting Mark's brother in a trial that would land him behind bars for a decade. And then, relief when David had magically come to my rescue, detaining Mark until the police arrived.

"We don't have to testify," David continued. "There won't be a trial. Basically he won't serve as much time, but he's still going to prison for a while."

"So I don't need to worry anymore?"

He cocked his head. "Have you been worried?"

"Yes," I whispered.

"Don't. I'm looking out for you."

"How can you be? You're not around."

He shifted against the counter. "I know. I meant you would have heard from me if I'd thought you were in danger."

"Oh."

"You know, the night in the alley, it was fortuitous that I was there. But the truth is, I had started driving by your office on my way home. I still do."

"David." It was a warning. I felt more comforted by his confession than I should, as if him driving by each night would keep anything bad away. Little did he know though, my demons were on the inside where nobody could save me.

He nodded and looked away. I picked up my glass and took a drink, waiting for his gaze to find me again. It didn't.

"You're looking for a house," he said flatly. I wasn't sure if he'd meant it as a question, so I just nodded. His laugh was empty as he shook his head at the floor.

"And you're dating Dani."

His chest rose with a deep sigh. "Not exactly."

I pursed my lips. "She seems to think so."

"We've been out a few times at Lucy's insistence," he said, pulling at his chin.

"You're here together."

He looked at me again. "I was invited before I even met her. You know Andrew and I are friends." I responded with a pointed look of skepticism, and his lips pressed together. "I suppose, in a sense, we are dating."

"Did it ever occur to you how that might make me feel?"

"You don't exactly get a say, honeybee."

My grip tightened around my glass. *Honeybee.* The hazy postcoital glow from our one night washed over me. "Don't call me that."

"Don't like it?" he teased.

"I love it."

His smile faltered marginally. After a moment, he took a measured step toward me. I pulled my robe closer as my heart skipped. Two more steps, and his ever-imposing frame was filling the space around me. The smell of liquor burned my nostrils as his gaze flitted down to me. "I'm serious about this shit," he whispered, tugging at the opening of my robe. "Start taking better care of yourself, or it's gonna piss me off."

"You don't get a say," I echoed. I held his gaze, but I could still see my breasts heaving with each breath.

"So this is it?" he asked. "Everybody just moves on? *We* just move on?"

I cocked my head. Isn't that what we'd been doing?

"Olivia?"

My heart dropped. David took a controlled step back. Behind him, Bill, in sagging boxers and a t-shirt, stood in the doorway. He looked between us briefly and rubbed his eyes. "What are you doing?" he asked.

"Just," I croaked and cleared my throat.

"She needed water," David said for me. He lifted the pitcher in Bill's direction and took my glass from the counter.

Streaming water filled the silence as he topped off my drink. Bill shifted on his feet. Long seconds ticked by until David calmly handed me the cup. I accepted it and walked toward Bill without looking back. "Let's go to bed," I told him.

He nodded at David and followed me from the kitchen. "How do you know him again?" Bill asked when we were out of earshot.

"Through Lucy. He was the one who helped me with Mark Alvarez. I never followed up so he was just updating me."

"Oh." He turned to look over his shoulder, and I quickly released the breath I'd been holding. "Maybe I should say thanks," Bill said.

"No," I said under my breath. "You shouldn't."

~

Tables were set up under the arches of a covered patio, replete with carafes of orange juice, platters of sausage, eggs and bacon and bowls of powdered-sugared fruit. It was like something from a bridal magazine, if they were to feature the morning-after festivities.

"Liv, grab the champagne?" Lucy asked.

I entered the kitchen just as David did from the opposite doorway. "Morning," he said. He sported a too-small striped polo and high-water khakis. I raised an eyebrow at his outfit, and he smiled awkwardly. "Andrew's 'tall' brother, as they keep calling him."

I gave a shallow nod and ducked by him to the refrigerator, infuriatingly conscious of his body heat despite the dopey clothing.

He cleared his throat. "We didn't finish our conversation from last night."

I yanked open the heavy refrigerator door and searched for the champagne. "I think we did. The idea is that we move on."

"Move on," he echoed.

"Yep."

"Olivia."

I leaned back to look at him from the other side of the door. We stared at each other a moment until I started laughing.

His eyebrows knit as he studied me. "What?"

"I can't take you seriously in that outfit." I turned back to the refrigerator and grasped the cold bottle of champagne by its neck. When I shut the door, he was at my side, his lips quirked into a mocking smile.

"You can't take me seriously?" he teased. "Do I have to make you?"

He leaned in to back me against the refrigerator, but I stepped forward under his nose. I tried to appear calm, even though my heart thudded in my chest. "How?" I breathed.

"It's not really something I can explain." His gaze fixed on my mouth and proceeded slowly downward. When his eyes jumped back to mine, he said, "I would have to show you."

"Show me?" My voice was raspier than normal, low. It didn't matter what he wore; he was all man and not a little predatory even, as he towered over me.

He leaned in further, and my breath caught. I'd been fidgeting with the cap of the champagne, and he took the bottle from my hands before straightening up again.

Gretchen's head poked through the screen door. "Hurry up, Liv, we need that for the mimosas." She looked between the two of us.

"We'll be right there," David said without turning around. He twisted the cork, and it freed with a loud pop.

"Um, no, everyone is waiting on you." Gretchen shot him a piercing look. "Come on, move it," she barked. She held the door open and ushered an irritated-looking David through. She grasped my arm as I followed. "Soon. We need to talk."

"Fine," I said, wrenching my arm from her grip.

I took my place next to Bill and filled my plate with whatever was nearest.

"What time do you guys leave tonight?" Andrew's mom asked Lucy.

"Late. We're sleeping on the plane so we'll be fresh for Paris."

"Ah, fresh for Paris," Dani mimicked. "Get over yourself."

"Don't be bitter, petite Dani," she said. "Your day will come."

Dani flushed red. "I've been to Paris," she muttered.

"That's not what I meant," Lucy said with a glance in David's direction.

I pushed food around on my plate, tuning the conversation out. My exchange with David replayed in my head, and I suppressed a smile that was trying to break through. He knew exactly how to draw me in, how to prick the bubble of numbness I lived in.

My thoughts wandered to the previous night. So he and Dani hadn't slept together. But that didn't mean they wouldn't. It was clear, to me at least, that she wanted it to happen – didn't he? Knowing how persistent he could be, I wondered what was stopping him.

When I blinked up, David was watching me from across the table. *Eat*, he mouthed, nodding subtly at my plate. I picked up a strawberry, bit off the end, and licked my lips. His eyes locked on my mouth as I slowly took another bite and dropped the stem on my plate. He swallowed and stared hard. I'd become uncomfortably aroused by his words in the kitchen, and it redoubled from the way he watched me.

I jumped when Bill placed his hand on my thigh and squeezed softly. He gave me a reassuring smile.

"And so," Lucy was saying, "I wanted to express regret for those who couldn't be here to help us celebrate. My aunt and my mother's sister, Grace, God rest her soul. As well as Olivia's mentor and good friend, Davena." I clenched my teeth and concentrated on steady breathing. Lucy's face contorted as tears welled in her eyes. "Two beautiful women who were taken from us too early."

She was crying now, along with her mother, and I just sat motionless. Andrew's mother leaned over and whispered as she rubbed Lucy's back. I inhaled and tried to wet my eyes as well, but I was drier than Death Valley. *Damn it, Lucy. Why are you bringing Davena into this?* The table looked at me with overwhelming sympathy, including Bill, which bothered me most of all.

"Say something, babe," he whispered in my ear, and my jaw tensed.

I scooted the chair back suddenly and dropped my napkin on the table. "Excuse me."

I passed through the kitchen and over to the backyard-facing window. My eyes scanned the lawn as workers packed up equipment. I thought of Davena. She would have loved the wedding because she loved all things extravagant and expensive.

"I'm sorry," Lucy said from behind me. I continued staring out the window, watching as the remnants of the night disappeared into the back of a van.

"It's fine," I replied.

"I only wanted to honor her memory."

"I said it's fine," I repeated gently.

"What's wrong, Liv?" she asked. "You never talk about her."

"There's nothing to talk about. I miss her, but that's all."

"What do you miss about her?"

I turned from the window and looked Lucy in the eyes. "She was a good person. She never judged anyone, didn't care what others thought, just lived her life. Davena was always on my side."

"We're on your side. Everyone wants you to be happy."

I smiled weakly. "You're a good friend. Let's go back before I ruin the weekend."

"You're not ruining anything. I just want things to get better. I thought they were getting better."

Even if David hadn't reopened the wounds, they were still painfully fresh. Something felt off, wrong, with the house in Oak Park and with life in general. But to have David in front of me, to smell him, to look into his eyes – it made my heart race, but in the right way.

"They are," I assured her finally. "Things are getting better." It wasn't at all convincing, but I was so tired of pretending. All the time. It was exhausting. What had David said to me? '*It's nothing compared to keeping it inside. I can't hide it like you.*'

I walked back to the patio without another word, knowing Lucy would follow. Everyone had returned to merry conversation, and nobody noticed our return. Except David, whose eyes were fixed on me. I allowed myself a quick glance in his direction. His expression was unreadable, which agitated me, but there was no pity in it. He looked almost angry when his gaze shifted over to Bill, who was chatting with Lucy's dad.

At a pause in the conversation, Bill kissed my hair. "All good?" he asked. He looked tired, I noticed. I only nodded with a quick smile.

As we spilled out of the Greenes' home, we took turns wishing Lucy and Andrew a good trip. I avoided David and took off for the car but immediately wished I hadn't. I watched from afar as Bill approached him. While I debated whether or not to interfere, David handed him something, and they shook hands. I bit my nail as Bill took eons to cross the pebbled driveway, rocks crunching loudly under his feet. The question burned at the tip of my tongue. Once we were driving away, I couldn't hold it in any longer.

"What did he give you?" I blurted.

"Who?"

I grasped my earlobe between my fingers and hesitated. "David."

"Oh, his card. We're going to try and set something up this week. Jeanine's been on my ass about what she should tell the owners."

"Can't we just hire an appraiser or something?"

"We'll do that too, but I need his expert advice on what it'll cost to renovate."

"Why?"

"Because, babe, I don't want to make an offer until I know what it'll set us back."

"No, why him?"

"Sounds like he knows what he's talking about, according to Andrew. Plus, if I don't have to pay someone, all the better."

"Aha," I muttered under my breath. I should have guessed, since saving money was one of Bill's favorite hobbies.

"Something bothering you, sweet cheeks?" he asked sardonically.

I huffed in my seat and looked away. I'd brought this on myself, so why was I taking it out on Bill? The threat of Bill and David getting to know each other was too real. *Fuck. Seriously, fuck. Now that he's dating Dani, will he be around all the time?*

Bill sighed, and I cast a sidelong glance at him. How could I have danced with David in front of everyone? Why didn't I leave when I'd found him in the kitchen? I was playing with fire, but when I was in his company, I didn't care. I just wanted more of him. I wondered what Bill had seen in the kitchen. Had he heard David's question about moving on? I flipped on the air conditioning in the suddenly stifling car.

Whether Bill knew it or not, I was hurting him. Directly, indirectly, it was my fault he couldn't perform the night before. I had changed something between us without him even knowing.

In the beginning, I had been drawn to Bill's confidence. He was independent and successful. Things with him had been simple, gradual. But the traits that had attracted me to him also had their downsides. He was attentive when it was convenient for him. He was even keeled, like our relationship. He was mild – like our relationship. He didn't dig, or probe, or question why things were the way they were because for him, it was enough.

David was not only attentive, but intuitive. Was he that way with all of his women? Though nothing had happened, I felt as though I'd misbehaved over the weekend. Everything about David felt intimate – the way he looked at me, his words, his touch. It wasn't realistic to expect that my feelings would have changed in only three months. What unsettled me was that they were as strong as ever.

Seeing David was a full-body experience. I felt heavy and light at the same time. *He gives me butterflies, but they aren't butterflies. They're bigger and darker and scarier, like crows. They're dangerous. And did Bill ever give me butterflies?*

My relationship with Bill had started slow. When we would meet downstairs in the middle of the workday, I would feel happy, anticipatory. I liked his company as well as our conversations. *Butterflies . . . . Were they there? Did I have them? Does it matter if I did? Since when do butterflies determine anything?*

I wondered if David gave Dani butterflies or worse . . . did *she* excite *him*? Had he been hoping to see her in the kitchen rather than me? My mind clouded. Did he, would he, touch her like he had touched me? I pictured how he would undress her, stroke her skin, run his hands through her long hair. My teeth gritted as I saw her in his apartment, sitting on the couch where I had. In his bedroom as I had been. Wrapped up in his sheets. Tangled in his – *Oh, God. It's too much.* I shuddered and shrank in my seat.

Maybe one day they would have their own wedding and their own honeymoon in Paris. Someone else would give a toast about finding 'the one,' and it wouldn't include me. David was my mistake and if they ended up together, I would be his. I would be the blemish. The wife's friend. The cheater.

CHAPTER 8

TAP, TAP, TAP. I stared down at the red pen jittering between my fingers and then at the clock: 11:20 a.m. *Tap, tap, tap, tap, tap.* I stilled and looked blankly at the list of article topics in front of me. I was across the office to grab my jacket in one motion.

"Early lunch?" Jenny asked as I whizzed by her desk.

"Yep."

I focused on the clicking of my heels against the pavement as I walked. Summer was ending, but it was warm and the sky was a clear blue. With each step toward my destination, I was a little lighter. Since the car ride home from Winnetka the day before, my mind had been in overdrive, and I needed . . . something. I didn't know what exactly, or even what I wanted, but I thought I knew where to find it.

A fifteen-minute walk; a lifetime hanging in the balance. A choice. I stopped in front of the sleek, modern doors of Pierson/Greer. Just inside was the one who haunted my thoughts, the one I couldn't forget. I reached out for the gilded handle and paused. After a moment, my hand fell to my side again. I backed away from the entrance and pinched the bridge of my nose. *Don't do this, Olivia. Let it lie. Let it be. Don't do this . . . .* I turned to pace the sidewalk. What did I want from David? What answers could he provide? I needed to know why this was happening. Why I was beginning to feel more and more like I was being torn in half.

I stopped my tread finally and sighed up at the tall building. With sagging shoulders, I turned around and idled back the way I'd come.

At the first convenience store, I ducked inside. I was craving comfort food in a way I hadn't been lately. I headed straight for the freezer, promising myself that things would get easier. I slid open the door and selected an ice cream sandwich, knowing I just had to stay strong. I walked to the cashier, determined not to break down in the middle of a convenience store. With one hand cradling my purchase, I used the other to fish out a couple dollar bills from my wallet.

"Hey, go easy on that ice cream, honeybee." My heart leaped, and I turned to see David filling the doorway. He tilted his head and smiled at me. "What are you doing here?" he asked. "Shouldn't you be over on Adams, making some Bachelors miserable?"

I just stared, blinking as sunlight illuminated him from behind.

His eyebrows folded. "Are you all right? You look like you've seen a ghost."

"No," I replied as his cologne slowly wafted into my orbit. "I mean yes, I'm fine. You startled me."

"Well, I do work right down the street."

"I know . . . ."

"Of course you do. Is that your lunch?"

I followed his curious gaze to my hands. "Um. No, I – I . . . ," I stammered. I fumbled to set it on the counter. I shouldn't be there. To run into him was one thing, but I had sought him out. Grasping the strap of my purse, I hurried to the doorway, where he swiveled to let me through.

"I never got to tell you how much I enjoyed the issue."

My head shot up, but I continued my stride. "What?"

"The *Most Eligible* issue," David said. "The feature had a fresh, creative touch. You deserve that promotion."

"Oh." I slowed fractionally to sync with his relaxed gait.

"Thanks."

He handed me the ice cream sandwich. "Here."

"Did you steal this?" I asked with widened eyes.

He laughed loudly. "No, of course not. I bought it for you."

After a slight hesitation, I accepted it and started to peel away the wrapper.

"What did you think of my part?"

"Hmm?" I asked as I took a bite.

"The article. What did you think?"

I swallowed and feigned interest in the sidewalk. "Your pictures caused quite the commotion."

"What did *you* think though?"

"I thought . . ." I paused, exhaling loudly. "I thought you looked very handsome. Lisa did a nice job."

"And the interview?"

I squinted ahead and took another bite of the softening ice cream. A young guy dropped his skateboard on the ground and zoomed by us. "I didn't read it."

We stopped at a corner and waited for the light to change. I looked up at him as vanilla dripped down my fingers. I tried to convey with my eyes what I couldn't with my words. That I hadn't read it because it was too painful. That since the day I'd left, I could never forget the hurt in his eyes. Even in my heels, my head was almost vertical when I said, "I'm sorry."

He sighed and nodded his head toward the green light. "This might be one of our last warm days," he commented once we were walking again.

I wanted to laugh. The things left unsaid were almost palpable between us. But it was better that way; so instead, we would talk about the weather. "That's fine by me," I said. "I love Chicago in autumn."

"Me too," he said with a smile. "What's your favorite thing about it?"

"Probably the way there's something electric in the air just as it starts to cool down. Also, that I get to wear boots again."

He laughed and rolled his eyes toward the sky. "Typical."

"What about you?" I asked.

"I take my sister's kid to pick apples a couple hours away. That's my favorite thing. That and the weekend mornings when you wake up and your bed is so warm and you have nowhere to be . . . ."

My face fell as the fantasy of waking up in his arms, pressed against his hot, hard body flashed through my mind. So much for a safe topic.

When I glanced up, he wore a roguish smile. "And who doesn't love the foliage?" he asked.

"Of course," I agreed immediately. "The foliage is just beautiful in the fall."

His shoulders shook with a silent laugh, and I looked away quickly.

"When my sister and I were kids," he continued, "one of our chores was to rake leaves. She hated it, but I didn't mind. It gave me a sense of order. It agitated me when they were strewn all over the lawn."

I pictured David as a young man, his posture straight and his movements concentrated as he worked.

"I guess you didn't really have that problem in Dallas."

I shook my head. "Not at my house, no."

"Did you like growing up there?"

"It was all right." I shrugged and took the last bite before sucking chocolate cookie off my fingers.

"How's that ice cream, Olivia?"

I tried not to squirm at the way he said my name. "Delicious."

"I like watching you eat it."

I arched an eyebrow at him.

"I mean because you look like you're enjoying it."

I nodded and licked my lips.

"I would buy you an ice cream every day just to watch you eat it."

I captured a deep breath. His low and manly voice made enjoying my ice cream sandwich sound sinful. And then I imagined dripping vanilla ice cream onto his abs and cleaning it off with a long, drawn out lick.

"Besides, you could use the nourishment."

I jolted back to reality. "What do you mean by that?"

"You're too skinny."

"Oh, David," I said, rolling my eyes. "Would you drop it?"

His voice deepened into a chastisement. "I meant what I said about your health. I don't know why you're not eating, but it stops now."

"Of course I eat," I replied cheerily. "If I didn't, I'd be dead."

His eyebrows met in the middle as he studied me, seemingly not amused. "What does he say about this? And your friends?"

"They know that I'm an adult with the ability to gauge my level of hunger." I crossed one arm over my stomach, and our steps slowed to a stop as we approached my office.

He turned so we were facing. "I overheard Gretchen say at breakfast yesterday that you're depressed."

I blinked up and pressed my lips together. I imagined punching Gretchen in the arm. "I suppose maybe they think so."

"Why?"

"Why do they think that, or why am I depressed?"

"Are you depressed?"

I wrapped my arm tighter and refrained from pinching myself. "They think I am because of . . . Davena. She's the woman who – "

"I know who she is. You didn't seem very pleased with Lucy's toast."

"It was silly of me. Melodramatic." I balled up the wrapper and ran the back of my hand over my mouth.

He leaned closer. "It's been hard, hasn't it?"

I took a step back and wondered why my heart was suddenly pounding.

"These past few months," he continued, "I've been worried about you."

"I have to get back to work."

"Olivia – "

"Thanks for the ice cream." I spun around before he could say anything else and booked it up to the fourteenth floor.

~

With a soft sigh, I flipped some hair over my shoulder. The computer screen blazed bright, but the entire floor was dark. I could almost feel myself burning out from another long day.

With a deadline in the morning, I couldn't leave until I'd hammered out the last few paragraphs in front of me. But it had been impossible to concentrate all day. Butterflies were perched in my chest, threatening to explode into a million fluttering wings if I let my mind wander. It was the reason I was the only person left in the office: I couldn't stop daydreaming.

How was it that Bill left the apartment in a suit every day, yet I barely noticed? David, in all his charcoal pinstripe glory, was far more distinguished than the rest of us plebeians who walked the planet. He was perfection in a suit. And somehow, I had his attention. His heavy brows joined when he watched words fall from my mouth, as though he might have to reach out and catch one.

Our short walk was a like a bookmark in the dark chapter I'd been living; a moment to come up for air when I'd been stuck just beneath the surface. It was like a dream that had never happened, except that it had.

I bit the inside of my cheek and leaned over to the bottom drawer of my desk. I rifled through it until I saw the issue of *Chicago M.* With a short breath, I opened it and flipped through the pages until I found what I was looking for.

Chicago Metropolitan Magazine
Most Eligible Bachelor #3:

David Dylan
Senior Architect, Pierson/Greer

Age: 34
Lives in: River North

David Dylan is the epitome of cool. From his made-for-Hollywood name to his devilish good looks, he holds more clout than a varsity quarterback dating the homecoming queen. To complete the package, he comes from a perfect family of four, owns a sailboat and has a vacation home in Spain. This highly sought-after architect, who was recently profiled for *Architectural Digest*, spends what little free time he has in the water – no small feat for an Illinois native. From surfing to swimming to sailing, it's no wonder his friends nicknamed him Fish years ago.

Looking for: Someone to settle down with. His well-known father's greatest accomplishment, he says, is marrying the woman he fell in love with almost forty years ago. Oh, and big, green eyes. "Eyes truly are the windows to a woman's soul," says Dylan. "Business has taught me to be tough, but when 'the one' bats her eyelashes at me just the right way, I will be putty in her hands."

Topic of interest: The Revelin Resort – he is the lead designer on the hotel that is set to open at the end of this year.

Oh, he is good. I wondered how Chicago-ettes would recover after reading that. After some consideration, I decided that my pity was for the male population. They'd have a hard time stacking up to someone like David Dylan. David Dylan and his affinity for big, green eyes. At the time of publication, he hadn't yet met Dani. I knew it was narcissistic, but I couldn't help clinging to the thought that maybe he had added that part for me.

I expelled a wisp of breath and texted Bill that I wouldn't be making it home for dinner. As I refocused on my project, I automatically swiped my finger across the phone's screen when it pinged.

Sep 4, 2012 7:19 PM
Good thing for the ice cream then.

My heart leaped with panic. I scrolled my eyes over the screen to find that I had texted David instead of Bill.

"Shit," I said, slamming the phone down. *That is* so *embarrassing!* I felt myself turning various shades of red. Quickly, I sent the same text to Bill and tapped my way back to David.

Sep 4, 2012 7:22 PM
So sorry. Wrong person!

Sep 4, 2012 7:23 PM
I believe that counts as a Freudian slip.

I was at a loss for words. Now it appeared as though I was actively looking for trouble. He would either think I had done it on purpose, or that I'd been thinking about him when I'd sent it. Which would be the truth.

Sep 4, 2012 7:25 PM
Didn't mean it. Working late & a
little tired.

Sep 4, 2012 7:26 PM
Mrs. Germaine, it's not advisable to
alert predators of your whereabouts
late at night.

My heart stilled as I melted into a puddle of desire. A memory of a dream wedged itself into my thoughts. I'd had it shortly after David and I had stopped contact, only once, but I hadn't forgotten it. We would meet accidentally in the same alley where Mark Alvarez had attacked me.

When my phone chimed again, I was already panting.

Sep 4, 2012 7:29 PM
That is, unless you're looking to get
caught.

I slid a tentative hand under my dress and into my damp panties. I relaxed back in my chair and remembered the dream, filling in the details where necessary.

I peer down the dark alleyway and am struck with fear when I see the silhouette of a big man. As he approaches, slow and cat-like, I turn to run the way I came but am met with a brick wall. He's bearing down on me now, filling the small alley so I can't escape. He looks incredibly strong.

It's David, I realize, but my sigh of relief catches in my throat. I'm afraid of him. He slowly reaches out and snaps me to him by my waist, like plucking a flower from the ground.

His lips are on mine, hard and unrelenting, and he won't budge when I push him.

73

"Don't fight," he says when we've parted.

He scares me, but I obey. I let him move my arms like a puppet master and fix them above my head so I am helpless in his grip.

"Say it," he prompts, as he shifts both wrists into one hand.

I fret because I don't know what he wants me to say. When I look down again, I'm naked. With his free hand, he unzips his pants and pulls them down.

I panic and look over the exquisite face that is now hard and unrecognizable, a David I don't know. Even his brown eyes are obsidian black to match his hair.

"Say it."

"I don't know," I reply, chewing the inside of my cheek.

He pulls my leg around him and positions himself against me. When he plunges into me, I cry his name, a word that is a mixture of fear and pleasure leaving my tongue.

He pins me against the wall over and over, and I am lost. I whip my eyes open. "I know what you want me to say!"

But he doesn't stop, and suddenly I have forgotten it again, but I don't care because I am falling . . . and coming . . . and coming . . . .

I came to, winded and slumped in my chair. I pulled my hand out from between my legs and glanced around the dark office shamefully. I'd written the dream off as anxiety following Alvarez's attack, but I had often wished it would return.

Say it. The words frequently ran through my mind. They were his last words to me the morning I had left. *Tell me you can forget,* he had demanded. *Say it, Olivia! Say it say it say it . . . .*

An alert told me Bill had responded.

74

Sep 4, 2012 7:36 PM
K. Jury prob out for a few days,
going to OP house tmrw if you want
to come.

Sep 4, 2012 7:44 PM
Why?

Sep 4, 2012 7:46 PM
Meeting David there. I can pick you
up.

I closed my eyes for a long moment as the information permeated my still fuzzy brain. Bill and David, alone together? I wanted to scream. I wanted to blame David, but it wasn't his fault, so I blamed Bill, but it also wasn't his fault. I was only left with myself. With unsteady fingers, I told Bill I would come along. What choice did I have? I couldn't forbid it, and I couldn't not be there. The two of them alone, talking, laughing, sharing. The thought of not being able to monitor their conversation made me want to pull my hair out.

I groaned to myself and put the phone away, ignoring David's last text.

CHAPTER 9

FIDGETING WITH THE COLLAR of my purple silk blouse, I craned my neck to watch for Bill's car. According to Bill, we had to see the house before David left for New York in the evening, so I was taking a break from work to be there. I didn't know what else to expect; whether David even knew I was coming or how long this hell would last.

Bill pulled up and screeched to a halt at the curb.

"We're late," I commented. "Are we picking David up?"

"He's meeting us there."

I worked my lower lip between my teeth in anxiety and excitement. Just a week prior, I knew I'd never see David again. And now this. I half-rolled my eyes out to the window.

"Look, whatever happens will be for the best."

"What?" I asked.

"With the house. If it's too far gone, we'll find something else. I don't want you to get your hopes up."

"I'm not worried," I said, looking back out the window. At least, it didn't make it into the top three of my current concerns.

When we pulled up, David was talking intently with an older, portly man. David gestured to the house, and when the man spoke, he listened attentively, his arms crossed and his thick eyebrows knit in concentration. His back was straight as a board and his shoulders taut. The small glimpses I'd seen of David in architect mode were especially disarming – there was something arousing about watching him do what he loved.

He looked up then and gaited toward us with calm confidence. I couldn't tell if he'd expected me because he was almost too collected. While I was near senseless with anxiety, his wide smile and sturdy handshake were signs that he was a schmoozer, a player, a charmer to the core.

"This place is a find," he said, sticking his hands in his pockets.

"I know it's not like the other houses," I said, "but that's why I like it."

"It certainly isn't, thank God for that," he replied, looking down the street.

Bill grumbled under his breath as he stole a look at the house behind us. "You must be the appraiser," he said to the other man, extending his hand.

"I've already been around the neighborhood and the outside of the house," the man said. "If you have the keys, I'll just take a look inside."

They took off for the front door, leaving David and I behind. I glanced up at him from the corner of my eye and gave him a half-smile, to which he responded with a friendly wink.

"What do you really think?" I asked.

"This is a prairie-style home, you can tell by the horizontal lines and overhanging eaves. They're reflective of a sweeping prairie," he explained, gliding his hand through the air to demonstrate. "It's a fairly popular style in Oak Park because of Frank Lloyd Wright's influence – he designed several homes around here. You're right that it seems out of place on this street, but it's not for the area. I meant what I said – it's a find."

I followed him through the door into the front room, where his eyes went to the ceiling and worked their way down. "Open floor plan," he observed. "My personal favorite. You could really do something unique with the interior."

My mouth warped skeptically. "I don't think Bill would like that. He's pretty traditional."

"This isn't a traditional home, Olivia. It would be an injustice to turn it into one."

I flushed. He said it with such conviction, I felt as if I'd insulted him. "Um," I said. "It seems like a lot of work."

"Right off the bat, yes, you're looking at a long renovation period. Maybe up to a year, depending on what you want to do." I followed his gaze down. "These floorboards have to go," he continued, "but the hearth is big and central – I wouldn't even touch it." He walked toward the wall of windows and peered into the backyard. "Bonus for great lighting. Wright loved nature. This house reflects that. The landscaping needs work, but once it's scaled back, it could take on a woodsy, earthen feel. Romantic, in a way. I'd run with that, maybe incorporate water somehow – a pond or fountain. Reminds me of my place in New York a little bit."

It was maybe the most I'd ever heard him talk, and I was hanging on his every word. He was even more devastating when he was passionate, and I fell in love with the house as he spoke.

Bill returned then, and it took a great deal of effort to peel my eyes from David. When I decided that their conversation was benign enough, I left the three men and headed upstairs to explore further. As I walked between rooms, I was overwhelmed by the amount of necessary work. I couldn't help but feel selfish for expecting Bill to go through with it. He'd just seemed so pleased with the idea, and now, I didn't want to give it up . . . .

"Hey," Bill said from the doorway. I turned around to find him panting. "The fucking jury is already back. I have to run, like five minutes ago."

"Oh," I said. "All right, let's go."

"Actually can you stay with these guys?"

"No, Bill, please, I have to get back to work."

"Just a few minutes longer. I talked to the appraiser already, and David has an estimate, but they haven't hit the second floor yet. I wouldn't feel right leaving the two of them alone since David is doing us a favor."

"He has an estimate? How much?"

He cleared his throat. "A lot. But not impossible. It helps that they're willing to work with us on the sale price. David says he works by you and can drop you after."

"What if he has plans or something?"

"Liv, I can't," he said, disappearing back into the hall. "Gotta go."

I twisted my hands nervously. Footsteps ascended, and David's voice resounded throughout the second floor. The voices drifted to the master bedroom and then back down the hall. I was still stuck to the same spot in one of the spare rooms when they entered.

"David, I'm so sorry," I blurted. "You're already doing us this big favor, and now you have to give me a ride."

"It's no problem. I insisted," he said before turning back to the appraiser, who was making notes.

He looked up and waved his clipboard at me. "Mrs. Wilson, would you like to have a seat and go over this?"

"Um, I'm not really – can you just talk to my husband?"

"Already did. There are just a few more things I'd like to cover, but I'll e-mail him."

"Can you CC me?" David asked, handing him a card. "Since I promised to help."

"Sure. I'll be in touch." He looked between the two of us before turning away.

I crossed my arms over my breasts, and David stuck his hands in his pockets. "The issues aren't just surface deep, but it's not the worst I've seen. The owners are giving you an extremely fair price. It's a steal. Honestly, they probably don't realize the value." He paused and cleared his throat. "But most importantly, it's obvious that you love it."

"I do. I think I really do."

"Follow me."

My heels clunked on the wooden steps as we descended. Back on the ground floor, he removed his jacket and set it on the covered couch. He rolled up his sleeves and crouched down to pull on a floorboard. My eyes followed as he walked over to a doorway and inspected it. He was talking as he moved, but I only heard the bass of his voice, felt the vibration of it inside me.

I realized in that moment that I never should have gone to the house. That I'd never be able to erase the image of him there.

The home I couldn't grasp before began to form in my mind. The room was sylvan, rustic; it smelled of cedar, like David. It glowed with a blazing fire on a cool autumn evening. Abundant, leafy maple trees just out back rainbowed from green to yellow to red. David was there, lifting me off my feet in a consuming hug after walking through the front door.

I squeezed my eyes shut and pressed the heels of my hands into my sockets. Pieces of the puzzle began to fall into place. Bill and I had seen almost ten places since we'd started looking and not one had been right. I pictured Bill at the apartment on our rundown couch, yelling at the TV. I pictured him in the late morning, goofing off as he fixed me breakfast. I'd never felt at home in the apartment, because I knew we'd eventually move somewhere permanent.

Davena's words from our last moments together floated back to me. *'It's about whom you're making a home with.'*

It wasn't that the places we'd seen hadn't felt like home. It was that Bill didn't feel like home.

"Come here," David said, ripping me from my heartbreaking realization. I obeyed with my eyes glued to him. "You could put built-in seating there under that window and a breakfast nook on the other side. And look." He pointed into the next room and said something. I leaned over to peer through the doorway, but I had no idea what I was looking for because my mind was whirring. Bill was so far, and David was so close. So close that if I angled slightly, I would whiff that earthy, subtle David-ness . . . .

"Did you just smell me?"

"What?" I blinked and shook my head. "No."

"Yes, you did," he said, a smile creeping onto his face.

I rolled my eyes. "I did not. I was just trying to get a better look."

"Don't lie to me."

"Well I'm very close to you, and – okay, you *do* smell nice, so it *is* possible that I sniffed you, I just . . ."

The look on his face stopped me. "You never answered my question."

"I just admitted – "

"Not that one." He paused. "Are you depressed, Olivia?"

I blinked in shock as I sought a response.

"Just answer, don't – "

"Do you ever think about that night?" The words tumbled out of my mouth before I knew what I was saying.

"Do you?" he asked.

"No. I don't let myself."

"Because of what you did?"

"No." I glanced down, ashamed.

"Do you regret it?"

"I hate myself for what I've done," I said slowly. "I think about how it would hurt Bill if he found out. It would wreck him. The guilt is almost unbearable." His expression turned something tortured before he looked at the floor. "But . . ."

He blinked up at me again, pinning me with intense eyes.

"But what I hate more," I continued, "is that I don't regret it. I don't think about that night because I'm terrified that nothing will ever come close to it again."

He inhaled sharply and locked his arms across his torso.

"That sounds crazy," I said, shaking my head and looking away. "I guess for you it was just – "

"I think about that night all the time."

My gaze jumped back to his. We stared at each other, the space between us vibrating. My hands began to tremble with the agony of months of wanting to touch him. Slowly, he unfolded his arms. His hands hovered in the air awkwardly before scooping under my hair to grasp my face. He ran his thumbs over my jawline, and when I didn't move away, he leaned in and pressed his lips to mine. We sat that way for a long time, both breathing heavily until he puckered his lips gently.

When he pulled back, it was to rest his forehead on mine. "I've been dreaming about that for fifteen weeks," he said quietly.

I laughed in a gust of breath. I felt his cheeks with my hands, relishing the rough, bristly spots. I ran my fingers through his obsidian hair, which felt even silkier than I remembered. I traced his lips reverently with my fingertip. "Why can't I forget you?" I whispered.

He leaned in and pecked me on the lips twice before nuzzling his nose into my neck. "The way you smell," he said into my hair. "It's irreplaceable."

I hugged him, feeling the muscles of his back through his shirt. He brushed his mouth down my cheek until reaching my lips. They parted for him, and he kissed me with careful movements, allowing me to appreciate every slide of his tongue and tremor of his lips. He tasted fresh but warm; he tasted like home.

As we kissed, he molded my arms around his neck to pick me up by my waist so we were level. I felt safe in his arms again, hidden from the outside world in our own private one. He untucked the back of my blouse and slid a hand underneath. It was a simple act, his hand skating over my back, but it was comforting. And then it was sensual, dizzying.

Without disconnecting our mouths, he set me on my feet and unzipped my skirt so it fell to the ground.

I pulled his shirt from his pants and undid the buttons with tremulous hands. I slid it over his shoulders. His pecs were hard and coarse under my palms, and I kissed them, breathing in the fresh, woodsy smell that had been muted by his shirt.

He undid my top button deftly. After each button, he glanced up and looked me squarely in the eyes. His hands glided under the fabric to hold my waist. We were looking into each other's eyes, my body securely in his grip as if it were made to be there.

He pulled me to his bare torso and wrapped me in strong arms. A hand over my hair pressed my cheek to his chest. Between his heartbeat and mine, I heard nothing else.

My desire grew, and my skin burned with the need to meld with him. I remembered how he had felt inside of me, driving me to the edge with the entirety of his focus. When I was sure I couldn't stand another minute, he let go.

Confusion cut through my euphoric haze. "What are you doing?"

He stepped back suddenly and pinched the bridge of his nose. "I don't know," he said up to the ceiling. "I wanted this . . . ."

I stood staring at him, wavering with my skirt pooled at my feet. The blood drained from my face. "Wanted?"

"It's so wrong. But I can't stop thinking about you, about that night."

"I *want* this," I whispered.

His face was still pointed upward, appealing to a higher power, maybe, I wasn't sure. Avoiding my gaze, he stepped forward again. He tugged the bottom of my blouse and fingered the last button for a long second before closing it. We both watched as his hands re-dressed me.

He crouched down and picked up the skirt. Methodically, he tucked in my blouse, smoothing his hand over my stomach, and reached around to zip me up. I just stood there as his smell taunted me, tempting memories on the verge. His fingers combed through my hair. They went to touch my lips, but he leaned in to kiss me desperately instead. I was still shocked into immobility, but my body responded on its own. My arms wrapped around his neck, and my mouth gave into him. I did not wonder why he stopped. I did not wonder why *I* couldn't stop. I blocked the thoughts from my brain and melted into his hands in my hair, his breath with mine, a kiss that was a different kind of passionate than I'd ever experienced.

But we broke apart when he tore his lips from mine. I fixated on a button rising and falling with his chest, trying to catch my own breath. My arms slithered down from his neck, and he caught my wrists. "I can't do this because I care, not because I don't. I can't do this again, and I don't think you can either."

He was wrong. I could do it. The realization came with a painful constriction of my heart. He had me so wound up in him that I saw nothing else. But his words made sense, so I nodded.

He dropped my wrists and backed away. I watched, transfixed, as he re-buttoned his own shirt and shrugged on his suit jacket. Watching him dress himself in clothing I couldn't touch – a chest, a face, hands that I couldn't feel – put my entire body on edge. I had almost been allowed to show him how much I had missed him, but it had been dashed away, disintegrating under my fingers.

My phone chiming from my purse relieved me of my torture. But relief quickly drained away, and my jaw fell as I read Bill's text message.

Sep 5, 2012 1:58 PM

Called Jeanine. Gave her our offer!
Champagne tonight, babe.

David was leaving the room when I finally looked up from the screen. I'd just thrown myself at another man. And worse, I'd realized only minutes before that Bill's and my problems might be deeper than I thought. And now –

David stopped short in the doorway, and I halted just short of colliding with him. "Jesus," he said, peering at his phone. "The appraiser already e-mailed."

"I know." He looked up, and his head cocked. Before he could ask how, I said, "Bill just made an offer."

His expression morphed. The grandfather clock chimed twice. It was as if every thought that passed through his mind were trying to break free, but his mouth remained set in a rigid line.

"David?" I asked as he stared down at me. "Are you all right?"

He cleared his throat and fixed his gaze over my head. "Yes. Yes, I'm fine."

He gripped the knob of the front door and hesitated a moment. I waited for him to speak, my eyes darting between his face and the handle. Instead, he turned it and stepped out onto the broken walkway. I followed him to a sleek, silver Mercedes-Benz.

I ran my hands over my suddenly cold arms, wishing for a sweater to curl into at that moment. With automatic movements, he opened the passenger door to let me in. I tried not to look over at him as we left the house behind, but after a few moments of silence had passed, I couldn't help myself. He looked back at me and smiled.

"Are you sure you're all right?" I asked.

"Yes."

I looked around the unfamiliar car. "Are you mad about what just happened?" I asked the dashboard.

He reached over confidently to squeeze my bare knee. "No."

I covered his hand with mine. There was nothing and everything to say. We were quiet the rest of the way home.

Our hands remained on my leg during the drive. I studied both of them, the way his long fingers and massive palm took up the whole lower half of my thigh. The gesture was meant to be comforting. But to me it was erotic. When he adjusted his grip, I silently willed his hand to slide up my skirt. But it didn't, and when I smoothed a fingertip over his knuckles, he flipped his palm up and took my hand.

There were no appropriate words: good-bye, see you soon, see you never – none of it felt right. So when he pulled up to the curb, I let go of his hand and climbed out.

"Olivia."

I leaned back into the car. His jaw was set, his eyes fixed on me. Then he said, "There are other options."

As I stared at him, blood drained from my face. I shut the door vowing to forget what he'd said but knowing it was now seared into my mind.

~

As soon as the front door shut behind me, Bill was in the kitchen.

"How was your day? Get back to the office all right?"

"Yes."

"How'd you like driving in the architect's car? It's a V12. I noticed it on my way out. Your dad would love it."

I looked up at him and set my purse on the counter. "Sure."

"He seemed impressed with the house. Did he say anything to you?"

"Honey, I just walked in the door," I said, untying the belt of my jacket. I removed it slowly and hung it up as Bill waited. "What happened with the jury?" I braced myself against the counter to slide off my shoes.

His smile was victorious. "We won."

"Oh, Bill. That's great news."

"I was worried that they came to a verdict so quickly, but it turned out in our favor. So aren't you going to say anything about the house?"

I sighed. "Yes, actually."

"I'm excited, babe. I know I was skeptical because of the amount of work it will take, but I'm on board now. I'm just so ready to get started with our life already."

"Yes, but you should have consulted me first."

"Consulted? Why would I? You're not my business partner, you're my wife."

"You know what I mean. We could've sat down and – "

"Whoa. What are you saying?" he asked defensively. "You told me you wanted this."

"I do, I just – you made the offer without discussing it with me. This is my home, my money too."

"Well, technically, babe, my money is going toward the down payment."

I drew back and crossed my arms. "So I don't get a say?"

"Of course you do, but we already discussed it," he said. "You said yes. Once I got the information I needed from the guys, I knew we were good to go."

"I know you're excited, I am too. But would it have killed you to wait one night so we could go over this together?"

"And give you another opportunity to back out? No way, babe. This is happening. It's done."

"I'm not going to back out. When you make decisions without me though, it makes me feel like you don't respect my opinion."

"I believe your opinion was 'yes, Bill, I want the house. Buy me this house.' I *believe* it took a good eight or nine houses for you to decide that."

I pursed my lips. "I *do* want the house."

"So what's the problem?"

The problem? I repeated to myself. *The problem is that I almost had sex with someone else this afternoon. The problem is that I'm not sure of anything anymore. The problem is that I don't know how to make a home with you!*

I shook the vicious thoughts from my head. How could I think that about this man who'd been nothing but good to me since the day we'd met? Of course I knew how to make a home with him. It would happen day by day – one thing at a time – we would build and build and build –

"I don't know," he said with exasperation, running his hand over his face. "I can't keep up with your back and forth. But it's too late anyway. You'll just have to trust that I'm making the right decision for both of us. The offer is made, and when they accept, that's it."

I nodded and took a deep breath. "Yes," I agreed. "Yes, that sounds right and good and . . . Yes."

"I have work to do. There's champagne in the fridge, you can help yourself."

"Bill," I sighed, but he disappeared. I leaned over the kitchen counter and put my head in my hands. Wasn't it enough that I had betrayed him? Been vile to him for months? Was I now *trying* to make him unhappy? I straightened my shoulders. I would have to try harder, or I was going to drive an even bigger wedge between us. This was important to him, and it was something that would change our lives for the better.

I found him at his desk, hunched over a stack of papers. My hand rested on his shoulder. "I'm sorry," I said when he looked up. "I am really excited about the offer. I know this means a lot to you, and it does to me too."

"This is the right decision. We have to move forward. I can't stay in this place any longer."

I nodded. *Move forward. Leave this place behind. Whatever is holding me back, I have to give it up.*

"Just think. We will finally have a home of our own. Who knows? We might have this house forever. We'll grow old together there. Down the line, we'll raise our children there – at that point, hopefully I'll be partner at the firm, and I'll be around more. I'll come home, you'll be cooking with the kids or getting them ready for basketball practice. We'll have family dinners, a Christmas tree by the fire, birthday parties in the backyard . . . . One day, we'll pass the house down to our children, and them to their children. It's the beginning of our future."

I took a small step backward, thrown by the idyllic smile on his face. He was so confident in what he was saying, as though he'd already glimpsed into the future. As if, in his mind, it were the past, it had already happened. He'd seen me there, baking pies in a ruffle-trimmed, red and white apron. In his fantasy, I wanted those things too.

But didn't I? I wanted a place to call home, somewhere that was mine, where I felt safe enough to let go of the past. To stop worrying about how things could disappear or break or end without warning. What he had described sounded like a place to be where I was. In the present. It sounded like a home – a warm, loving home with a steadfast husband and not only a child, but children. *Plural.*

"All right," he said, and I lifted my eyes back to his. He made a show of getting out of his chair. "One glass of champagne to celebrate, but then I really do need to get back to work."

~

After Bill had gone to bed, I stayed up at the kitchen table, staring into the abyss. I envisioned over and over again the life he had described. Someone else's life. Dread surfaced in the

form of chills over my skin. I had promised those things to
Bill in front of everyone we loved years ago. I never knew if I
wanted them, but I had promised them forever with two
words: *I do.*

What scared me most was that I might give him those
things because I was supposed to. And had David never come
along, I might not have questioned the path I was on.

Because now, something else was developing inside of
me. Maybe there was another way to love. A selfless, open
way, where you took the good with the bad and the ugly with
the beautiful. A way where, in order to experience bliss, you
had to risk pain – you had to risk everything.

I can't think of this now, I decided. *Tomorrow, with fresh
eyes, things will be better.* I rose from the table and went to
bed.

~

As Bill and I waited for our realtor's call, things became
increasingly stressful. The harder I tried to forget David in that
house, the clearer I saw him. Each night after Bill had fallen
asleep, I found myself somewhere in the house, staring
straight ahead.

In our bathroom, I had sat against the tub, tormenting
myself with the meaningless details of my new life. Like what
time I would wake up to catch the train to work. And was
there a coffee shop on the way? Would being a mom mean
that I'd have to cut my hair shorter? I wondered how to
change a diaper, what types of friends I would have in the
suburbs, whether or not there was an animal shelter nearby.

A different night, on the couch with the TV muted, I
worried about the bigger things. I wondered if Bill expected
me to quit my job, and how had we never discussed that? Or
how often Gretchen and Lucy would make the trip to see us,
or at what point we should start saving for a college fund . . .

or this, or that.

And David. David. *David.* There was no night to think of him, because he was always there, telling me there were other options when I just didn't want to admit that there could be.

CHAPTER 10

HE WAS A BLUE-EYED, blond-haired prince in the lobby of *Chicago Metropolitan Magazine*. A mischievous smile kinked one corner of his mouth, complementing the gleam in his eye. My mouth, on the other hand, hung open as I blinked in disbelief.

"Olivia Germaine," he crooned.

I shook my head as a smile forced its way onto my face. "Greg?"

"The one and only."

Before me stood Greg Theo, my ex-best friend and legendary breaker of Gretchen's heart. I took a tentative step forward, and his arms opened for me. My mouth was still agape when we hugged. "What are you doing here?" I asked.

He pulled me back by my shoulders and held me at arm's length. "It's so good to see you. You look fantastic, even better than I remember. A little thin, but – "

"Greg."

He slid his hands down my biceps. His eyes, though equally as captivating, were not the same blue as Gretchen's. They were carefree pools, colored like the sky. "A position with my company opened up in Chicago, and I jumped at the chance. I got here a few months ago."

"Shit," I muttered, rubbing my forehead. "Gretchen is going to flip."

"She already knows."

"What?" I screeched, and he stepped back. "She knows? She hasn't said anything to me."

He nodded once. "She doesn't know I came to see you."

"What do you mean?"

"We've started things up again – "

I sucked in a sharp breath and grimaced. "Oh my God."

"I missed you guys like crazy, Liv. Gretchen – I was stupid to give her up. I want to make things right. I came to Chicago for her."

I shook my head rapidly. "Why didn't she tell me?"

"She doesn't think we're ready. But I just couldn't wait to see you and Lucy."

"A few months, you said?"

"Yes."

"Well that explains why she was dateless to Lucy's wedding."

He nodded. "We fought over that. I wanted to be there, but she refused. She's worried I won't stick around."

"Oh, Greg," I said, steepling my hands over my mouth. "Please be careful. If you hurt her again . . ."

"Was it bad?"

"Awful. I don't think she could take it."

"I can tell. She's different – harder or something. But I'm not going anywhere this time. I still love her."

"You do?" I asked, dropping a palm to my heart.

"I do. And you guys, too." He reached out and touched my cheek. "I'm sorry I left. I shouldn't have. Remember late nights in the dining hall, goofing off when we were supposed to be studying for Bio? Or when Gretch would visit, and we'd all go out? One of us would inevitably get busted with a fake ID." He smiled. "I miss that."

"I missed you too, but Greg?"

He dropped his arm. "Yeah."

"What makes this time different?"

"I realize now what we had. Not just me and Gretchen, but all of us. Friendship, love. It's important. I gave it all up for my career."

"For your career?"

"Yes, Liv. For the job in Japan."

"Is that really why? I always thought you left for other reasons. Because you were scared."

"No. I went for work. I knew it would hurt her, so I didn't say anything until it was confirmed."

"But now you realize that that was the wrong way to go about it."

He flashed me a smile. "Of course. I should have been upfront."

"Well, you know I can't lie to her about seeing you."

"I know. It's okay."

"So, what are you doing? Where are you working?"

"An accounting firm over on Monroe. I'm close enough that we can have lunch together."

"I'd like that."

"We should take a trip up to Notre Dame this weekend, visit a few of our old haunts."

I gave him a sympathetic smile. "I can't, Greg."

"Right," he said, nodding. "How's married life? I got your e-mail. Sorry I couldn't make the wedding."

"Don't worry about it. I just wanted to reach out."

"Bill, right?"

"Yep. I'm excited for you to meet him."

"Gretchen's got this big work party coming up, we could all go."

"That sounds fun," I said.

"I'll let you get back to work then."

"It's so great to see you," I whispered as we embraced again.

He handed me his card. "Anytime you want to grab lunch, dinner, drinks, whatever. Just let me know."

I clasped it between my palms. "I will."

With a kiss on the cheek, he was gone. Immediately, I ran back to my office to text Gretchen.

~

"Without experiencing a Chicago winter, you cannot call yourself a true Chicagoan." I paused and stared at the screen as I thought. "What better way to appreciate our city than to endure a Chicago winter?"

I tore my gaze from the screen when I felt eyes on me.

"You have impressive powers of concentration." David's deep voice resounded through my office, almost as imposing as he himself.

I fluttered my eyelashes, waiting for him to fade away. When he didn't, I asked, "How long have you been standing there?"

He smiled and peeled himself from the doorjamb. "Not long."

I glanced behind him quickly as he crossed the office. "What are you doing here?"

"I just had my follow-up interview."

"Follow-up?"

"For *Most Eligible*."

"I don't know anything about it."

"With Lisa. She e-mailed me some questions, but," he paused, a faint smile forming on his face, "I thought it would be more convenient to stop by."

"I nixed that idea, but I guess they're doing it anyway."

He leaned long arms on my desk and peered at me. "What're you working on?"

"Editing an article. *Fifty Things to do in Chicago This Winter*. Serious stuff."

"There's enough serious stuff out there already," he said.

I meant to reply, but I was distracted. His gaze, probing, seemed to make contact with my skin, pushing, pervading me. My attempt to avoid it was futile as I cleaned my desk off, but I managed not to shiver.

From the corner of my eye, I saw him check his watch.

"Done for the day?"

"I'm meeting Gretchen for dinner."

"Where?"

"Just over the river."

"That's on my way. I'll take you."

"I was going to walk, actually. It's a nice evening."

His eyes narrowed. "By yourself? It'll be dark soon."

"That's all right."

"Not with me, it isn't."

I looked up at his definitive tone and couldn't help the smile on my face. "David, I'm a big girl."

"I'll walk with you," he said, ignoring my declaration. He pushed off the desk and waited with his eyebrows raised expectantly.

I shook my head at him and made my way across the office. "Do you always get what you want?" I asked as I shrugged on my jacket.

"That is yet to be determined."

I rolled my eyes but laughed.

"After you." He motioned me through the door.

"David Dylan, I thought I recognized your voice."

We turned, and David nodded at my boss, Beman, as he scurried to catch up with us.

"Mr. Beman," I started, "I wasn't aware of a follow-up piece on the *Most Eligible* feature."

"It was a good idea, Olivia, and Serena said you turned it down. Tsk, tsk."

"Because I think it's a waste of resources. It's important to keep things fresh."

"*Most Eligible* draws a large reader base. They become connected with the subjects, interested in knowing more about them. In a way," he said, smiling playfully at David, "they're local celebrities."

"That may work for the website, but not the publication."

"I will keep that in mind." David held the glass door

96

open for me. "Are you two off together?" Beman asked with a hint of amusement.

"No," I squeaked quickly.

"I see. Good evening, David. Hope to see you around."

David only raised his eyebrows and followed me out. "That guy is a piece of work. Do you like working for him?" he asked, punching the 'Down' button.

I shrugged. "Not particularly, but a job's a job."

He only frowned.

In the elevator, I picked an invisible piece of lint from my shoulder. Tension mixed with David's distinct air. It was hard to forget the confusing elevator ride from that night. I remembered my internal battle, knowing it was the moment to stop everything. But I hadn't. I hadn't said no, I hadn't said anything. I almost felt guiltier for that moment than all the things that came after.

Now, it frustrated me how relaxed he looked. I wanted to shake him, to ask him what he wanted, why he couldn't just walk away. I wanted to scream at him and kiss him all at once, anything to crack that perfect exterior.

And then the doors slid open, so I did the only logical thing I could and exited the elevator. We crossed the lobby and turned right onto Adams, as though we did that sort of thing every evening.

"Relax, Olivia."

"What?"

"Relax. Your shoulders are at your ears. We're just walking."

I took a deep breath and released an exhale that deflated my shoulders. He was right; my hands were balled into fists, and I felt the stiffness in my neck. "I'm sorry, I'm just . . . stressed."

"I can tell. Why?"

"Just things, stupid things."

"Such as? Work? Home?"

"The house, for one. There's so much to be done, and it just feels like everything is moving so fast." I glanced up at him. "Do you really want to know?"

He nodded once, shoving his hands in his pockets. "I do."

"Buying a home is a commitment. Bill is making such a big thing of it. Of what it symbolizes."

"What does it symbolize?"

"Our future. It's like he's been waiting and waiting for it to start, and now it's finally here. That's a lot of pressure. I feel the opposite – like it snuck up on me. One minute I'm twenty-two and graduating college. Suddenly, I'm almost thirty, and I'm supposed to be this other person. An adult, a wife, a homeowner, a mother."

"Mother?" he blurted.

"One day. Isn't that why people move to the suburbs?"

"Are you . . ." He paused, swallowing. "Are you having second thoughts?"

I folded my arms into myself as we waited to cross the street. To say yes would be admitting the worst thing possible to the worst person possible. "I met Bill right out of college," I said carefully. "I was so young. I mean, I don't know if twenty-five is too young to get married, but maybe it was."

When I looked up, the cool expression David normally wore had slid from his face. "What?" I asked.

His reply was disjointed, as if his throat were constricting. "I meant second thoughts about the house."

"Oh," I breathed in a rush of air, too conscious of the flush creeping up my neck. "No. I was hesitant to move out of the city at first. Maybe I still am. It's not the house, though."

His hand shot out and yanked me back when I stepped off the curb. "Can't you see there's a car coming?" he chastised.

We both looked at his hand on my arm, and he dropped it after a moment. "Continue."

I sighed. "It's boring."

"It's not the house, you said. Then what is it?"

Once I'd made a show of checking for cars, we continued across the street. "I guess I just don't know when everything happened. I don't remember choosing this. I knew it would eventually come to this, me on the brink of my life, about to dive in, but I expected to be more ready."

"You keep saying that you two are starting your future together. There's no *start* to your future. It's already happening. Finding you should have been the start of his future."

"When you say things like that, I can't tell if you're being authentic, or if you're just so used to feeding lines."

He laughed, but his smile slipped from his face quickly. "If I had found you first, there would be no waiting. When I looked into your eyes at that theater – "

"David," I admonished quietly, scanning the faces of passersby. His words hit me forcefully, diffusing as much guilt through me as disbelief. If he finished his sentence . . . If I let myself believe him for even a moment . . . I knew I'd fall quickly and painlessly under his spell. "Don't say those things to me. Save it for your girls."

"You don't have to go through with anything you don't want to," he said over me.

"Yes, I do," I said resolutely. "We've put the offer in. There's no reason they won't accept it. And anyway, I want it. I just said I wasn't quite ready."

"It's just money. Don't let that get in the way. If you're not ready, if you don't want – "

"*I want it*," I snapped.

A tourist with an upward-pointing camera momentarily split us apart. My gaze spanned the city around us. I wondered why he didn't just leave me right there on the sidewalk. I sighed and looked over at him in the falling dusk, noting how powerful he seemed with the steely buildings as his backdrop.

As if, with a snap of his fingers, Chicago would bow at his feet and heed his commands.

"What are you thinking?" he asked in a disarmingly gentle tone.

"That the city looks different depending on whom I'm seeing it with."

He nodded easily, as if this same thought had occurred to him.

"I notice different things," I continued. "Like with you, I pay more attention to the details of the buildings – the textures, the colors, the people standing in front of them. The reflections are different."

"Reflections?" he asked quietly.

"They are." I watched our bodies morph and distort in the window of an empty bank. "You're there," I said. "That's how they're different."

I wanted to ask him why he was walking with me after he'd told me he couldn't fuck me again. Didn't he know it was impossible for us to be anything other than what we had been that night? A sweeping and powerful force of passion and insatiable hunger?

Without missing a step and still looking ahead, he touched me. "Relax," he instructed.

My muscles melted under his hand. He removed it once my shoulders were back in place, but the warmth lingered. "Clearly I need a vacation," I sighed.

"Where would you go?"

"I'm joking."

"But why not?"

I made a face.

"Don't you ever travel? Everyone likes to vacation."

"Not Bill."

"I remember. So what?"

"So maybe I don't like to either."

"That's impossible."

"Vacation is always, like, idealized. It becomes something huge in your mind, like all the other days in the year are leading up to this one week. You're going to dine grandly and spend hours in the sun forgetting that you have a real life. You're going make love sweetly – maybe on the beach, maybe under the stars or by candlelight. But those things don't happen. Your flight is delayed. You spend the next three days in a state of permanent jetlag. You never remember the sun being as strong as it is. You eat too much and – and you have to undo the top button of your jeans."

He looked confused, as if that were a new concept to him. "Eat too much?" he asked.

"I never stop thinking about work, no matter how hard I try. I'm always thinking about how the vacation is setting me back. So is Bill. The one trip we took, he brought paperwork with him, and he worked a few hours a day because he had to. I checked my e-mail so I wouldn't miss anything important. But the thing is, I never did miss anything, because at the end of the day, life goes on without me."

"You think so?"

"Yes. The office runs, and life goes on. When I was an assistant editor, I undertook most of my boss Diane's workload. I always assumed that if I didn't do it, nobody would. But somehow it got done during that one vacation."

"And making love?"

"What?"

"There's the plan to make love *sweetly*."

"Oh, you think you will. And you try. But when you're stuffed, burnt and exhausted, making love suddenly doesn't seem so appealing."

"So it doesn't happen?" he asked, hope dripping off the question like honey.

"No, it happens," I said. "But it's not how you imagined it. On the beach, it's scratchy and painful. Sand gets places it should never be. And that's the last time you'll ever make that mistake."

"Mistake," he repeated with a snort. "Sounds like you're doing it wrong."

I swallowed hard. "We're here."

He peered into the restaurant, scanning the crowd. When his eyes returned, they were calm.

I touched my hair. "I probably shouldn't say this, but . . ."

He arched an eyebrow, an amused smile tugging at his lips.

"I like spending time with you," I confessed. "I know I'm tense. But around you, I feel . . . better." I bit my bottom lip. "I shouldn't have run out on you the way I did. It was childish. I guess what I'm saying is, I'd really like it if we could be friends."

He looked up at the sky and laughed.

"I'm serious, David. It's the only way to be in each other's lives. Can you manage that?"

He broke into a wide, shit-eating grin. "Can you?"

I stuck my hand out between us. "Friends?" I asked.

My body practically shook with his answering handshake. Any amusement on his face was then replaced with purpose. "How are you getting home?"

I thought a moment. "Probably the train."

"You could also take a cab."

I smiled. "I'll consider it."

He smiled back at me. "Okay, Miss Olivia." In one swift movement, he leaned in and froze. My breath caught as his face hovered just above mine. After a long moment, he rerouted his swoop and planted a gentle kiss on my cheek. "Goodnight, friend," he said softly.

"Goodnight," I echoed with my heart pounding in my ears.

I wasn't sure how long I stood there after he'd walked away. Gretchen appeared, somewhere from the shadows, and gave me a strong hug. I hadn't divulged the reason for our emergency dinner so when she pulled back, I shook my head at her. "You big, fat liar."

Her eyes widened fractionally and then narrowed. "That asshole. He went to see you, didn't he?"

"Yes."

She groaned and pulled open the door to the restaurant. "I knew Greg would do that, even though I specifically said –"

"Pause. What the hell is going on?"

"Liv," she said, her tone softening. "You know I could never say no to him." She smiled automatically at the hostess and told her cheerily, "Two for dinner."

"So what does this mean?" I asked, tailing her to the table.

"Well, we're – I don't know, trying again. He moved here this summer, but I didn't agree to see him until a few weeks ago."

"Why didn't you tell me?"

She stopped behind her chair and sighed. After a moment, she pulled it out and sat down. "You haven't exactly been available lately."

Understanding quickly set in. It was my fault she hadn't told me. I'd barely even asked about her life the past few months. "Oh," was all I said as I plopped into my own chair.

"But I'm relieved that you know," she continued. "I've really been needing someone to talk to."

"Isn't it going well?"

"Yes." She grinned. "But it's hard keeping it to myself."

I nodded knowingly. "So tell me then."

She gave me the short history of their new relationship. I wasn't surprised by the way he'd worn her down; he'd always been charming and despite her cool exterior, she'd always had a soft spot for him.

"It's weird," she said, dipping a chip into chunky

guacamole. "Things feel both different and the same."

"What's different?"

"We're both more mature. He seems more open to a relationship. It was his idea to become exclusive right off the bat."

"So you're not seeing anyone else?"

"No. I guess he's like my boyfriend."

I laughed. "When was the last time you had a boyfriend?"

"Nobody noteworthy since him," she replied, laughing with me.

"How's the sex?"

"We haven't done it yet. Er, again."

"What?" I screeched.

"If we sleep together, then I'm really in it."

"If I know the two of you, that's not going to last long."

"I know. I just want to be as certain as possible."

"Do you trust him?"

"He insists that this time is different, but . . ."

I set my chin in my palm and told her I hoped it would be. Greg was a decent guy, and the way he'd abandoned her was out of character. Still . . . there were no guarantees when it came to matters of the heart. If that was what she wanted, she needed someone like Bill, not Greg.

Unable to give her the assurance she needed, I changed the subject. "Greg mentioned a party?"

"The PR firm is hosting a soft opening next weekend. I'm supposed to invite people."

"All right, count us in."

"Really?"

"Yeah, why not?"

"You haven't wanted to do anything lately, and I know Bill doesn't really like that sort of thing."

"Well, I said I would try, didn't I? What's it for?"

"That gigantic new hotel on the River. Revelin, I think?

They're doing a test run to make sure the staff and everything is up to standard."

"Oh." *Revelin. David's hotel.* I rolled my lips together and nodded, trying to hide my surprise. Her eyes skimmed my face knowingly.

"What?" I asked when she didn't speak.

"I saw you earlier."

"Where?"

"Out front, with David."

"Oh." My body warmed with embarrassment, and I tucked some hair behind my ear.

"He kissed you."

"No," I said, shaking my head. "It's not what it looked like. It was just a peck on the cheek."

"Um, that's exactly what it looked like. Why are you even together?"

"I don't want to talk about this."

"Olivia, are you guys . . . Is this . . ." She paused and shifted in her chair. "Are you having an affair?" she asked with a lowered voice.

"No," I insisted.

"I don't believe you."

I gaped at her. "We are not sleeping together."

She nervously rotated her glass of water on the table. "Please tell me you aren't going to do anything stupid."

"No," I said, but it came out as a whisper.

"Are you thinking about it?"

I shook my head emphatically.

"Are you lying?"

I just blinked at her, trying to look offended.

"I know his type," she said, her tone heavy with warning. "He's a player with a capital 'P'."

"I know that."

"Do you? I get that it's tempting, he is a *god*. And yes, you clearly have chemistry. But I'm afraid he sees you as some kind of challenge. Guys like that have fucked over me and many of my friends. But you have way more at stake." She paused, searching my face. "Think of what it would do to your marriage. You would regret it."

How could I tell her that I'd already done it, and that I didn't regret it at all? At least not for the reasons I should? I looked down. Grains of salt were scattered over the table. I studied them, forming them into abstract patterns.

"Olivia?"

I nodded finally. No one had more concerns than myself. I knew I wasn't the only person under his spell; he could have anyone with the snap of his fingers. Why, then, was I tempted to put everything on the line for him? Gretchen was right. But I feared I'd wandered too far down that path to find my way back.

"So I guess you still have feelings for him," she said, sighing.

I opened my mouth, gulping for air. "I don't know. He's helping out with the Oak Park house."

Her eyebrows joined. "Isn't that weird?"

"Of course it's weird, but you were there after the wedding. What was I supposed to do when Andrew brought it up? Forbid them from seeing each other? That wouldn't raise a red flag *at all*."

"Well, look. He's with Dani now anyway, right?"

"Seems that way," I said, directing my scowl at the table.

"So let her have him. If he's going to break someone's heart, I'd rather it was hers than yours."

I smiled so she wouldn't notice my dejection.

"Speaking of the house," she continued, "any news?"

"We should hear back any day now."

"Are you ready for all that?"

"I don't know, I guess so." My conversation with David, fresh in my mind, hadn't given me any answers. But as usual, opening up to him was easy and left me feeling better. It also left me more confused.

"Well, I hate that you'll be leaving the city, but I am excited for you. This is a big step."

I nodded. "You'll come visit, won't you?"

"Of course," she said, but her smile waned.

CHAPTER 11

BURGUNDY LEATHER AND DARK WOOD made up Bill's office, and it smelled intentionally rich. Sturdy, essential-looking volumes lined the room like wallpaper. It had been a few nights since my dinner with Gretchen, and I hadn't seen much of Bill that week because of a big case. Knowing he was in for another late night, I'd decided to surprise him.

"This is a treat." He rounded the mahogany desk to embrace me. "Everything okay?"

"Yep. I haven't been here in a while, so I thought I'd make sure you've still got my photo up."

He plucked a frame from his desk and showed it to me. It was from the one time I had agreed to go on the fishing boat, and we were smiling from behind sunglasses and goofy hats.

"Great," I said. "So I'll stop by again next year."

"Har-har." He pulled me back into his arms. "Actually, I'm glad you're here. I have something to tell you."

"Okay," I prompted.

"I just heard back from Jeanine about the house. We didn't get it."

"Oh." I exhaled loudly. "Why not?"

"She didn't say, but she's going to find out and get back to us."

"Well, that sucks," I said.

"Yeah, it does," he agreed. "I'm sorry."

I looked down at his arms around me. "It's not your fault. You were so sweet to go through the trouble. Thank you."

For some reason, the tense way he rubbed his eyes made me feel overwhelmingly guilty. I'd spent late nights trying not to wish that life away, and maybe on some level I had willed it. Was this my fault?

"I know we'll find something else," he said. "I'm just so tired of this whole process."

"Maybe we should take a break for a while," I suggested.

"No, I don't want to do that." He paused for a deep sigh. "How was your day?"

"It was all right. I missed you."

He smiled. "Me too. Speaking of fishing," he said, gesturing to the photograph behind him, "Hugh and the guys invited us on the boat next weekend. Interested?"

"Gretchen's party is that weekend. I mentioned it a couple days ago."

"Oh. I don't remember that. I'll tell them no."

"No, it's okay. You should go, sweetie."

"Without you?"

"I won't be any fun without Lucy, and she'll still be on her honeymoon."

"True. What about the party?"

"Well, maybe I'll go with Gretchen and Greg. Gosh, that is so weird to say. I still cannot believe they're back together."

"Which one is Greg?"

"Honey, seriously? I also told you this the other night. Greg, from college. The one who ditched Gretchen to move to Japan."

"Yeah, sorry. I've had a lot on my mind with work and the house. That's exciting, I guess."

"You guess?"

"Just don't get your hopes up."

"Why?"

"You know her. She's a floozy."

"A floozy?" I repeated.

"Come on, she's always with a new guy. If I knew this Greg, I would warn him," he said with a chuckle.

"You would not. This is different for her. They're like college sweethearts."

"Whatever, Livs, I don't want to talk about Gretchen. Are you sure you don't mind that I go fishing?"

"No," I said, clearing some hair from his face. "I don't mind. Tell them yes."

"Great." He kissed my cheek. "You're the best."

"Do you want to go get dinner?"

"Shit, I really can't. If I don't keep on track I'll have to come in this weekend."

"Okay. I'll see you at home then."

"Liv?"

"Hmm?"

"I'm really glad that you're, uh, doing better. I hope losing the house won't change that."

"Um." I felt the color leave my face. I could only think of one terrible reason for the change. "Yeah," I said. "I mean no. I don't think it will."

"Good." He kissed me on the cheek again and glanced at the closed door. "Also . . ."

"Yes?"

"It's been a while since we . . . you know."

I nodded in agreement. "It has been a long while."

"Think we could give it another go?'

"Of course," I agreed. "Now?"

"No." He laughed.

"Why not?" I touched his crotch, and his shoulders stiffened.

"Liv, no," he insisted, trying to push my hand away, but I was already undoing his pants. I raised an eyebrow and backed away to lock his door.

"I'm not sure this is a good idea . . . ," he protested.

"The office is almost empty," I pointed out.

I went to sit on his desk when he stopped me. "Jesus, not on the legal briefs. The couch."

He walked over and lay lengthwise across it. I climbed up and settled into a straddle over his hips. He bunched my skirt up to my waist.

"Honey," I said, leaning over so we were face to face. "I want to go slow."

"I would like that, too." He pecked me on the lips and tucked some hair behind my ear. He smiled sweetly and pecked me again. When I drew back, his smile had fallen away. He pressed his lips to mine, holding the nape of my neck. I felt the passion behind his kiss, but there was something ghostly about it; a shadow of a kiss, a kiss that seemed to go right through me. It made me feel suddenly tired and dry, like my eyes had been open for days.

He ran one hand up my blouse and massaged my breast. My nipple swelled into his palm, and he put it in his mouth. His lips kissed down my sternum, and he sat up to urge me onto my back. His mouth continued over my belly until finding its way under my skirt. I could count on one hand the number of times that he'd gone down on me, so I gasped when his mouth closed over my mound.

"How's that?" he asked after a moment, glancing up at me.

"Fine," I exhaled. "Actually, you can be less . . . gentle," I instructed tentatively. *I can do this*, I thought. *I can make this happen.* I reached down to spread myself wider and circled my other hand over my clit.

I can do this, I recited to myself. I remembered Bill as my boyfriend, my fiancé, my husband now. We had history. We had a present and a future. His touch was familiar; it was just for me, and mine was for him. I bowed my back and moved my hand faster, frustrated that my body didn't respond the way I wanted it to. "Finger me . . . Yes," I breathed when he touched me. "More."

"More what?"

"More fingers."

"Are you sure?"

"Yes."

It took a moment until I felt the pressure. I was still rubbing myself, and he pulled his mouth away to watch. *Come on, come on*, I pleaded. After what felt like ten minutes, but what could have been two, I told him I was ready.

He was over me in a moment, groaning as he entered me. "Shit. Why don't we do this more often?" His face distorted with pleasure as he found his rhythm. He kissed his way down my neck, and then up to my jawline. I appealed to the ceiling, praying for more than what I had to give.

But my body was still broken.

I wasn't sure what inside of me had surfaced that night with David, but it wasn't present now. An orgasm wasn't even within reach. As Bill worked on top of me, sadness settled over me.

"Oh, babe," he said between gritted teeth. "I can't wait, I'm so sensitive. I'm going to come."

"Bill," I uttered, gripping his arms. "Pull out."

"What?" he exhaled. "Why?"

"Just pull out," I said, feeling panicky.

He dropped his head into the crevice of my neck and breathed hotly onto my collarbone. "Oh, God."

"Bill, don't come inside me," I said more forcefully.

"Aren't you . . . Shit," he cried and sat back. He grabbed himself and rubbed his crown against my stomach, groaning until liquid heat spurted over my skin. He remained that way for a few seconds, breathing heavily. "Damn. That was kinda hot." He stood to pull on his pants before swiping a tissue from his desk. "You're on birth control though," he said as he passed it to me. "Why'd you want me to pull out?"

I focused on wiping away the stickiness to avoid his eyes. "I don't know. I got nervous."

"That was a rush, huh?" He yawned. "Imagine if someone had caught us? I would've been toast."

I kissed his nose and got dressed. When he yawned again, I told him he was coming home with me. He readily agreed.

~

When I received an e-mail from David telling me how much he had enjoyed our 'friendly' walk, I knew exactly how he felt. The simplicity of our time together was refreshing. And when he asked if I wanted to do it again, I was ashamed of how little I hesitated before replying that I did.

I met him downstairs after work. Even though I had spent the afternoon convincing myself that I wasn't doing anything wrong, I still scanned the lobby to make sure there wasn't anyone I knew.

His arms were crossed over his broad chest as I approached. "Good evening," he said with a wide, contagious grin.

"Good evening," I repeated. I walked out through the lobby door when he held it open.

"You're nervous," he said.

"Maybe a little."

"I don't make you uncomfortable, do I?"

"No," I said. "I just feel like I'm doing something wrong."

"We're just two friends walking," he reminded me.

I nodded. "It's nice, just walking."

"Yes, just walking is nice. But I can think of nicer things."

I blushed and bit my bottom lip. I could also think of nicer things. When he winked playfully, I pretended to search for something in my purse to hide my embarrassment.

The city was our soundtrack for the first few blocks. As the sun set, the evening grew colder, and I buried my hands in the pockets of my jacket.

"What are your plans this weekend?" he asked eventually.

"I'm thinking of going to the animal shelter. It's been a while since I volunteered."

He smiled. "Of course. I remember that you like to walk the dogs. Where do you take them?"

"Usually just down to the water or the park. The shelter isn't far from my apartment."

"Lincoln Park?"

"Yes."

"I'll be there this weekend. My parents are driving in, and we're taking my sister's kid to the zoo."

"That sounds really nice."

"We're barbequing in the park afterward." He went to say something else, but stopped himself.

"Oh. Will Dani be there?"

He chuckled. "I was wondering when you'd bring that up again."

"I'm just curious." I hazarded a casual shrug. "Like, has she met your parents?" I asked, fingering a lock of hair.

"You think we're more serious than we are."

"When was the last time you went out?"

He cleared his throat. "A few nights ago."

"A few nights?"

"Yes."

"After I saw you? But you and I . . . We walked, and . . ."

"And what?"

"Nothing." I watched the sidewalk disappear under my feet. After a moment, I said, "I forget how good you are at that."

"At what?"

"Juggling women."

"I wasn't juggling women. We're just walking, remember?"

I nodded. "But you do . . . juggle women. Because you're a player. Aren't you?"

"So you keep saying," he said. "You called me that at the Meet & Greet that night."

"But isn't it true?"

He frowned. "I don't have time to pursue women."

"You could be pursuing someone right now instead of walking with me."

He covered his heart with his hand. "Ouch. But yeah, you have a point."

"So if you don't pursue women, does that mean you and Dani are in a relationship?"

"Relationships also take time."

"So you just have . . . flings."

"I generally don't deny myself a beautiful woman if she's offering. If that makes me a player, then I guess that's what I am."

I was surprised when an arrow of jealousy shot right through my heart. Jealousy was the ugly monster that lived in my mother – up until recently, it was something that I rarely felt. "Does Dani know that?" I asked.

"Listen," he started, "I like her. She's a sweetheart. But you don't need to worry. Lucy has been very persistent in trying to set us up. Nothing will come of it, though. I've told Dani so, but she's stubborn. Lucy's given her this idea that I want to be tamed, and I just don't know it."

My jaw tingled as I clenched it. The thought of them together crept back into my head. I wasn't sure I believed him – after all, it wasn't the impression Dani had given us. "Are there others?"

"What?"

"Are you seeing anyone else?"

"Maria."

Oh, of course. Maria. Gorgeous, straight off the catwalk Maria. Since the first time I'd seen them together, her image had been seared into my memory. Maria, mocha-skinned with ribbons of caramel hair, in her siren red dress; Maria, his go-to girl, the one who was ever-present in his life – available for events, work functions and *other things* . . . .

"Well, obviously there's Maria," I said snidely. "*That* is a given."

"As my friend, you should be happy that I have someone I can call when I'm lonely."

"As your *friend*, that isn't a reason to sleep with someone random."

"Maria and I have been close for years," he argued. "She's far from random."

I scowled.

He stopped short in the busy sidewalk, sending pedestrians scattering around us. "What did you expect, Olivia?" he demanded. "You ran away and literally left me empty-handed. I didn't know if I'd ever see you again."

The world whirred around us, but we stood like statues, facing each other. "I don't . . . expect anything. I *do* want you to be happy, but . . ."

I tried to read his expression. His eyes remained hard until something flashed in them. "Maria, Dani – they don't mean anything. You have to know that I would," he stopped, his face darkening. "But when I think about . . . about you and . . . you and *him* – " He shook his head, and his jaw hardened noticeably. "I can't go there."

I grasped his forearm and dipped my head toward him, alarmed by the look on his face. "Me and Bill?"

"This isn't how it's supposed to be," he said with conviction.

It was my first indication that Bill and I weren't the only casualties in this unfolding mess. That maybe David was hurting more than I realized. There was something sinister in his face; a tempest brewing inside him. I wanted to reassure him that I was also scared, that I had a dark place, and I went there too often.

As I looked at him, everything around us fell away. I had a powerful need to comfort him, to care for him like he was mine to make happy. I *needed* to tell him what I'd felt in the house; that my feelings for him might be morphing into something else, something deeper.

"The house," I started.

He glanced up and fastened anxious eyes on mine.

"The house – " I stopped, swallowing dryly. His entire presence narrowed in on me, intensifying the expression on his face. "We didn't get it," I croaked finally.

He blinked his gaze up over my shoulder and cleared his throat. His face closed again and after a moment, he pivoted slightly to resume walking.

"Maybe I was being unrealistic," I said, shuffling to catch up with him. "I mean, who has time for a project like that?"

His expression was tight when he looked down at me. "That place would have been a lot of work," he said with a hint of irritation.

"I know, but there was just something about – "

"I really don't want to hear about the house," he snapped.

"Oh. All right." I cleared some hair from my shoulder and made a point to look forward or at other people for the next few blocks.

It was dark by the time we approached Michigan Avenue Bridge. I pulled my jacket closer against the wind as we crossed the Chicago River. He asked if I was cold, and I said no, because what good would it do to admit that I was? He couldn't hold me or give me his blazer, because it was all just too intimate knowing the things we had done together.

He stopped in the center of the bridge and motioned back toward the Loop. "Can you imagine the Great Chicago Fire on your heels, driving you across the river?"

"I don't want to."

"Your only objective is to get to the other side – but so is everyone else's. All those people trying to cross at the same time. Panic is a phenomenal thing. You know that it went on for two days?"

"All because of a stupid cow."

He smiled down at me. "Yes, that stupid cow."

It felt so natural for him to brush his knuckles over my cheek that it happened before either of us had realized it. It was only a second, and he pulled back immediately. But it left my skin singing.

"I'm sorry," he said.

"You can't *do* that," I said. "You can't just do that."

"I know. It just happened. I'm sorry." He left down the other side of the bridge.

But oh, I wanted it to just happen again. My reprimand was not because I didn't want that too, but because I was always on the verge of making a mistake with him. His touch was intoxicating, burning like wildfire through my body and straight to my core.

Helplessly, I followed, unsure of whether or not he wanted me to. When I caught up to him, I gestured to the right. "I'm going this way."

"I didn't know we had a destination," he said, turning with me.

"I promised Lucy I would check on things while they're away."

He slowed to a stop. "And here we are."

"Here we are," I echoed, watching him closely.

He pulled a hand from his pocket and rubbed his chin, as though debating. He went to stick his hand back in his pocket but pulled the lobby door open instead. I looked from him to the door and back.

"I'll walk you up."

There was no question in his voice, and I didn't protest. I hid my face from the doorman as I waved in his direction, and we rode the eight floors up in silence. I located the keys and turned to him, leaning my back against Lucy and Andrew's apartment door. "Thank you. I don't know why, but I enjoy walking with you a lot."

"I know why," he said.

"Okay," I prompted, fighting back a smile.

"I'm not telling."

I arched an eyebrow at him. "Really?"

"I'm omniscient when it comes to these things. A good guy to have around."

"It doesn't do me any good if you withhold your great knowledge."

"True," he said, placing an outstretched hand against the doorframe. "But I'm withholding it for your own good."

"Well, now you have to tell me."

"Sorry, honeybee," he said throatily. "Privileged information."

"Friends don't call friends 'honeybee,'" I pointed out.

"Sure they do."

"It's flirtatious."

"You can't possibly think that I don't flirt with my female friends."

"You shouldn't," I breathed. "You might give them the wrong idea."

"And what idea is that?"

I flushed at the many wrong ideas that occurred to me.

"It's okay," he said when I didn't respond. "You don't have to tell me. I can guess based on your pretty pink cheeks."

I narrowed my eyes at him, angry that my fair complexion was giving me away. "Now you're intentionally misbehaving."

He laughed wolfishly. "This is not misbehaving. There's a whole world of misbehaving that we're not doing."

Goddamn if I couldn't help the way my body shuddered. "You didn't answer my earlier question. Why is it like this when we're doing something as simple as just walking together?"

His face turned serious. "Are you really prepared to have this talk?"

I hadn't realized, but my heart was pounding. I shifted the keys in my sweaty palm. I knew I should look away, but my eyes wouldn't obey. "What talk?"

"You know what talk, Olivia."

The talk, I guessed, was about us. About what we were doing. And about why just taking a walk was so nice, but also so wrong. He was leaning closer now. His gaze lingered at my throat, and his tongue flickered over his lips. Just on the other side of the door was an empty apartment, our own private escape. On the other side of the door was the potential to make mistakes – over and over again . . . . I touched my fingers to the base of my neck, sure that he could see my pulse racing.

"Answer me. Are you prepared for what I have to say?"

"No," I blurted. "I'm not ready."

He pushed off the doorjamb with aplomb. "Well when you are, let me know."

He turned and walked back down the hall. I fumbled with the keys, cursing when I dropped them at my feet. I wanted to call after him, invite him in and drown in the fantasy of us, just for one night.

Instead, I entered the apartment before I made an enormous mistake. I slammed the door shut with both hands, bracing myself against the barrier between us.

CHAPTER 12

LATE SUNDAY MORNING, I slid behind our breakfast bar and grinned at Bill.

"You're in a good mood," he said cautiously.

"I'm going to the shelter."

"Great, babe, you haven't been in forever."

"Come with me."

"Nah, you go have fun. I should catch up on some stuff."

"Come on," I prodded. "It will be fun. We can get lunch after."

"I don't think so. Sounds nice, but I really can't blow this off," he said, waving an overstuffed folder in my direction.

"But you've never even been."

"Well, that's because I'm swamped," he snapped. "There are no breaks when it comes to this job. And because of the fishing trip, I have to get as much done as possible this week."

"All right." I held up my palms in defeat and bent over to lace up my tennis shoes. "I just think you'd enjoy it. You work so much."

"So do you."

"I know," I called from below. "But I'm going to try and cut back, now that I'm more settled in this position."

"You know I don't have that option. The partners expect us to bust our asses."

I sat back up. "Okay. I get it. I'm going to go then. Don't work too hard."

He kissed my forehead and tossed the folder on the kitchen table. "I'll try not to."

Twenty minutes and five M83 songs later, I had arrived at my destination. The manager, George, greeted me with a warm smile and told me they'd missed me the past few months. He set me up with an older golden Labrador mix, who lovingly nudged me with her snout when I asked if she was ready for her walk.

Out front, I threw my hair into a quick ponytail and led her toward the park. I pulled my phone out twice on the way, only to put it away again. Finally, I took it out a last time and opened the text message David had sent me the day before.

Sep 15, 2012 3:30 PM
Meet us in the park tomorrow.

I hadn't responded, and now I bit my nail nervously as I stared at it. Finally, I replied.

Sep 16, 2012 12:22 PM
How was the zoo?

As soon as I'd sent it, I cringed. My nerves flared, knotting my stomach and causing me to pull hard on my earlobe. What was I thinking? And what if he'd brought Dani after all? What if he didn't want to see me? Why should I care if he did or didn't?

Sep 16, 2012 12:25 PM
Chaotic. Are you in LP?

Sep 16, 2012 12:26 PM
Yes.

Sep 16, 2012 12:28 PM

*Come to the Lily Pool, Fullerton
entrance. On my way.*

I looked down at the dog. "Don't judge me," I told her.

At the gates to Alfred Caldwell Lily Pool, we waited. My heart rate accelerated when I saw David in the distance. He spotted me, his stride quickening. His muscles stretched a short-sleeved black t-shirt. I let my gaze wander down his basketball shorts to his long legs. They were brawny, tan like his arms, and I guessed it was because when he flipped houses, *he* flipped them. As in, him, hammering, lifting, moving, ripping, tearing, sweating . . . .

"Hey," he said, a smile spreading across his handsome face.

I squinted up and easily returned his smile. "Hey."

"Who's this?"

"Sofie from the shelter."

"Hello, Sofie from the shelter." He crouched down and took the dog's head in his hands, scratching behind her ears. "Canyon's with us, they can play."

"She's sort of old."

"Canyon too. Have you been inside?" he asked, motioning to the Lily Pool.

"No." I looked at him sheepishly. "I've walked by but never noticed it. I had to look it up on my phone," I admitted.

He took the leash from me and looped it around the nearest tree. "Come inside with me. Sofie'll be fine here for a minute." With a hand on my shoulder, he guided me through the gates and into a peaceful, rustic oasis. A sprawling pond was dotted with floating lily pads and bordered by large stone slabs.

"Wow," I muttered. "Are we still in Chicago?"

He grinned. "I come here when I need to cool off."

The leaves rustled with a breeze, carrying the soothing water lily scent under our noses. I inhaled a fresh breath of air, and the wind danced in my hair. I could feel the city fading in the background as we stood together, soaking in the serenity.

"This reminds me of the house," I mused aloud. "The Oak Park house," I clarified.

"This park was designed in the prairie style, just like the house – notice the same horizontal lines. Alfred Caldwell was an architectural landscaper who was influenced by Frank Lloyd Wright. They both loved nature and knew how to incorporate it to make the space come alive."

As I had been in the house, I was arrested by the way he spoke. His love for architecture was inspiring, and I listened avidly as he recited a quick history of the Lily Pond's recent restoration.

"A lush, green sanctuary modeled after this would be perfect in the backyard," he said as we exited.

"I told you we didn't get it, though."

"I meant that it would have been perfect."

"Oh." I untied Sofie and took off along the path, rapt as David dropped facts here and there about the park.

"Liv!" I heard from ahead of us.

"I forgot to mention," David muttered, "your friend Brian Ayers is here."

"Why?"

"Sometimes we run Lakefront on the weekends. I knew he'd be around, so I invited him to eat with us."

Brian waved at me as he ran over in basketball shorts and a sleeveless tank. A lock of long blond hair fell into his eyes, and his toothy grin stretched from ear to ear. "We must stop meeting like this," he teased, referring to the first time we'd met. He was dressed exactly the same as that day, when the shelter dog I'd been walking had knocked me off my feet. Brian had rushed over to help me up, giving me an adorable smile that only deepened my embarrassing blush.

"Ah, sure," I stammered.

Brian laid a heavy arm over my shoulders. "Come on, the grill's already fired up."

"Mom, look! A Lab!" A young boy came running over, and David leaped forward.

"Hang on, buddy," he said. "What did I tell you about big dogs? Nice and easy, let her smell you first."

The boy slowed and held out his hand to Sofie. He beamed when she sniffed and licked it.

I identified David's family immediately from my brief moment of Internet stalking. David's sister, Jessa, introduced herself with a bright smile and a sturdy handshake. I liked her instantly. She looked about my age, younger than David, but warm brown eyes gave her sharpness away. "Is this your pup?" she asked.

"No, she's from a shelter nearby. I volunteer there some weekends."

Her smile widened. "I like you already. We're a family of animal lovers. Mom," she called behind her, "come meet a friend of David's."

I looked nervously at David's retreating figure as he took Sofie over to the Dylans' dog Canyon. A petite black-haired woman glided toward us, wiping her hands on the seat of her jeans. She looked mildly confused, but wrapped me in a tight hug and said, "I'm Judy."

"Olivia Germaine," I replied when she'd released me.

"Gerard, come meet a friend of David's," she called over her shoulder, never taking her eyes off me. I had to stifle a laugh. I was beginning to feel like I'd just landed in a spaceship.

David's dad had the same rigid bearing as him, and he commanded that I sit down at the picnic table in the same tone that David would have. Jessa had a plate of fruit in front of me in moments, and I didn't know who I should look at as they all stared at me.

David appeared suddenly and fell onto the bench next to me. He handed me a bottle of water. "You should always carry water when you're exercising. It's important to stay hydrated," he said, his tone edged with a scolding.

I opened my mouth to thank him when Jessa cut in. "So how do you two know each other?" she asked, looking between us.

"Mutual friend."

"Work."

I laughed nervously as David and I exchanged glances.

"Olivia here was the one who put us in the *Most Eligible* issue," Brian offered.

"Oh!" Jessa exclaimed, clasping her hands together. "I'm so glad David finally agreed to do it. He looked so handsome," she gushed. "You did a wonderful job."

"I actually didn't work with David, my colleague did, but I agree. She did a great job," I said, clearing my throat self-consciously.

"I see." Jessa smiled mischievously.

"David, sweetie, you never said – has anything come of it?" Judy asked. Her eyes darted conspicuously between him and me.

"Uh, no, not really."

"Come on, Fish, we both had a ton of responses," Brian volunteered. "Didn't you take any of them out?"

"No," David snapped. "I don't need a magazine article to find dates."

"No one said you did," Jessa pointed out. "You're being rude."

By now, I was sure that I was beet red. "It's okay. David was candid about what he expected from the article. My boss was more than pleased to feature him anyway."

David gave me an apologetic look as his parents excused themselves to check on the grill. I watched Judy loop her arm around Gerard's lower back, and he gave her an adoring smile.

It had been some time since I'd seen any of my friends'
parents looking so smitten; even at Lucy's wedding, her
normally affectionate parents had seemed frazzled.

"So was it intentional that the issue came out on David's
birthday?" Jessa teased.

"Come on," he said, rolling his eyes.

"No." I broke into a smile. "I had no idea."

Jessa nodded her head emphatically. "June twenty-
second. What's your sign, Olivia?"

"Jessa," David warned.

"I'm a Taurus. May twentieth."

"Oh." She was quiet for a moment. "That's interesting."

"How come?"

"Don't ask," David said. "She's into this astrology
bullshit."

"David is a Cancer."

"Like my friend Gretchen," I said.

Brian laughed to himself. "That explains a lot," he
muttered with his chin in his hand.

"Brian, did something happen between you and
Gretchen?" I asked.

"Oh." He looked up. "No, nothing at all."

"Are you sure?"

"Are you asking me to kiss and tell, missy?"

"So there was a kiss?" I exclaimed.

He looked embarrassed. "It was very brief. I stopped it."

I raised an eyebrow. "Why? Don't you find her
attractive?"

"Exceptionally. We aren't well suited though. She seems
to have something to prove. And that's not me."

I shrugged at his cryptic answer and turned my attention
back to Jessa. "So why is it interesting that I'm a Taurus?"

"It's not that," she mused, touching a finger to her lips.
"Both you and David are on the cusp of your signs. In fact,
you're both on the cusp of Gemini."

"Is being on the cusp bad?" I asked.

"No, no. But two Gemini together can be, well, explosive. Volatile. Not usually a good combination. On the other hand, Cancer and Taurus is a great match."

"Oh." I smiled at her before glancing over at David. "Well, we're not . . ."

She raised her eyebrows at me. "You're *not*?"

"No," I said, shaking my head in confusion. I looked to David for backup, but he was stoic as he stared at his sister. "I'm married," I said, holding up my hand. All three pairs of eyes dropped to my ring, and her face fell instantly.

"Oh," she said quietly. "I'm sorry, I just assumed . . . Crap, I'm really sorry."

"It's okay, no big deal," I said with a reassuring smile.

"Uncle David!"

David bolted upright, knocking his knee on the table and cursing. He shot us a quick look before jogging over to the boy. Brian shifted uneasily. After a moment, he mumbled an excuse and took off after David.

"Well this is uncomfortable," Jessa said.

"Not even, don't worry. I'm sure it's hard to keep track of all his girlfriends."

She cocked her head at me, and my hand flew to my mouth. "I'm sorry, I didn't meant to imply anything. Just that he's so charming, I'm sure he's had many girlfriends."

Jessa released a fluid, heartfelt laugh. "Don't worry, I know David's something of a ladies' man. But 'girlfriends' is the wrong word." I waited for her to continue, but she just popped a grape in her mouth and looked over to the grass.

"Is that your son?"

"Alex – sorry I didn't introduce you."

"It's okay, he's busy. How old is he?"

"Just turned ten."

I nodded and watched as David scooped him up effortlessly and spun him around until Alex started screaming.

As soon as he released him, the kid stumbled sideways and fell to the ground laughing. David leaned his hands on his knees and said something to Brian, who burst into laughter. David's head swung in our direction then, a carefree smile plastered on his face. He really was blindingly beautiful when he smiled, especially when it was directed right at me.

"I'm surprised."

"I'm sorry?" I asked, reluctantly breaking from my adulation.

"That you're married. You and David seem to have a connection. I certainly haven't seen him look at someone like that . . . *ever.*"

Breath rushed from my lungs. I fingered the hem of my spandex tank top, trying unsuccessfully to avoid her stare.

"Brian has the idea that your being here today is a coincidence. Is it?" Her eyes were alive with questions, and I was afraid of the answers she might read in mine. I felt scarily close to confessing everything to her; she seemed so warm and understanding and disconnected from my life. I grasped at words, opening and closing my mouth like a goldfish.

Judy appeared suddenly, rescuing me from any spontaneous confessions. "Hot dog or burger, girls?"

"Burger for me," Jessa chimed.

I nodded my agreement.

"Two burgers," Judy called to her husband, and she climbed onto the bench. She sat up straight, brushing dark hair off her shoulder and flashing a colossal ring that dominated her slender fingers. "So, Olivia, where are you from?"

"I grew up in Dallas, but I moved here after college."

"Oh? You don't strike me as Southern girl."

"I get that a lot," I said with a laugh.

"Where'd you go to school?"

"Notre Dame. Your husband went there, right?" I recalled my conversation with David the last time we'd had burgers. "My dad too."

"How funny!" she exclaimed. "Ger, Olivia here went to Notre Dame."

Gerard brightened visibly and called, "A fellow Leprechaun! That's my girl!"

I couldn't help but smile back at his enthusiasm.

"We tried to get David to go there, but for some reason he chose Yale instead," she said, laughing.

"You must be so proud of him. He's done very well for himself."

"We are, but we never had any doubt he would succeed. David has always excelled at the things he puts his mind to. He's always been very motivated, sometimes to a fault."

"It's true," Jessa said. "When we were in elementary school, he cried when he found out he could only receive the Student of the Month award once."

I giggled into my hand just as the three boys descended on the table. Alex climbed up between me and Jessa, as David and Brian sat across from us.

"Who are you?" Alex asked.

"I'm Olivia." I smiled down at him. "Nice to, um, meet you," I said, offering my hand.

He made a sputtering noise with his lips, sending spittle onto my top.

"Alex," Jessa scolded. "That's not polite."

"It's fine," I said, waving him off. "He can't possibly get more saliva on me than Sofie already has."

Alex gave me a narrow-eyed look before grasping an iPad from the table and diving into it. *What was that for?*

"Watch this," David said. "Alex."

"Huh," Alex snorted, his fingers gliding across the screen expertly.

"How old are you?"

"Huh."

"Where do you go to school?"

"Huh."

"Alex."

"Huh."

"Do you have a girlfriend?"

He jerked his head up. "No way, yuck," he exclaimed before returning his eyes to the screen.

We laughed. David was a good uncle, that much was obvious. It hit me that perhaps he liked children and wanted some of his own one day.

"Come and get it," Gerard said, indicating to the barbeque.

I went to stand, but David waved me down. "Burger?" he asked, and I nodded. He left the table, clapped his dad on the back and loaded our burgers onto two plates.

Brian fixed his twinkling eyes on me just as David set my plate down. "Ah, the question of the hour. What *does* the mysterious Olivia Germaine take on her burger? Can I guess?"

With all eyes on me, I nodded. He rubbed his hands together.

"Ketchup," he said, moving the bottle in front of me. "Because red is the color of love." He paused, and David rolled his eyes before taking off almost half his burger in one bite.

"Not onions," Brian murmured, "for that would make her lovely eyes cry." I blushed furiously as Jessa giggled. "And sauerkraut is much too sour for such a sweet creature." He hummed to himself as he looked over the offerings. "Yes to relish, because I know she has a naughty side." He winked at me. David was openly glaring at Brian now, and Jessa watched her brother intently. "To top it off, lettuce, extra crispy, and a touch of mayo. How'd I do?"

I was about to respond when David swallowed his food and cut me off. "Wrong. Ketchup, mustard, pickles, tomatoes."

"Yep." I smiled and emptied some ketchup onto my patty. *He remembered.* "David wins."

"Bummer."

"Dude," David said, "what the fuck is naughty about relish?"

Brian looked thoughtful. "Haven't you ever relished a lady?"

"Boys," Judy admonished, gesturing at Alex.

"You just pulled that out of your ass," David mumbled and Brian grinned, seemingly pleased with his quick wit.

I sighed happily. I couldn't remember the last time I'd been to a family barbeque, and I was enjoying the warmth of the Dylans' bubble. When it came time for me to go, I was reluctant. I thanked them for their hospitality while David brought Sofie and Canyon over.

"I'll walk you," he said, fisting both leashes.

I nodded and turned to wave once more at the group.

"He's gorgeous," I said, stooping to run a hand along Canyon's black and tan fur. "I wanted a German Shepherd when I was younger."

"I'd get one of my own if I could."

"I've never had a dog," I said wistfully. "My dad didn't have the time or patience to take care of one. But I love them." I sighed.

"Everything all right?" he asked.

"Yes. You're great with Alex."

David shifted the leashes from one hand to the other. "He makes it easy."

"I like your family."

"They like you too."

"You don't know that," I teased, bumping him with my shoulder and then withdrawing, embarrassed by the contact rush.

"Of course I do. I never would've invited you if I didn't think they would."

"Okay," I accepted, because I desperately wanted it to be true. That this lovely family might think I was a good person meant a great deal to me. When David's and my naked and entangled bodies flashed before my eyes, the blood drained from my face. *Good people don't cheat on their husbands*, I reminded myself. I held my hand out for the leash. "I have to go."

"Thank you for coming. I'm glad you did."

I held up my open hand before turning and retreating down the path.

I was also glad that I'd gone. There was an element of the afternoon that had been long missing in my life. Any time spent with David seemed to emphasize the things that hadn't been there before. Simplicity. Effortlessness. And on the other end of the spectrum, passion. I'd learned today that the passion between us didn't only live between the sheets. It was a different kind of passion, but it was there. The desire to be around him, to feed off his energy. When he wasn't next to me, I longed for him. I thought about it all the way home with a smile.

When I got back to the apartment, I wiped the arrogant grin off my face. Bill glanced up to greet me before turning back to his paperwork. Remembering the other night in his office, it occurred to me that Bill and I didn't have a very passionate relationship. It was loving and stable. But Bill wasn't the type to get passionate about much, except maybe sports. And even then, it was passive in its own way.

I had seen what passion could do to a relationship. My mother had been irrational, senseless when it came to my father. She let her emotions dictate her life, and that had ultimately driven their marriage into the ground.

I'd never questioned which way was the right way before. I'd always known I would choose reliability and stability over the alternative. The alternative meant a lifetime of mess; fights, pain, insecurity. I tried not to picture that kind of life with David as I watched Bill at the kitchen table. Could David even be faithful to one person? Did the spark between us come from him, because it was the type of person he was? And did that mean everyone felt it in his presence?

Sure, for two people with as much heat as we had, there was bound to be mess. It was inevitable. But there'd also be intensity, craving, impatience. There would be passion.

CHAPTER 13

IN HER BABY BLUE PARTY DRESS, Gretchen twirled when I called her name. "I'm so glad you're here," she said as I approached the hotel entrance. "I need another drink."

"Don't you have to work the door?"

"No, not my client," she said, crooking her elbow in mine. She guided me inside with a quick step. "And don't try to tell me you didn't know this was David's project. Sneaky bitch."

I bit my lip and considered feigning innocence, but I knew she'd see through it. We were at the soft opening for David's resort hotel. I'd been there once before with David, when it was under construction, and the exterior alone had had me envisioning sultry black sand beaches. That concept was even more prevalent now as I scanned the interior. The hotel had onyx-colored marble floors veined with pearly silver. Large aquariums with unnaturally blue water flanked the lobby. Even the fish matched the interior.

Someone dressed in head-to-toe black directed us toward a doorway situated between aquariums. We passed under the glass bottom and into a sensual lounge. It was darker than the lobby with low-hanging glass chandeliers that gave the space an ethereal glow. Red velvet seating lined the room, inviting and attractive against shadowy walls.

"I see sexy Liv came out to play tonight," Gretchen said, raising her eyebrows at my outfit and waving down a bartender.

I smiled. With heavy eyeliner and glossy pink lips, I was channeling my inner-retro. My black strapless jumpsuit was skin-tight and proudly displayed my slight but full cleavage.

After Gretchen handed me a drink, we clinked glasses. "Where's Bill?" she asked as she took a sip.

"He went north with some friends for the weekend."

"He fucking loves fishing, doesn't he?"

I laughed. "He loves getting out of the city and yes, fishing too."

"You'd think he grew up in the country or something." She checked her phone. "Wait here. I have to get Greg at the door."

I drifted over to the aquarium that separated the lounge from the lobby, drawn in by the comforting blue glow. I sipped my Belvedere and cranberry while gazing at the aimless fish.

Something about Gretchen's comment stuck with me. Bill had actually grown up on a small farm an hour outside the city where his very Catholic parents still lived. He worked hard now because they'd instilled that in him as a child. His weekends were spent with his parents, tending to things around the farm. During the week, they had him booked solid with all sorts of lessons, tutoring and a part-time job.

He'd had one long-term relationship before we met. He didn't talk about her often, but I knew that he hadn't been the one to end it. In the beginning of our relationship, he'd given me the impression that he'd intended to marry her. Like any girl learning about her boyfriend's ex would have, I wondered how things would be different if she hadn't broken it off.

I brought my glass up to my lips and started when I felt a presence behind me. Alcohol splashed down my cleavage, drawing a curse from me.

"Olivia," David greeted, drawing up next to me.

"How do you that?" I mumbled, accepting a napkin from him and mopping the fabric with it.

"What are you doing here?" he asked, his voice frayed with irritation.

I balled up the napkin and tucked some hair behind my ear. "I don't know."

"You don't know?"

I sighed and snuck a glance up at him. "Gretchen invited us."

His expression was unreadable as his gaze followed the fish intently. He blinked down, letting his eyes leer over my outfit. They swooped up to my face, and he took a measured sip from his glass. "Well, you never fail to impress, Olivia. Never."

I didn't know how to take the wryness in his voice. He remained impassive with one hand deep in his pocket and the other curled tightly around his glass.

"Um," I said, trying not to sound intimidated. "The hotel turned out wonderfully. You must be so pleased."

He snorted and nodded to my near-empty glass. "What are you having?"

"Trying to get me drunk, are you?" I teased. "That's not very gentlemanly."

"Who gave you this idea that I'm such a gentleman?" He leaned in closely and whispered, "Because they were entirely mistaken."

I inhaled deeply at his liquor-spicy breath on my skin. A wolfish grin before he strolled away let me know he had noticed my reaction. This wasn't the same restrained David I had been dealing with lately. This was the David in Lucy's doorway, who was growing impatient. David from the cold stairwell, who took what he wanted.

I followed him to the bar, lured by his words, hooked by his trailing scent. "How's that view at night anyway?" I ventured.

He cleared his throat and looked over my head. "Where's your husband?"

"Fishing," I said flatly. His brown eyes dropped to mine, and he surveyed me like a predator would – with a tense jaw and a lusty, narrow-eyed stare. His maleness was in full force, and I wavered slightly in the fog of his virility. The thrill he inspired in me held as much fear as it did excitement. He scoffed and uttered something to himself.

"What?" I asked.

He only handed me my drink and turned to tip the bartender.

"Hey, you must be Bill," Greg said from behind us. David turned and stared at Greg's hand as it hung between them. "Incredible," he continued. "You are exactly as I pictured."

"That is most definitely *not* Bill," Gretchen muttered as she walked up.

I introduced them, and David finally shook his hand with a firm pump and a curt nod. His mood was noticeably dark and edgy, as if he might explode any moment. It made *me* feel edgy and slightly out of control; I wanted to know exactly what it would take to make him snap – and what would happen when he did.

"Great, what's he doing here?" Gretchen's voice wormed its way into my thoughts. I followed her glare to Brian Ayers, who escorted a pretty girl our way. He adjusted his patterned bowtie and pushed a hand through his blond locks.

"What happened between you two, anyway?" I asked quietly.

"Absolutely nothing. I only needed one date to see that he was just another self-absorbed artist trying to cram his shitty photos down everyone's throats."

"Whoa. You saw his photography?" I asked with an arched eyebrow.

"I didn't have to."

"So nothing happened at all? Not even a teeny-tiny kiss?"

"No," she insisted, but she fidgeted with her purse. "Give me some credit. Like I said, he's a prick."

When I looked again, Brian was at my side with a scowl that told me he'd heard her last comment.

"Hello, lovely Olivia." He kissed me on both cheeks. His mouth drooped. "Gretchen," he acknowledged before looking away.

"Isn't there some fabulous art exhibit you should be at?" she asked, batting her eyelashes with exaggeration.

"Yes. This is my work." He motioned to a series of black and white photographs displayed on the walls. They were entirely different from the ones I'd seen in his apartment. In the one nearest to me, a nude woman leaned against a doorframe, her body curved like an 'S' and her head resting against her raised arm. She stared at us with all-knowing eyes, amusement dancing on her parted lips.

"You took those?" Gretchen asked skeptically.

He nodded. "Sure did, princess." She responded to his endearment with a frown. "David recommended my work," he continued, "being the good friend that he is."

"It's just business," David replied stoically.

"Well, you certainly are a lovely crowd this evening, but if you'll excuse us," Brian said, winking at me again.

"So where's Dani tonight?" Gretchen asked loudly. She sipped her drink through a tiny straw, avoiding my glare.

"Lucy's sister?" Greg asked, turning to David. "Are you two dating?"

"No."

I raised my drink to hide the smile that was forming.

"Oh. I was under the impression that you were." Gretchen's statement pitched at the end, conveying her piqued curiosity.

He shrugged. "We've been out, but we're not really looking for the same thing."

"Which is?" Gretchen prodded.

Irritation marked his face, though I knew better than to think that would deter Gretchen. "She would prefer something more . . . permanent."

"Oh, hmm," Gretchen said, nodding. "Well gosh, that's really too bad. Dani is a catch. She's *definitely* worth becoming exclusive for."

I fingered a piece of hair and bit my lip near bloody as Gretchen threw me a hasty smirk.

"I agree completely," David said. "She will make someone very happy."

"Someone else?" Gretchen ventured.

"Someone else," he agreed. "I have yet to make it official though, so I would appreciate your discretion."

"Scout's honor," Gretchen said, holding up three fingers. "So then where's your date tonight?"

I gave her an exasperated look.

"If you'll excuse me, this is Maria now," he said, pulling out his phone.

When he stepped away, I pinched her. "What are you – " I stopped to glance at Greg. "Greg, can you give us a minute? What are you *doing*?" I asked when he'd left.

"This is for your protection, Liv. I told you already, he's bad news. I don't know why you're still consorting with him."

"We're friends," I said defensively.

"He can't even stick with one girl for more than a few dates."

"I don't care who he sticks with," I retorted. "It's none of my business."

"Then stop eye-fucking him, and get it together. Anyone can see that you're ready to jump each other's bones."

I gasped and covered my mouth. "I am doing no such thing!"

"He doesn't look very happy with Maria at the moment," she observed over my shoulder. I turned and noticed his drawn features as he held the phone to his ear. He stood rigidly with one arm crossed over his chest as he appeared to be listening.

"Come on," she said. "I have to break the seal."

"I'm good," I replied with a smug smile. I picked a quiet spot amongst the velvety cushions to people watch and wait for Gretchen. I was not alone long, for an attractive man of considerable height was suddenly looming over me.

"May I?" he asked, motioning to the space next to me.

"Sure," I said, scooting aside.

"Are you part of the PR team?"

"No, just a guest. You?"

"We handle the advertising for this place. Steve," he said, offering his hand.

"Olivia."

"So, Olivia, what do you do?"

I told him, and he smiled genially, remarking on how much he'd enjoyed an article the magazine had just published. He was good-looking, I noticed as he spoke. I fleetingly thought that I should introduce him to Gretchen before remembering that she was no longer available. He laughed at one of my comments and touched my knee.

"She's with me."

We glanced up at the same moment, my eyes taking a little longer to travel up David's towering body.

"I'm sorry," Steve said, making a show of getting up. "Just being friendly," he added.

David did not move aside. When Steve stood, the men were almost nose to nose, except that David still held a couple inches over his imaginary adversary. *And my David is infinitely more handsome*, I thought. *Wait – my David?* Steve shuffled around him and slinked away as David took his place beside me.

"Is it necessary to remind you," I started, "that we are *not* together and that implying so could give people the wrong idea?"

"He was bothering you."

"He was being a perfect – we were just chatting," I squeaked. I inched closer to him, hoping to get a whiff of the David cologne cocktail.

"Regardless, he should have checked your hand before embarrassing himself by trying to pick you up."

"Like you did?" I asked, pursing my lips.

"That's different."

"How?"

He leaned back against the cushion so that I had to shift marginally to look at him. I was close enough that I wouldn't have to move much further before my lips would land on his. His eyes traveled down my neck to my breasts before shooting back up to my face. "It just is."

"That's not an answer."

He only grunted.

"Why is it all right for you to hit on me and not him?"

"Damn it, Olivia," he hissed. "Don't provoke me. It's inappropriate for me to answer that."

I reeled back, and he reacted instantly, pulling me back by my upper arm. A familiar thrumming ignited throughout my body, and I gasped softly.

"Is there a problem here?" I looked up reluctantly to see Steve glowering at David's hand on my bicep. He loosened his grip slightly and then dropped his hand.

"No, it's fine," I answered hastily.

Their eyes locked on each other, and I sensed David's breathing deepen beside me. Steve looked between us, wariness etched in his fine features. I dismissed him with a thank you. I had experienced David when he was cross, and I didn't want to be the cause of any problems.

"I'm sorry," he said, pulling on his collar and glaring after Steve. "I didn't mean to frighten you."

"You didn't," I said softly. "You're upset. Does it have to do with Maria?"

142

He looked confused. "What?"

"You seemed angry on the phone."

"Irritated is more like it."

"Did she stand you up?"

He snorted. "No. For some unknown reason, she was upset that I didn't invite her. But that's not what is bothering me."

"What then?"

"I don't really feel comfortable talking about it."

It was his turn to brush me off, but I didn't intend to let him. Unfortunately, Gretchen picked that moment to drop onto the bench across from us.

"Hey," she said with a stretched smile.

"Hi," I said cautiously.

"Who's the hottie that won't stop staring at you?"

"Who?"

She indicated across the bar.

"Oh. That's Steve."

"Steve," David muttered to himself, rubbing his eyes with his thumb and index finger.

"He is s-e-x-y. But you probably don't think so, do you?" she asked me.

I shifted and gave her a look.

"Liv never did go for the blonds," Gretchen explained to David. "But that's okay, more for me."

"You smell like tequila," I told her.

"I took a couple shots." She leaned forward and put a finger over her lips. "Shh. Don't tell Greg."

"Aren't you working?"

"No, no . . . I'm just here to party."

"Okay," I said, stifling a laugh.

"I'm going to talk to Steve."

"Steve? What about Greg?" I asked.

"Oh, he won't care," she said, waving her hand at me. "Look but don't touch, right?" she shouted and bolted upright.

She swayed slightly and steadied herself on David's shoulder. "Be back in a minute."

I searched the room for Greg until I noticed that David was staring at me. He shook his head and swiped a hand over his face. "I'll be a saint if I get through this night," he muttered.

"You're upset."

"*You* are who's pissing me off," he said suddenly. "Not Maria. You."

"Why?" I asked, trying to pinpoint anything in particular I might have done.

"You show up here, looking like that . . . ."

"Like what?" I asked, glancing down at the jumpsuit.

"I want to rip that fucking thing off you."

I sucked in a breath and flushed. His brazenness fired a sharp thrill through me. "David," I exhaled.

"Fuck." He sat forward abruptly, scrubbed his face with both hands and looked over at me. "I should go."

"You're leaving?" I asked as he stood.

"Hey, Liv, over here!" Gretchen called, waving me over.

I lifted a finger in her direction.

She said something to Steve and hurried over. "We're all going upstairs to see the view from one of the rooms," she told us. "You can come too, David," she added with a smirk.

I glanced at him. "David was just leaving, actually."

"Great," she said, shrugging. "Let's go."

"Wait." David caught my forearm gently. "Is he going?"

Gretchen and I looked in the direction he had jutted his chin.

"Who, Steve?" she asked. "Why, yes, it's his room." She grinned.

David blinked slowly and released my arm. With another glance at Steve, he said, "I'll take you to the roof."

"What about us?" Gretchen asked.

"You, as in, all of you."

"Great," she squealed and ran off.

"Mercurial much?" I muttered to myself as I trailed him out of the lounge.

David and I piled into one elevator with Gretchen's co-workers while she hung back to wait for Steve. The girls had been rowdy in the elevator bank, but now they were silent.

Perfume filled the tiny space, and one girl flipped hair over her shoulder. "You're David Dylan, right?"

He nodded.

"The place looks so good. I was just telling my friend that it's gonna be *the* hottest hotel in Chicago."

I was about to smirk when he gave her a prize grin. "What about the country?" he asked.

She giggled nervously. "That too." There was whispering from the back of the elevator.

I looked away and crossed my arms. The whispers stopped when I felt David clear some hair from my neck. I whipped my eyes back to him, and he smiled barely. Just the ghost of his reassuring touch sent chills over my skin. The elevator dinged, and everyone waited as we held each other's gaze.

I blinked and stepped out when someone cleared her throat. The girls tore across the hall to the penthouse suite. Despite their excitement, David was calm as he extracted the key from his pocket and opened the door. I glanced up and around the large, dimly-lit space. When I looked back, it was just us in the foyer.

"Flirt," I accused.

"You know I don't give a fuck about them," he replied without missing a beat, his voice low with bass.

I bit the inside of my lip. "I thought you were leaving."

"Not while *Steve* is around."

There was a thunderous knock on the door behind us. Another group flew by me when David let them in, and Gretchen grabbed my hand. "This is bananas," she said. My eyes scanned the expansive suite quickly as I let her drag me onto the roof. Outside, an elongated swimming pool ran the length of the deck, glowing turquoise on the otherwise dark roof. Glass partitions edged the perimeter, allowing for an unobstructed panoramic view.

"Look," someone called, "you can swim out over the city!"

Gretchen dropped my hand and rushed off, giving me a chance to admire my surroundings. What I'd seen with David on our previous trip to the roof was nothing compared to now. The pool jutted off the side of the building, hovering over the world below. As if you were floating. The opposite end of the pool showcased the first floor of the suite.

"Beer?" David asked from next to me.

"Where'd you get that?"

He leaned in. "My secret." He twisted off the cap and handed it to me before taking a swig from his own bottle. "Cheers."

"Thanks," I said hesitantly, trying to read his fluctuating mood.

We slowly followed the edge of the pool toward the group, as if we didn't actually want to get there. He looked into his beer bottle. "My family . . . They really liked you. Jessa especially. She says you have an amazing energy or something."

"I liked her also. A lot. Too much."

"And that means . . . ?"

One of the girls squealed ahead of us. "Just that I had a strange urge to tell her all my secrets."

"Secrets, huh?"

I nodded fractionally.

"That girl has a way of getting people to open up."

"Must run in the family." I cursed silently, knowing the comment hedged dangerous territory.

He didn't respond right away, but eventually asked, "Do you feel like I've opened you up?"

"Ah, well . . . Maybe a little," I said, embarrassed.

"I only wish it were more," he said casually. Even in the dark I could feel him peering down at me, trying to see me clearer, the way he sometimes did.

Without even looking at him, I said, "That's the problem."

"What?"

"The way you look at me. The way I look at you. It gives too much away. That's what your sister told me. For Christ's sake," I said, turning to face him. "She thought we were dating."

"So I can't look at you anymore?"

"Just don't look at me *like that*."

"Like what exactly?"

"She said she'd never seen you look at anyone the way you look at me."

He took an audible breath but didn't respond. We stood back from the crowd, watching them in silence.

"Are you really going to stop seeing Dani?"

He tilted his eyes upward to the sky and groaned. "I shouldn't have said anything. But yes."

"I'm sorry," I said. "I do want you to be happy, I just . . ." I bit my lip to keep the words from coming out. "You know."

"No, I don't know," he clipped. "I didn't do it for you anyway."

"I know."

"This is too much, Olivia, you know that?"

"What is?" I asked, taken aback.

He shoved a hand through his hair. "Nothing. Just never mind." With one last look, he turned and walked away.

I fought with myself, angry that I was doing this to him, to all of us. I wanted to go after him and make things better, but his departure had an air of finality. Instead, I took the last few steps to where everyone else had congregated. Steve smiled shyly at me and commented on how inspiring the skyline could be. I looked across the roof at David's shadowy figure. He faced Lake Michigan while taking a long pull from his beer bottle.

"Is that your boyfriend?"

I looked back at Steve. "No, just an overprotective friend."

"Oh," he exhaled, looking relieved. "I'm glad. I know this is forward, but I was hoping you might like to go out sometime."

I gave him a sympathetic look and held up my left hand.

"Oh, geez," he said. "Sorry. I didn't realize."

"It's all right. My husband isn't here tonight," I said with a friendly smile. "Anyway, where did you say you work?"

He stepped backward. "Actually, I think I'll head down for a refill."

"There might be drinks up here," I said, showing him my beer.

"Er, I . . ." His sentence trailed off as he mumbled something and then fled.

"Oh, okay. Goodnight," I called after him. I laughed at the unfailing powers of a wedding ring. *Well, almost,* I thought, and my laugh vanished. I peered down at my ring, wondering pointlessly how things might be different if it weren't there. I slipped it off and studied my hand without it, expecting to feel different somehow.

"Where'd Steve go?" Gretchen demanded, and I furtively slipped the ring back into place.

"He left." I frowned. "Who cares though? The question is, where's Greg?"

"That *is* a good question, smarty-pants. I should go find him," she slurred, pulling out her cell phone. "Yeah, he texted me like five times." She held the phone up inches from my face. "See?" I nodded, and she poked the girl next to her. "I've seen enough, let's go get another drink."

"And look for Greg," I reminded her.

"Yep. Let's go."

The girl announced that they were leaving. Gretchen gestured for me to follow, and I glanced back at David. The group retreated as a unit with Gretchen leading the way.

"Come *on*, Liv," she called over her shoulder. "It's time to *go*."

"Time to go," I repeated quietly to myself. *Go, Olivia . . . . Go.*

CHAPTER 14

THERE WAS A PART OF ME that wished David would tell me he was done and put an end to this. Then I wouldn't have to ride this emotional rollercoaster every day. I felt guilty for hurting both Bill and David. For the fact that maybe I was standing in the way of both their versions of home.

Why did I keep returning to this ridiculous concept of home? Is it not enough to have love and be happy? At thirteen years old, my home had broken in half in one fell swoop, and I'd never found that sense of belonging, that sense of security again. What was it about David that had me longing for that?

Bill was the only future I had ever known. He was supposed to be my rock, my love, my life. I wondered if knowing he was supposed to be all those things was still enough. Would I have eventually realized my doubts even if David hadn't come along?

Do I have doubts?

I blinked from my daze to find I was glued to the same spot on the roof. The voices in the penthouse suite faded away. I looked across the way at David's almost invisible silhouette; the ache to be next to him was deep. To feel his hardness through the softness of his cashmere sweater, to rescue him from disappearing into the black horizon.

I clenched my hand around the beer bottle, fighting against what threatened to devour me. Did I even have a choice? It felt bigger than me, this thing. I wanted to bask in his warmth, feel his mouth on my neck; I wanted to see him gaze at me again like I was the only girl he couldn't resist. Because he was that person for me. Of all the men, and, ashamedly, that included Bill, David was the one who I felt in my core, as though I only existed as an extension of him. I wanted to fall just so he could catch me.

I set my beer down and walked to the edge purposefully. With each click of my heel, my mind chanted *mistake, mistake, mistake*, but my heart . . . .

He stood unresponsive with his back to me and his hands in his pockets. I stopped and took a deep breath before slipping my arms around his stomach. My cheek pressed against his back.

He inhaled sharply, but said, "Don't."

"I can't not," I said back.

He put his hands over mine and squeezed them hard before removing them. I didn't fight him, though I wanted to. After a long moment, I backed away. My hand curled into a fist over my thumping heart. I longed for him with my whole being; I had never wanted anything more than to feel him now. But it couldn't be. There was a wall between us. I told myself over and over that it couldn't be, that it was a mistake, that the day would come when not being able to touch him wouldn't hurt *so bad* . . . .

I turned and left, focusing on anything but the sting in my chest. My whole body flinched when he hurled an angry, thunderous curse into the night. But I kept walking until I hit the exit. My fingers enclosed over the handle. I rested my forehead against the door. *Breathe. Breathe.* My body was turning against me, the longing both physical and painful. In that moment, I wanted to give it all up just to feel him one more time.

My head snapped up when swift footsteps echoed behind me. My chest constricted. It was seconds before I felt that familiar heat on my back. I swallowed dryly, staring at my white knuckles still on the handle, willing my feet to walk out the door. David's arm curled around me. His hand went to the lock. I closed my eyes. The deadbolt slid into place with a deafening click.

"Turn," he demanded. "Look at me."

My body obeyed on its own, as did my eyes. He slipped cold hands underneath my hair and grasped the nape of my neck. *You are my escape,* I said silently. In his arms, nothing could touch me; not fear, pain, monsters under the bed, attackers in the alley, the judgments of others.

He found my impatient, wet lips with his and calmed them with a sweet, close-mouthed kiss. His tongue gently coaxed my mouth open. I responded slowly but desperately, snaking my arms around his back and clutching him close as though he might disappear if I didn't. My weight sank against him, and he sucked air sharply from my parted lips.

"Oh, God," he said into my mouth. "I want you so fucking bad. I never stopped wanting you."

"Don't make me go," I pleaded quietly.

His arms tightened around me. "How could I ever make you go?" Our lips collided with the heat of reunited lovers, his tongue, hands and mouth taking over. Lovers who had just overcome their agonizing, crawling enemy: time.

His hand slid up my back and tangled in my hair, pulling slightly to expose my neck. He licked and then kissed a spot under my ear, and I wilted against him. Every part of his body was hard, from the arms that held me, to the abs that supported me, to the erection that begged me. I moved my hips into his, encouraged by the small groans that escaped the back of his throat.

With one hand still in my hair, the other dropped to my ass and squeezed me against him. His lips returned to mine with urgency, and he kissed me like he owned me. Like I was made to be kissed that way by him.

He was lacing his hand with mine, and tearing himself away to lead me from the exit. The dark master bedroom was a curved stretch of seamless windows; he placed me in front of them, the cityscape at my back.

"Take it off," he instructed and backed away to watch.

After reaching back to lower my zipper, I stepped out of my shoes and onto the cold marble floor. The jumpsuit peeled from my body like I was shedding a second skin. I wavered in my lacy black strapless bra and matching thong, awaiting instruction.

"Christ." There was anguish in his voice as he reached and turned me around. He ran a hand down the length of my spine. "You're nothing," he breathed.

I turned my head over my shoulder and responded instantly, "I'm nothing without you."

He kissed my palms reverently and then the insides of my wrists. His lips moved up my left arm and over my shoulder, moaning my name softly against my skin. "I never stopped thinking of you," he said into the curve of my neck. "My beautiful girl. I've dreamed of having you again over and over."

His words were bittersweet pangs in my heart. Pangs that I squashed by fumbling with the button on his pants until it gave. When I nudged my head under his clothing to kiss his stomach, he squeezed my shoulders and muttered. He pulled his sweater off, and I admired him in his undershirt and boxer briefs; a wall of man before me, stripped down to the basics.

He extended a hand to me, and I took it without hesitation. My legs wrapped around him when he lifted me. Yanking back the covers, he placed me atop buttery sheets against a mountain of pillows. I stayed secured to him as he ran a firm hand along my leg, fueling the ache. We stared at each other, me communicating with my eyes what I couldn't with my words.

"You know why I get that way, don't you?" he asked suddenly. "It's torture to be next to you and not be able to even touch you. I can't stay away from you, and I can't have you."

I nodded, hearing his words but nearly blind with lust. "Take this off," I commanded, fisting his shirt.

He stood and tugged at the collar to yank it over his head. His boxer briefs were next. I bit my lip at the enormity of him, solid and real, *finally so real,* and me, trembling with anticipation for him to relieve the heavy emptiness between my legs.

He was back on the bed, and I pulled at the ends of his velvety hair so he would settle his weight on me. His long body felt right covering mine.

I arched into him while his deft fingers released the clasp of my bra. His immense hand skated up my stomach. His fingers were coarse against my nipples, which tightened as he pinched them. With a hand on one breast, he lowered his head. I gasped, my breast swelling into his open mouth as he swirled his tongue around it.

The longing between my legs tormented me, impatient to be acknowledged. He explored me leisurely though, with his lips and his hands, revering each curve of my body. In some spots he grasped me urgently, and in others, his touch was so gentle that I was sure I'd imagined it. I kept my hands tangled in his hair for fear that I'd wake up from this dream empty-handed.

"Olivia," he moaned into the space between my breasts. Goose bumps lighted across my skin as his hand slipped into my panties. "Christ," he grated. His other hand grabbed mine. "Feel how wet you are," he demanded, pushing my hand between my legs. He guided our fingers into me.

"David," I begged.

"For me, baby. Does he get you dripping like this?"

I bit my lip and shook my head, my body tensing with arousal.

He released my hand, but his fingers continued sliding in and out of me. "Does he make you come?" he asked, his face hovering over mine.

I shook my head again.

He growled from his chest. "I'm still the only one. That part of you is mine." He withdrew his hand, and I lifted my hips as he removed my panties with unnecessary concentration.

"David," I begged again.

He kissed the inside of my knee. "What, baby?"

"I'm ready. Now."

"You are more than ready," he answered. The panties dropped, and he climbed back over me. He locked his lips on mine and made love to my mouth, softly and sweetly, ignoring my demand. "I was rough with you last time." His words were careful, like his kisses and caresses. "Now that I have you again, I'll fuck you slow so I can savor every second of it."

I gasped, growing even wetter from his words but also with frustration that he wasn't already inside me. My frustration grew when he stood up. I rose onto my knees and watched him pluck his pants from the floor, raiding the pockets.

I waited at the edge of the bed. We were playing with fire, and what scared me most was that I was lucid enough to stop it. But all I wanted was to cover myself in his broad, defined shoulders and spend our precious moments nestled in his smattering of chest hair.

I reached out for him. There was a crinkle of foil, and he produced a condom.

"I want to feel you, David, all of you, everything single thing," I ranted as he rolled it over his cock.

"You will, baby, you will. In time. When you're mine." I bit my bottom lip eagerly, and in that moment, I believed him. I never removed my eyes from him, scared even to blink and miss a millisecond of his beauty.

He crawled over me, forcing me onto my back. He placed his lips on mine and then trailed kisses down my neck as his hips found their place between my legs. My hands rejoiced over the hot skin of his hard, muscled back. He cupped my jaw and looked down on me. "Are you sure about this?" he asked with surprising tenderness.

I'd wanted to be this close to him for so long. The thought of losing him now chilled me to the bone, triggering a tremble through my body. "I've been empty since I left you," I whispered to him. "I need this – I need you, one last time."

"But I need more." Unable to comfort him with words, I reached between us. "I need more," he repeated. His low whisper rumbled into a groan when I touched him, and he grew stiffer in my hand.

He reached down too and wrapped his hand around mine. We both watched our hands rub the crown of his cock against my opening. "Please, I'm so ready," I insisted, because my folds were quivering. I flexed my hand around him, urging him in.

He looked back at me. "I like you slow," he said. "I can see on your face how bad you want it."

"I want it," I breathed, "bad."

With our eyes locked on each other, he eased into me until he was buried to the base. I exhaled with a loud moan. He was so swollen and hard inside of me, the thought alone coiled my insides. His thrusts began short, like he wanted deeper than our bodies would allow. He gathered me in his arms and flipped us over, keeping me against him. One hand splayed against my lower back, and the other higher, pushing my compliant breasts against the hard surface of his chest.

I straightened up to deepen the angle and stilled, drowning in the feeling of having him wholly inside me. I lifted and sank back onto him while bracing myself on his abs. I felt them flex as he sat up and secured my body in his big arms.

"You're beautiful," he said, clearing hair from my face. I could see into him, read the adoration, the desire, the hurt in his eyes.

"It's you," I breathed. "You're what I need, David. Make me whole again."

He groaned and covered the sides of my face with his big hands. My mouth parted, and I sucked in a breath as I began to rock onto him. He touched the tip of his nose to mine, and I transferred every heartbeat from my mouth to his while he lapped them up greedily.

His hand slid behind my neck and stayed there, demanding my eyes on him. "Wrap yourself around me," he said. I squeezed his shoulders and crossed my legs behind him. He gasped in a way that sounded almost pained when I undulated faster. "That's it," he panted. His hands fixed possessively over my hips and guided me onto him.

I dropped my head into the crook of his neck. Giving the control over to him drove me quickly to the edge. "Yes," I breathed against him. Without thinking I bit his shoulder, and he let out a guttural groan. His hands jumped up to my waist, urging our bodies to meet faster as his fingers flexed into my skin.

"I can feel your body reacting," he whispered fiercely with the tightening of my insides. "I can feel you getting close."

I looked into his face. Everything I had been bottling released into my bloodstream, seeping into my bones, begging for an outlet. "David," I cried with stuttered breaths, crushing his shoulders with my hands.

"I'm here, baby," he responded, his own voice ragged and shallow. "Let go. I'm here." Our fingers dug into each other at the same moment. Holding my gaze, he growled from his chest, and I bore down on him. His muscles tensed and contracted underneath my hands, and I watched, rapt, as he gave in. The raw pleasure in his face as he climaxed pushed me over the edge. I came onto him with a body-wracking orgasm that shot waves from my core to the surface of my skin. As my body heated with bliss, I called out for him. Months of simmering loneliness bubbled over, and I collapsed into his arms with unsolicited sobs.

He wrapped me up tightly as his shoulders heaved with deep breaths. "I'm here, baby, I'm here," he repeated into my hair. "I've got you."

I tangled my fingers in his chest hair and released the pain the only way I could: all at once and with unstoppable force. His hands stroked my back, my hair, but his clutch never loosened. His arms easily engulfed me, and though I was aching, I'd never felt safer than curled into his embrace.

"I'm so sorry," I said finally, when I'd caught my breath.

He let the words hang for a moment. "Never apologize," he responded, rocking me against him. "Do you hear me? How can you apologize for that?"

"Oh, David," I moaned into his skin. He rested his forehead against my sternum, rubbing the still-tingling skin of my back. "What are we going to do?" I asked in a rush of breath. I wasn't sure if he heard, because he never responded.

Eventually, he rolled us both to set me on my back. He disconnected from me, tossed the condom aside and propped his head above mine with his hand. His fingers played with my hair, pushing it back on to the pillow as he looked down at me.

"I don't always cry after sex," I said, an empty attempt at humor. "Just with you apparently."

"You can't help your reaction."

I studied the man above me, still in disbelief that he was, in fact, above me. He concentrated on my hair, raking his hands through the tangles as best he could. "I wish I could help it," I said.

"Why? Just let go. You don't need to manage yourself with me."

I sighed and dropped my gaze. "*With you*, I have no control."

"I told you before, I like you this way. Unguarded. Undone." I bathed in his adoration; his fingers in my hair, his sweet but fleeting words. Already, the guilt was building inside of me, demanding my acknowledgment, trying to break the moment. As if he were listening to my thoughts, he said softly, "I want to take all your sadness away."

My chin quivered, and I pressed my fingertips to my eyes to stem any more tears. *It's been so hard, David.*

"I know," he said. He encircled my wrists and carefully pulled my hands from my face. "I know."

I blinked up at him. Had I said it aloud?

He placed a hand on the base of my neck and kissed me, claiming me with that one gesture. "But I can't fix it if you won't let me." His eyes searched mine, and I looked away. "Don't turn away from me."

"I can't," I whispered. I went to sit up, but his hand on my chest pushed me back into the pillow.

"I said don't turn away. Look at me."

My jaw clenched; in that moment, I wasn't strong enough to keep the hurt off my face, and I didn't want him to see it. But his hand slid up to my chin, and he turned me to him. His expression was stern, but there was concern in his eyes. "I want to make it better."

With my face locked on his, I said, "You can't. You can't fix it. This can never be anything but broken."

"To hear you say that . . . It kills me."

"But it's true. We're headed for disaster. Even if I walk away right now, too much has happened already."

His brows dipped. "Are you going to walk away?"

My chin was quivering again, and he rubbed it with his thumb. "How can I?" I whispered. "How can I not?"

"These have been the longest months of my life."

"For me too," I said in a breath.

"I don't think I could give you up again."

"But you *have* to. We're all going to get hurt."

"I'll do whatever it takes so that you don't."

His hand slid away, but I held his gaze. "Even if it means letting me go?"

He cleared his throat and looked up at the headboard. His answer sounded far off, as if from a distance. "Would that make it better?"

"It's just too late," I said, unwelcome tears spilling from the corners of my eyes. "I did this to myself. But I don't know how to make it stop. It – it hurts to be away from you."

His face folded, and he cupped my cheek. "So don't be away from me."

I curled under the shelter of his broad shoulders, hiding my face from him. "You don't know what you're saying," I said, holding in the tears with everything I had.

"I know exactly what I'm saying."

"No," I said resolutely, clutching the pillow. *But it hurts so much.* He enclosed around my quaking shoulders, littering my hair with kisses until I slept.

CHAPTER 15

I WOKE ABRUPTLY and shot upright. I was in the very big bed, and the breathtaking city sprawled around me, but I didn't care because I was alone. I eased out of the bed and stood slowly. Had it not been for my surroundings, I would have sworn it was all a vivid dream. I slipped into an oversized terrycloth robe and slid open the door to the deck.

Hanging my toes over the edge of the pool, I watched David complete a lap. He whipped his hair off his face to look up at me. "Did I wake you?" he asked from below. "I couldn't sleep."

"No." I shook my head dreamily. Steam spiraled upward from the water; I was dizzy just from the way his wet, glistening body was backlit by the glowing pool.

"Why are you smiling at me like that?" he asked.

I sat and dipped my feet in the warm water. I reached out to push wet hair from his forehead. He moved between my knees and skimmed his hands down my calves to shackle my ankles. Leaning back on my palms, I closed my eyes at the feeling of his skin against mine.

Our rooftop was completely silent, only water splashed as his hands glided back up, over my thighs and underneath the robe. My breath quickened as he pulled the tie open, grasped my waist and slid me to the edge. His head buried in my lap while I fingered his dripping, inky hair. He eased my thighs apart to nuzzle me. His breath was soft and tantalizing, and I exhaled a moan.

With his first firm lick, my arms buckled. He tasted me slowly, stopping now and then to suck and kiss. With an ankle in each hand, he bent my knees so my feet curled over the edge. His arms wrapped around my hips, securing me to him. When his nose nudged into my clit, I jerked against his firm hold. He inserted and spread two fingers to open me wider. His tongue probed inside of me quicker, with more pressure, and my legs began to shake.

At some point I'd fallen onto the concrete and was now clenching the lip of the pool with tense arms. With his mouth working its magic and his thumb on my clit, he coaxed me into rippling, full-body orgasm that had my back bowing off the ground and my throat surrendering to soft moans.

As I lay limp, he pulled my arms from the robe and lifted me. He slid me down his body and into the pool until I was submerged. When I resurfaced, his hand touched my face for a deep, penetrating kiss. He was hot, tasted like me and like him. The night was cold but the pool heated, a heady mix that had my mind spinning.

"Look down."

"Oh," I gasped. I instinctively clung to him when I saw that he had swum us to the overhang.

"It's safe," he reassured, but he held me close. A thrill spiraled through me as I peered down at the city. His feet planted firmly on the glass bottom, but I knew I would be treading water if I let go.

He was looking at me strangely. Something fiery, but deep and sensual. "You're so beautiful," he told me softly. "Do you have any idea what you do to me?" I wanted to look away; it was too much – but his burning brown eyes, his dripping wet lashes, his razorblade jawline . . . He was so arrestingly beautiful in that moment. He licked his lips, curled a hand into my wet hair and pulled. "Christ," he murmured. "I need you now." Hearing him voice his desire turned my insides liquid. He devoured my neck with hard, unforgiving kisses that strayed over my shoulders and up to my earlobe.

He cut us through the water and out of the pool, depositing our bodies onto a lounge chair with an outstretched hand.

"Cold?" he asked, breathing heavily over me.

"No," I replied, because when I was underneath him, I could never be anything but warm. I wrapped my legs around him, and he dropped his hips. I cried out as he drove into me with a grunt.

His face fell into the curve of neck, and he stilled. "You feel amazing wrapped around my cock," he panted. "You're so warm."

When a breeze blew over us, I locked my ankles at his lower back, pulling him closer. "*Christ*, Olivia." He rolled his hips into me and pulled back to the tip. His eyes locked on me, and his next stroke was firm but slow. My face flamed feeling his every inch move into me and then out again. His hand moved to my hips, steadying me for his next powerful plunge. He rooted himself there, gritted his teeth and squeezed me against him. "Deep enough?"

"It's d-deep," I stammered, because I was so full with him I thought I might split apart. "Don't stop."

His thrusts continued steady and firm, the perfect complement to his soft and buttery voice. "I'm so hard for you," he muttered, nibbling my ear. "So hard, and you're so hot."

I was still thrumming from my first orgasm, and my climax built quickly. I almost came when he began to swivel his pelvis, feeling all of me with each rotation.

"You're close," he said as he switched from swiveling to short, fast drives. "Kiss me."

Our lips clashed hungrily, and I could taste his desire for me. "Show me how it feels," he ordered into my mouth. "Come, Olivia." My name rolled off his tongue with command, turning my world on its side. I clenched around him as he pounded me through a pulsing orgasm. Despite the cold, I was warm and flushed when I fell back against the cushion.

"You feel too goddamn good," he said through a set jaw while grinding faster into me.

I dove my hands in his hair and pulled. "I want you to come, David, come inside me, make me yours."

"Not without," he paused as his face contorted with pleasure, "a condom."

"Then come in my mouth."

He groaned loudly and jumped up before I'd finished the sentence. I went to touch him, but he stopped me with a hand around my wrist. "I want you on your knees," he growled. I climbed down onto the hard concrete, and he took my chin in his hand. "Open."

I obeyed, and he slid into me. He threw his head back when I closed my lips around him. I circled my tongue around the tip before taking him as deeply as I could.

"That's it, baby," he praised. His fingers threaded in my hair and pulled. "How do you taste on my cock? Hmm? Look at me."

I blinked my eyes up to his.

He hissed and jerked slightly but held my stare. My tongue ran over every glorious inch I could reach. I pushed him to the back of my throat and stroked with my hand whatever I couldn't taste. "Hands behind your back," he admonished.

Oh, God, I love the way you rumble when you tell me what to do. Take me, use me, have me, David, I'm yours . . . .

He fisted my hair tighter and with one thrust, he took over. I sheathed my teeth with my lips, and he pushed himself to the back of my throat until I gagged. He pulled back but continued fucking my mouth, his moans low and throaty.

"Fuck, I'm gonna come so fucking hard," he warned. My tongue flattened against his crown, and his body shook as he began to ejaculate. I lapped up the first few drops before he yanked my hair and erupted into my eager mouth. I swallowed him as I could get him, letting the saltiness fill my mouth and run down my throat.

"Holy shit," he breathed, loosening his grip. I waited on my knees while he caught his breath. He hauled me up by my armpits and kissed me hard. "That was so good," he started, "it should be illegal."

"I'd go to jail for that," I responded seriously.

He laughed and kissed me again, his hands falling down my arms. He interlocked his fingers with mine and ran his other hand over my hair, tugging softly on the ends. "Are you cold?"

I nodded. He led me back into the suite and gestured once at the toilet. Remembering his rule about peeing after sex, I rolled my eyes but sat down anyway.

"How about a nice hot shower?" he asked.

"Yes, please," I rasped, not yet recovered.

I found him moments later cloaked in billowing steam. "Come on, pretty girl," he said, opening his arms. The heat of both the water and his hard body was heavenly after the cold. He planted a sweet kiss on my lips when I looked up at him. "You drive me mad," he whispered.

I smiled into his mouth and just said, "Likewise."

His hands moved over my face, and my eyelids drooped shut. He smoothed my hairline repeatedly and kissed me carefully. "I never want to let you go," he murmured.

Though his words were warm, a chill wound through me. Our bond was strengthening alarmingly fast. He ran his thumbs over my eyebrows. I opened my eyes cautiously, because I knew what I would see on his face: something stronger and more intense than I was prepared to accept. As water dripped from his long lashes, I remembered when our eyes had met for the first time and the jolt of electricity I'd felt. *What does he see when he looks at me that way?*

I rested my cheek against his solid pecs and clung to him as he massaged shampoo into my hair. I was content to just listen to his heartbeat while he cleansed me.

"I need conditioner," I said against his chest when he'd finished.

"You *need* conditioner?" he teased, but he ran it through my strands, lovingly working out the tangles. I still didn't move when he washed his own hair. My eyes squeezed shut as the suds slithered down his skin and onto my face.

When he shut off the water, I let him go reluctantly. He wrapped a large white towel around his waist and held another open for me. *I prefer his skin,* I thought, but let him envelop me in it. He ran his hands over my covered shoulders to warm me and moved some hair from my face. "We should get your hair dry."

"It's all right," I said and yawned. "I'm tired."

"You can't sleep with wet hair."

"It'll dry before I get home," I reassured him.

His face fell, and he stepped back with my shoulders still firmly in his hands. "You're going home?"

"Well, yes, I have to. I can get a cab."

"Isn't Bill . . . ?" His mouth distorted as though he'd bitten into a lemon. "Isn't he out of town?"

"He'll be back sometime tomorrow." I glanced away.

"Well," David said and exhaled an irritated laugh, "if you think I'm letting you go home alone at this time of night, then you'd better think again."

I furrowed my brows and turned back to him. "I'm not a child. I can get myself back in one piece."

He raised an eyebrow at me. "Think about that one."

I nodded. "Okay, you have a point, but the confrontation with Mark Alvarez was a fluke. He's behind bars, and that's all over."

He shook his head. "Not going to happen. If you must go, I'll drive you."

I shifted on my feet, weighing my options. I was so sleepy, and David was so warm and comfortable . . . . Guilt and desire were constantly battling inside me, overcoming one another, tormenting me in the process.

"Come on," he said with a sigh. "One step at a time." He pulled a hair dryer from a drawer and motioned me over. I stood in front of him tilting my head upward as he raked a hand through my hair. "Just tell me if I hurt you."

His eyebrows dipped as he concentrated, careful not to pull while he detangled my hair. It made me smile to think that he'd just been pulling it much harder without a second thought. And I'd loved the uninhibited rawness of it.

"Keep smiling like that, and I might have to bend you over this sink." He gave my hair a playful tug when I widened my eyes. I rewrapped the towel under my arms and took the rare moment to appreciate the man in front of me. The shampoo made him smell fresh like early morning. His pecs flexed in unison with his biceps as his arms moved over me. I admired the lines of the square jaw just inches above my head that gave way to a long neck and sprawling, muscled shoulders . . . .

I quivered and ducked backward, hoisting myself onto the counter. I wrapped my legs around him and pulled him to the sink. "Your turn," I said, taking the hairdryer.

He inhaled appreciatively when I stuck my fingers in his hair, which was really only damp. He kissed my nose.

"Now, now," I scolded. "I take blow jobs very seriously. No one goes to bed with wet hair tonight."

He laughed with his whole body, and I secured him closer, locking my feet against his lower back. We were level now, and his eyes watched me closely; I could feel them even though I kept my focus on his silken hair. Once I'd finished, I set the blow dryer on the sink and styled his hair away from his eyes. My own hair was messy, but it didn't matter. How could it be bad when he'd fixed it himself?

He pulled on my towel so it fell open. His eyes closed, and he leaned in to inhale deeply, as if committing my smell to memory. He placed a kiss on the underside of my jaw. Curious hands explored me, touching wherever he could reach. I flinched when he passed over my scar.

His eyes dropped to my lap, and he gripped my thighs. "You taste so good," he uttered, licking his lips. He pulled me in for a hug, and his finger trailed goose bumps down my spine. "Did you eat tonight?"

"Hmm?"

"Did you eat? Aren't you hungry?"

"I'm fine," I sighed into his neck. "And I should go. It's late."

He stepped away, and I shivered instantly. My face distorted as I looked at him. "I'm so cold without you."

"I'm sorry, baby," he said. "It is cold tonight."

I shook my head. "All the time. I've been cold since that night. I can't get warm."

"It's probably all the goddamn weight you lost," he said. "This is unhealthy. What happened to the girl I took for burgers a few months ago?"

"She was lost," I said, my voice hitching as I looked at him.

He embraced me again. "Oh, baby. If it were up to me, you'd never be cold."

"I know," I said, because I thought I did. I thought I believed that he really did want more from me, but it terrified me when he said it.

"I'll take you home," he said, pulling back. "But for the love of God, Olivia, please let me make you something to eat."

"How?"

"We had an event up here last night. There are some leftovers."

"Will you be shirtless?" I asked, knocking my heels against the cupboard underneath me. My mouth formed into a circle. "You're blushing."

"No, I'm not. If those are your conditions, then fine. I accept."

I blinked at him and hopped off the counter. "All right," I said, shrugging my robe back on.

"Can I put underwear on?"

"Hmm . . ." I closed one eye as I thought, and he laughed.

I went to leave, but he pulled me backward and into his arms. With my back to his front, he leaned into my hair and murmured, "How's that for a reflection?"

I looked up at the mirror. He made me beautiful. Together, we were beautiful; a puzzle with only two pieces. I shifted my eyes to his and nodded. He held my stare a moment and let me go with a kiss on the cheek.

I snuggled into the warmth of my robe as I wandered to the kitchen while he changed. "Are there plates?" I called.

He appeared, tutting at me. "I'll prepare it."

"I don't mind."

"Go on, and let me make you something to eat." He furrowed his brow at the contents of the refrigerator. "There isn't much, but I'll come up with something."

I propped my chin in my hand and watched him navigate the kitchen. "Do you like to cook?"

"No. I usually eat out or my housekeeper makes something a couple times a week."

It was my turn to tsk. "You do need a woman in your life."

He answered with a grunt, but I was comforted that there was at least one thing he wasn't proficient in. I smiled like a schoolgirl as I watched, enjoying the view of his spectacular, ridged torso and taut ass. His muscles were hard but not bulky, and they became more defined as he moved. I was tempted to show my appreciation by exploring them with my tongue. Once, after he stuck something in the microwave, he stole away for a chaste kiss on the lips.

He set down two plates of day-old hors d'oeuvres and pulled his chair to the corner of the table so we were close. "Next time *you'll* be topless, right?" he teased.

I forced a laugh, but I had caught his slip. *Next time.* "However you'll have me," I responded, deliberately gulping down the nagging guilt.

His eyes darkened with the dilation of his pupils. He reached out and slipped his hand in my robe, tugging it open slightly to reveal my breast. "I'll have you any way I can, until you beg me to stop."

At his touch, I sighed, deflating against the chair. If he were mine, I would have told him that I'd never ask him to stop. That he could take me any way he needed me. His fingers grazed over my nipple and under the curve of my breast. I arched toward him as his hand dropped behind me, caressing my lower back and sliding over my ribs. He pressed my waist, and his thumb ran over my scar. His eyes burned when he said, "Tell me."

CHAPTER 16

HE WANTED ME TO OPEN for him again, and he had a way of making me. But didn't he understand that it made everything harder? I sighed heavily. "The best way I know how to deal with it is to forget, David."

"The best way or the only way?"

I smirked at him. He grabbed the seat of my chair and pulled me to him in one quick jerk. With a firm hand under my jaw, he thumbed my cheek and then kissed the corner of my lips.

"Even when you smirk, you have the prettiest mouth I've ever seen." His breath was hot on my skin as he said, "I think about it all the time."

My heart stopped, and I was sure I'd blown a circuit. "All the time?" I exhaled.

"All the time. To see your mouth wrapped around my cock earlier is something I will never forget."

My nipples tingled and tightened. I swallowed. His mouth brushed over my skin, and he pressed a lingering kiss on my temple. When he drew back, he maintained contact with a hand over my hair.

"You're safe with me," he said quietly, and I scrambled after his mood shift. After a beat, and without removing his hand, he said, "Forget about the scar. Tell me about growing up in Dallas."

"What?" I breathed.

"I don't get much time with you, indulge me."

I waited for my heart to calm while he stroked my hair. "I was a happy kid," I said. He nodded encouragingly, so after I dipped a buffalo wing in blue cheese dressing and took a bite, I continued. "That's how I remember it anyway. We lived in a nice home, which actually had a white fence." I smiled. "Gretchen and her brother John were my best friends. They lived around the corner."

"What were you like as a little girl?"

I dropped my eyes. Why was I telling him this? What was the point in learning about each other? It could only lead to more pain.

"Hey," he whispered, and I looked up again. "What were you like?"

I closed my eyes and the memory began to seep in – the memory of the girl I was before the divorce. It was a place I rarely let myself go. "I was *alive*."

There was a hint of concern on his face when I opened my eyes again. "Alive?" he asked.

"I was always doing something. John would tease me about being a chatterbox, and when I wasn't talking, I was making up stories or games. I wrote everything in journals. I always had a pad of paper with me."

David's forehead creased with a deep 'V'. "I thought you didn't like writing."

I searched my brain, trying to remember when I had said that. "I used to. A lot. A teacher told my parents that I had a knack for creative writing and grammar skills above average for my age. My mom wrote for our local paper and had published a few books before I was born. Sometimes she had two or three novels in the works, and as soon as I was old enough, she would have me sit and edit them. When I told her I liked writing and not editing, she would make this face and tell me that I didn't have what it took to be an author. Editing was what I should focus on.

"Anyway, regardless, Gretchen and I started an unofficial school newspaper. I would write short little articles, sometimes about our classmates, sometimes fiction, and she would illustrate it." I blinked a few times and took a sip of water. "My dad would photocopy it, and we'd pass it out every couple weeks or so. John called us nerds, but he always stole a copy."

"Did you ever think, as you got older, about writing your own book?"

"Only when I was a kid. That's my mom's thing."

He dropped his hand and sat back in his chair. "And you don't want to be like her."

"No."

"Why not?"

"My mom was, and continues to be, difficult. She . . ." I studied the table as I thought. "She could be distant. And mean. She was very jealous and sometimes, when my dad went on business trips or stayed out late, she would drink. It made things worse. My dad stopped allowing alcohol in the house, but when she got in a mood, it didn't stop her."

I paused, and he placed his large hand over my lower ribs, consuming the small scar. "Is that how this happened?"

His hand was incredibly warm and comforting, and I covered it with one of mine. "That night . . ." I paused and closed my eyes. I inhaled deeply and deflated against the chair with a long exhale. The last fifteen years flashed behind my lids. "That night was hard, but everything that came after was worse."

"Why?"

"Thirteen isn't the best time to have your life flipped upside down. I was still figuring out who I was, and it was easy to shut down. I stopped playing, stopped writing, and I just . . . was different afterward. I had to grow up fast. Suddenly everyone expected me to be an adult about the whole situation, but I was just a kid. And after, I wanted to take care of my dad the way my mom had. Better, actually. So I had to grow up. I had to take control."

"You like to be in control."

"If I'm not, I feel . . . helpless." I picked at something on the table with my free hand, while the other one still sat atop his.

"Is that why you don't like people touching you?"

My eyes darted up to his. "What do you mean?"

"Sometimes you flinch. Not with me, I mean. But for instance, that jerk-off earlier."

"Steve?"

"Don't say that name to me again, all right? Yes, him, or the bartender from Lucy's engagement party."

This way he had of figuring me out, I didn't know if it bothered me. It was as if I had no secrets from him, and there was nobody in my life that I let get away with that. "I just don't like when strangers touch me. That's not unusual."

"Well, might it have something to do with wanting to be in control all the time? Or even what happened that night?"

"I don't think I want to talk about this," I said, trying my best to sound indignant.

He looked disappointed but nodded. "Do you ever read what you wrote as a kid?"

"She destroyed everything."

"Your mom?" His expression was horrified.

I shrugged. "After we left. It was childish stuff anyway."

"I refuse to believe that."

"But it's true." I smiled warmly. "I bet you were a perfect kid."

He took a moment to respond. "I was." I laughed, and he shook his head. "I was pretty good, but I had my moments."

"What does that mean?"

"It means that I would sometimes get overly excited about the things or the people I loved."

"You're being vague."

He narrowed his eyes at me playfully. "I was good. I got straight A's, and I didn't party too much because I played sports. But I can be a little hotheaded, and it was harder for me to control as a kid."

"You don't say," I responded without thinking.

He looked at me a second and then raised his brows. "You might not believe me, but I'm usually pretty level-headed. I hate bullshit, and I don't let it get to me. Certain things just set me off, especially when I feel . . . protective or possessive of something."

"Something?"

"Or someone."

"Did it ever get you into trouble?"

"I got into a couple fights, yeah. One almost landed me in juvie."

"Over what?"

"That particular one happened at school when this guy called Jessa a bitch. I got lucky though; his parents were pretty fair and dropped the charges. I think they were secretly happy that I laid him out, because he was an asshole."

I giggled.

"I almost killed Alvarez that night," he said seriously. "If I'd known what he said to you," he swallowed, "I would have."

I believed him. Mark had pinned me against a wall, hissing in my ear how he would show me a good time when David found us. I remembered the anger that had radiated from his body that night as he pushed a gun into Mark's neck.

"Does that scare you?" he asked.

We searched each other's faces in the late hour, as the city slept around us. "I don't know. No," I said softly. "You don't scare me."

"Even though I can be a little . . . intense?"

I twisted my lips and considered this. Nothing about him frightened me, so I shook my head.

"Good." He exhaled, looked down at my plate and grinned. "You ate."

My answering smile turned into a yawn.

"I guess I should get you home."

I nodded. "It's been a while since I stayed up all night."

He leaned in and kissed me. With his face an inch from mine, he said, "Know that you would be spending the night in my arms if things were different. I wouldn't let you leave." He delivered the last line in a firm, almost angry manner. Before I could respond, he said, "I'm parked in the garage. We can take the elevator straight down so there's no chance of running into anyone."

"Thanks for taking care of me."

His lips pursed, and he turned away. I followed him from the kitchen to reluctantly change back into my jumpsuit. While I waited for him, I checked my phone, bracing myself for Gretchen's reaction, but there was only one text from Greg.

Sep 5, 2012 11:17 PM
Heard from Gretch?

I shrugged it off and when I looked up, David was watching me. He walked over slowly and cupped the side of my hair. "Ready?" he asked. I nodded into his palm.

"Why's it so cold?" I grumbled on the way to the car.

"Didn't you bring a jacket or anything?"

"Did you see me in a jacket?"

"I think I might have something." He stopped at the Mercedes, popped the trunk and rifled around until he produced a pink hoodie. "Here."

"What is this?"

"A sweater."

"Whose is it?"

"Who cares? You're cold, I have a sweater, put it on."

"No." I handed it back to him.

"Olivia, put it on," he ordered with finality and closed the trunk. He opened the passenger door and raised his eyebrows at me. I shrugged into it before climbing in sulkily. Flowery perfume assaulted my nostrils, and I sneezed. I hated the pink sweater.

"Whose is it?" I asked again once we were driving.

"It's Dani's." He glanced over at me. "Isn't she a friend of yours?"

"Yes."

"So why are you making that face?"

I sighed. "Because she's a friend. I've known her for a long time. And it's weird . . . ."

"Maybe you could return it to her for me."

I glared across the car at him and then narrowed my eyes when his shoulders pulsed with a suppressed laugh. "It's not funny," I said. "The idea of you two together makes me sick." I dropped my head between my knees, and he was silent. I knew I was being unfair, but I didn't care; when it came to David, none of my reactions seemed to be in my control.

"I'm sorry," he said graciously, grasping the back of my neck. "Nothing's happened though."

"Have you broken things off?"

"No, but – "

"Then it still I could," I clipped.

He sighed heavily. *Why isn't he reassuring me that it won't?* I ran my hands over my face and decided not to let it ruin one of the best nights of my life. I took a soothing breath and looked over at him. "I'm sorry. It's not my place."

His gaze remained fixed out the windshield when he said, "It could be."

I reached out and put my hand on his thigh, and he rubbed my forearm.

"So what now?" I asked. Outside, the sky was gradually lightening to pink with the rising sun.

"I don't know. I'm going back to New York though, I need to spend some time on that project."

"For how long?"

"A week or so."

"Oh." A week suddenly felt like a lifetime.

"I'll e-mail you when I return. At work?"

I sighed and looked out the window. Even without my veil of lust, why couldn't I just say no? And why did it feel like not saying no was almost worse than anything I'd done up that point?

Even when he sat across from me, I yearned for him. I felt myself being pulled in opposing directions, crumbling under the pressure of two men. Bill, who I loved and who had been there for me whenever I needed him. And David, who drew me in so completely that I didn't see anything but him. But it wasn't just the way he physically consumed me, it was an emotional, intense, overwhelming consumption of my body, mind and heart.

"Here we are, Miss Olivia."

I squeezed his thigh and looked back at him. "Thanks for driving me."

"Wait."

"Oops, almost forgot," I said, zipping out of the hoodie. "You're crazy if you think I'm going to return it to her."

"Not that. Come here." He reached out a long arm and pulled my jaw to him. A palpable silence settled around us when he gave me a hard peck that softened into an open-mouth kiss. When he pulled back, he wore a goofy grin.

"I'll miss you," I blurted.

His smile faltered, and he swallowed hard. With a nod, he said, "I'll miss you too."

CHAPTER 17

DAVID HAD MEANT TO CONVEY SOMETHING with the way he'd looked at me Saturday night, but I wasn't prepared to learn what it was. Nonetheless, being looked at that way was addicting. In fact, I couldn't get it, or other intimate things, off my mind the remainder of the weekend.

After an agonizing Monday morning, I took a break to call Gretchen. "Are you still asleep?" I asked when she picked up the phone.

"Maybe," she rasped.

"Why aren't you at work?"

"It was a long weekend."

"Lucy is back from Paris. Should we do happy hour tonight? We can surprise her by having Greg show up."

"Um, no."

"Why not?" I pouted, thinking it had been a very clever idea.

"Greg . . . We're off. I think it's over."

"What?" I screeched. "Oh, honey, what did he do?"

"He didn't do anything. It was me. I left with someone else on Saturday night."

"From Revelin? Who?"

"Does it matter? I didn't even really know the guy."

"Why would you do that?" I waited as I heard her shifting around, most likely sitting up in bed.

"I don't know," she said finally, her voice cracking. "I just freaked, I guess."

"Freaked?"

"I spent years hating Greg for what he did, and all of a sudden I'm supposed to forgive him?"

"You aren't supposed to do anything."

"Things are just moving too quickly. I think maybe this is for the best."

"I'm really sorry, Gretch."

"Why? It's my fault."

"Because I know how much he means to you. And I know it's not just about some other guy."

"Um. Why are you being so understanding?"

The question caught me off guard, and I hesitated. "Listen, I'm coming over tonight and bringing something really bad for us to eat. We can talk about everything."

"I would like that," she said. Her tone made me realize how much she needed to talk. And I hadn't been there for her. I hadn't even asked her how things had been with Greg, the one who broke her heart all those years ago.

~

Gretchen answered the door in her pajamas, and I wondered if she'd been wearing them all day.

"We come bearing gifts," I said.

"Really?" Gretchen asked when I handed her a DVD. She stepped aside to let us into her apartment. "*My Best Friend's Wedding*? That's like the worst thing you could have picked."

"Why?" Lucy asked, clearly hurt.

"No, it has nothing to do with you," Gretchen said. She plopped onto the couch, and we followed. "I'll just put it out there. I've been seeing Greg again."

"What? Greg as in *Greg*?" Lucy's eyes doubled in size. "I think I need to sit down. Liv, wine, *now*," she instructed.

"He called me a few months ago to say he'd taken a job here."

"Here as in Chicago?"

"Yes."

"Oh, my," Lucy said, shaking her head.

"I didn't call him back at first. After several attempts to get in touch though, I finally gave in and agreed to see him."

"Seriously?"

"Yes. It started with a drink, an apology for what he's put me through. He said he'd made a mistake by leaving. The second time we met up, he said he wanted to try again. Of course I protested, but you know how it goes. One thing led to another, and well, we've started dating again."

Lucy clamped a hand over her mouth and muffled, "You've been keeping this to yourself?"

"Yes. I guess I was afraid he'd change his mind again. It was mortifying the first time being dumped like that. I don't exactly want witnesses if it happens again."

"He's the one who should be mortified," I pointed out.

"Why is he moving here?" Lucy asked.

"There was an opening with his company, but . . ."

"What?"

"Well, he says that's not the reason. Something about wanting to be with me," she said, reddening. "Because he misses how we were."

Lucy sighed and rested her chin in her hand. "Wow."

"I'm not sure I believe it, though," Gretchen added.

"Why wouldn't you?" Lucy demanded, her tone teetering on outrage.

"He doesn't exactly have a squeaky clean record," I reminded Lucy.

"But maybe it's different this time," Lucy countered. "People change, they want different things as they get older."

"That's putting a lot of faith in him," Gretchen grumbled.

Lucy looked thoughtful as she took a sip of wine. "So let me get this straight. He left his entire life behind and moved across an *ocean* for you. Geez, that's like right out of a movie."

Gretchen looked skeptical. "I don't know if I would quite say – "

"This is like, super romantic," Lucy chirped over her. "He realized he made a huge mistake and couldn't spend another day without you."

Gretchen rolled her eyes, but a dimple appeared in her cheek.

The corner of Lucy's mouth tugged, and she broke into a large smile. "This is major."

"It is?"

"This could be it."

"I don't follow . . . ." Gretchen's eyes narrowed as she focused on Lucy.

"He might be 'the one.'"

"Jesus Christ," Gretchen blurted. "It's only been a month!"

"Gretchen, he moved here from *Japan* for you. It's not like he drove over from Indianapolis. He couldn't stop thinking about you for, like, five years or whatever. That's true love. You're the one that got away."

"I think you have that the wrong way around."

"Don't you love him?"

"I think so."

"You think?"

"After all this time, how do I know if I still love him? Is he the same person? Am I?"

"Of course," Lucy stated.

"But how can I know that?"

"You can't, Gretchen. Love means having faith." Lucy swirled the wine in her glass and looked off into the distance. "Of course you still love him. That doesn't just go away."

"Maybe not . . . but what if it lessened? I'm not really sure how I feel."

"Love doesn't have levels," Lucy decided. "It just is."

"So you can't love one person more than another?" I asked.

"No, I just mean that love doesn't change or morph into something else. It just is, you either love him or you don't. Of course I love Andrew more than anyone else, but that doesn't mean I love you guys any less. I just love you in a different way."

"What about loving two people at the same time?" They both looked at me. "In the same way," I added.

"You mean like friends?"

I felt suddenly warm and pulled at my collar. "No . . . not friends."

"I don't understand," was all Lucy said while her eyebrows met in the middle.

"Like what if Gretchen had met someone else when Greg was away. What if she were married now? When Greg shows up, does she love them both?"

"Well, no."

"Why not?"

"Because that's just not plausible," Lucy said crossly. "You can only love one or the other."

"Never mind," I said. I knew better than to point out that maybe her theory had some holes.

"Shit," Gretchen said. "This is much too philosophical for my state of mind. I think we are getting way, way ahead of ourselves. Marriage is not even in the equation, trust me."

Lucy pursed her lips to show that she didn't approve. She looked at me. "I'm not even going to ask what you think."

"I'm with Gretchen. Anyway, there's one very important detail that makes this whole discussion pointless: they are breaking up."

"Wait, back up," Lucy said. "What?"

Gretchen fidgeted with the fringe of the nearest pillow. "I ditched him for another guy on Saturday night."

Lucy cocked her head at Gretchen and shook it slowly. "Gretchen, how could you? After all this time you've waited for him to come back."

"Waited? I haven't waited for shit. I thought I'd never see him again, and I'd made my peace with that. But then he comes waltzing back into my life, in true Greg fashion, and expects things to go back to the way they were. Do you think I want to put myself through that again?"

I slanted my lips at her. "But you should have discussed your feelings with him like a mature adult."

"You're one to talk, Olivia."

My jaw dropped, and my eyes darted over her.

"What does that mean?" Lucy asked.

"Nothing," Gretchen said with a sigh. "I'm just upset. You're right, I could have handled it better."

"She hadn't even slept with Greg," I told Lucy.

"You didn't?"

"No. And I didn't hook up with the Saturday night guy either. I couldn't bring myself to do it."

"So just tell Greg that," I said.

"It doesn't matter, what matters is that I left him. I've been avoiding him ever since, and I'm sure he's pissed. I don't even know if I want to work things out. What if he leaves again?"

If I'd had more faith in Greg, or love for that matter, I would have told her not to be afraid. Even though my marriage had been happy, the disappointment of my parents' divorce was always fresh in my mind. There was no guarantee that people wouldn't suddenly change their minds. And to tell Gretchen that Greg wouldn't leave again was a reassurance I couldn't give her. I grabbed her hand instead. She tilted her head at me but didn't say anything.

"If you love him, then you have to try," Lucy said, her voice an octave above a whisper. "Don't give up because of fear."

Gretchen rubbed her temples. "Liv, I don't think I can go to the ball this weekend."

"Ball?"

"Um, yes, the animal shelter charity event that you hounded me to buy tickets for."

"Oh, right. The masquerade ball. I completely forgot that was this weekend. It's fine, you already paid. They'll get the money."

"Dani will be in town, I could give them to her," Lucy offered. My ears perked at the mention of her name.

"She can have them."

"So, can we talk about my Parisian honeymoon now?" Lucy asked excitedly.

~

Droplets of turquoise water, the smell of chlorine, skin slick against skin, hovering above the rest of the world, wandering fingers, curious tongues, fistfuls of hair . . . . Heat pooled inside of me, turning me warm and tender. He'd cradled me on his lap and held me close. He'd not only listened but had heard me, and when he watched me, it was with attentive eyes. I tried to forget the feeling of his lips claiming mine or of him swelling inside of me.

I jumped when the front door slammed. I picked up the nearest magazine, hiding my flushed face behind it.

"Hey."

"Hi, honey," I said from behind an article on graceful aging. "How was work?"

All week had been that way; on the train, in my office, at the deli – I couldn't stop the scorching memories from infiltrating my life. Between work and home, I hadn't even been able to relieve myself, and I was feeling full to the brim with no outlet.

"Liv?" Bill asked.

"Yes?"

"I asked how your day was."

"Oh, fine. Do you want to see your mask for the masquerade ball this weekend?"

"I don't really care. Thanks for picking it out. Jeanine has a couple houses she wants us to see. How's Sunday?"

Shame. It was red and ugly and written all over my face. No, I could not see houses with Bill, because I was gutless and afraid. How could I tell him that things were moving too fast when for him, they weren't moving fast enough?

He came and sat next to me on the couch. "Are you all right?"

"Yes, why?"

"You look pale," he said, holding the back of his hand against my forehead. He brushed some hair from my face. "I'm worried that you're slipping away again. You've been quiet this week."

"Oh," I said softly. "No, I'm okay."

"I think . . ." He paused and looked over at the coffee table. "I think it might be time to see someone."

"Someone?"

"Therapy. I know what you're thinking, and yes, I still think it's sort of bullshit. But I'm running out of ideas, and this is getting to be a little much."

Glossy pages crinkled when I clenched the magazine. "Therapy?" I repeated angrily. "For me or for us?"

"For you," he said, drawing back. "Why would we need therapy?"

"I don't know," I said. "Why would I?"

He hesitated. "One minute you're up, the next you're down. At this point I'm willing to try anything."

"I – I . . ."

"I don't know what else to give you, and it's messing with me."

"I'll go see Mack," I blurted. *Mack.* His wife had died, and I'd been neglecting him out of my own selfish fear of what he'd be like without her. Without the love of his life, Davena. I sighed. "Maybe that would help."

"That's a great idea, babe. Really great. I think that would be a good start." He took my hand and kissed the back of it. "How about Saturday morning? I'll take you."

I nodded. "I'd like that."

"Great," he said again. "What should I tell Jeanine?"

"Actually," I said, looking at him over the magazine, "I promised George I'd put in some time at the shelter on Sunday."

"Okay. Maybe next weekend, then," he said. He smiled, but his mouth drooped at the corners.

~

Mack had been very gracious over the phone. After four months, I was ready to see him, but a knot sat heavy in my stomach. It had been too long.

I almost didn't recognize the man who opened the door. He'd lost weight, and his sallow skin drooped, but it was lively eyes that gave Mack away.

"Come in, come in," he coaxed to us.

I handed him a plateful of brownies I'd baked the night before. "I know these are late, but I wanted you to have them."

"My favorite, dear, thank you," he said, setting them down.

"I'm so sorry," I rasped. I felt my eyes flooding as I stepped into his embrace.

"It's okay," he soothed, petting my hair. "It's okay. It's been hard for all of us."

"I'm sorry," I repeated as tears spilled onto his shoulder. "I miss her so much," I whispered. "She was so good to me, and I never deserved it."

He pulled back to look me in the eyes. "How can you say that? Of course you deserve it. She loved you like her own, and there's no reason she shouldn't have. You brought her so much happiness."

I shook my head. "I've been terrible," I said through blurred eyes. "I'm awful."

Mack raised an eyebrow over my shoulder. "What is she talking about?"

"She's taking this very hard. It's been a rough few months, Mack. In fact, this is the first time she's cried since she found out."

"Can you give us a minute?" I choked out. There was a hesitation before Bill agreed, but when he did, his voice pitched with a hint of bitterness.

Mack guided me to the same couch I'd sat on with Davena during our last visit. I fell rather than sat and bawled rather than cried into my hands. He handed me a box of tissues, and when I could, I looked up to face him.

"I think about her every day, Mack, and you too. I hope you know how much you mean to me. There's no excuse for not coming earlier."

"I know. People grieve in different ways. You made her happy, and that's all I could ever ask for."

I sniffled and looked at my hands.

"Is there something the matter?"

"What kind of person am I for not visiting? You've been there for me through everything, and this is how I repay you? I'm terrible," I said quietly and erupted into tears. "Terrible, terrible," I ranted, "I've done something terrible."

He scooted closer and wrapped me in his arms, rocking me back and forth. "That's it, just let it out."

Mack's love was overwhelming. I wondered how it could be so strong. It hadn't diminished in the absence of his wife, even though she'd been, and still was, the center of his world. It was my greatest fear, here in front of me. To love someone the way he had loved Davena and to lose him suddenly to something that was so wildly out of my control.

"How do you get up every morning?" I asked into his shirt.

"Reluctantly, like everyone else," he kidded. "Really, life is too short to be so unhappy. You have to let go of the past or you're denying yourself a future. Whatever is holding you back – whatever you've done – you must forgive yourself."

"What if what I've done is unforgivable?"

"Olivia, nothing is unforgiveable. But only you can figure out how to move forward. I can't tell you how."

"Did you ever doubt your love for Davena?" I asked softly.

He squeezed me closer. "We fought a lot, dear, we were very different people. Did I ever tell you that we separated once?"

I pulled back to look at him. "No."

"We did, a long, long time ago for a few weeks."

"So even you had doubts?"

"Doubts?" he repeated. "No. I never doubted that I wanted to be with her. Not since the moment she agreed to have dinner with me. Those few weeks were the worst of my life. I was miserable without her. I know it's cliché, but I felt incomplete, and not until we got back together did I feel whole again."

Goose bumps sprang over my body at his words. *Whole. 'You're what I need, David. Make me whole again.'* He continued before the meaning could sink in. "We separated because it felt necessary at the time, but I would've died before I let her get away."

I looked away and held a tissue to the corner of my eye.

"Now, now. That doesn't mean it's not normal to have doubts about your partner. It's not common to be so sure. Dav and I were different. We had an exceptional love."

He drew me back to him. I had declared to Lucy that I didn't believe in soul mates, but contrary evidence held me in its arms. Did I have any doubt that Mack and Davena were meant to be? Or even Lucy and Andrew for that matter? *What if I've been wrong all along? What if there is such a thing as soul mates, and what if . . . ?*

David recalled something unidentifiable in me that I'd been missing since my parents' divorce. His embrace, his scent, his adoration felt natural, effortless. When I was away from him I was cold and empty and longing for something more. *Why then is it so wrong?*

I'd been trying to rationalize away my fears about making a home with Bill. But the image he'd painted for me was different than what I'd seen in the Oak Park house. He had seen us, children, a warm and open home. And what had I seen? *David.*

It was true, I thought. I'd done a terrible thing. I'd led Bill to believe that he could trust in us.

Was there a wrong way to fall in love? I couldn't remember when or how it had happened with Bill. Gretchen had called him safe. He couldn't hurt me because I wouldn't let him close enough for that. He couldn't hurt me because he wouldn't, and I had known that from the start.

Bill didn't deserve to be loved with my hands on the wheel, controlling the direction we took. Even though he couldn't understand the depth of it, I was hurting him – I had been even before I'd met David. And the way David opened and closed to me, as though he was fighting himself, I saw that I was hurting him as well.

Things could not continue as they were.

There was only one option. The idea of losing David constricted around my heart like a snake. When he returned, I would have to end things for good. I'd taken a vow, and even if David thought he wanted more from me, it wasn't mine to give. And not only that, but he, as a lifelong bachelor, couldn't understand what more meant.

I wanted to tell David everything. Every feeling I'd experienced since the moment I had met him; what it had meant to make love with him and how it felt to become one with him. But saying those things to him was even worse than my physical betrayal, and so I had to bury it.

Mack never once asked what it was I had done because to him, it didn't matter. He loved me regardless. "Come now," he said into my hair. "Let me make you some tea, and we can catch up."

The three of us spent the morning remembering Davena. The despair I'd been holding in over her death flowed from me finally. Mack told us about her foundation, and how he'd been coping by pouring himself into it. We talked about work, and he congratulated me on my promotion, assuring me that Davena would have been proud.

On the walk back to the car, Bill was quiet. My time with Mack had been cathartic in many ways. And though I knew what I had to do, I felt no clarity from my decision.

As the silence dragged uncomfortably between us, I chewed my cheek anxiously.

"You never cry in front of me," he said finally, squinting ahead.

I swallowed, unsure of how to respond. But he didn't look like he wanted me to. On the way home, I sought the words to comfort him but came up short. I didn't know how exactly I would proceed, only that something had to give.

~

Bill crossed the bathroom and raised his eyebrows at me. "Wow."

"I hope that's a good wow."

"Where'd you get that?"

"The costume shop." I looked down at the ivory floor-length ball gown that billowed out from a tight corset. My breasts were trussed up, and I had pinned half of my hair back and curled the rest into soft, brown waves. "Do you like it?"

"Yeah."

I brushed my hand over the fabric of the skirt. "Do you really?"

He straightened his tie and smoothed back a few stray pieces of his hair. "I said yeah. I like it. It looks expensive though."

"It's a rental," I said with a shrug.

"A rental," he said with a scoff. "For tonight? Is that practical?"

"It's a special occasion, babe."

He grabbed his mask from the table and slid it on. It skewed left a little, a black piece of plastic with two cutouts for his eyes. I'd bought it for ninety-nine cents, knowing he wouldn't wear anything elaborate.

"How do I look?" he asked.

"Good." I picked up my own mask and fingered it. It had come with the dress and was more intricate: ivory lace overlay, glass pearls at the corners of the eyes and a spray of white feathers off to the side.

"What's wrong? Are you still upset about this afternoon?"

"No." I gave him a reassuring smile.

"K." His shoulders slackened, and he smiled goofily. "Tonight's going to be fun. I'm looking forward to it."

I nodded, wondering at his shifty mood. As of late, our dispositions had rarely been on the same page. So as I stretched the mask over my hair and fixed it on my face, I promised myself that I would be in high spirits for the night. No matter what.

Come Alive

CHAPTER 18

TICKETS TO THE BALL had been expensive, but Bill knew how much supporting the shelter meant to me. It was held at a private mansion just outside the city, a lavish home with curved staircases and velvety gold décor that reeked of luxury. Bill and I circled the silent auction table, joking about how much we would bid on an eighty-two-foot yacht or a ten-day Jamaican vacation. We found Lucy and Andrew hovering over courtside seats for the Bulls, and I shook my head at Bill as soon as he gave me a pleading look.

"You look stunning," Andrew said, appraising me. "Well done!"

"Thanks," I said with a sheepish smile. "You guys too."

Lucy donned an ornate sky blue dress that matched both Andrew's tie and her Venetian mask.

"Your waist is so tiny in that dress," I heard from behind me.

"Oh. Hi, Dani."

"Really Liv, you're so little."

"I'm not *little*," I said with a hint of irritation. "Lucy is barely five feet – *she's* little."

"You know what I mean – skinny," Dani said, waving her hand nonchalantly. Her chocolate hair was long and luxurious in perfect ringlets, and her eyes were especially green behind a brown mask. A pang of envy washed over me, and I remembered the stupid pink hoodie. Hadn't David broken things off? Why did she look so happy?

"Not much of a mask, Bill," she quipped.

He shrugged. "Better than Phantom of the Opera over here."

Andrew visibly blushed under his mask. "What's wrong with mine?"

"You look very handsome, honey."

We all laughed and headed into the ballroom to take our seats. I waved at Lucy from across the room and texted her to save me a dance. The director spoke about the shelter's mission and their goal to spread the word about animal adoption and the plight of homeless animals. Bill squeezed my knee. He whispered that he was proud of what I did, even though I knew in my heart it wasn't enough. When her speech concluded, the room filled with applause.

"That was nice," Bill commented.

I gave him a close-lipped smile, but he was watching the dance floor where people had begun to gather. When the music started, he turned to me and grabbed my hand. "Come on."

"What? I don't know how to dance to this."

"Just come," he said, pulling me to the dance floor.

I started laughing, more from nervousness than anything. "Bill," I protested between giggles.

He whirled around and stood in front of me before bowing at the waist and offering his hand. "May I have this dance?"

I adjusted my mask and put my hand in his. "Certainly."

He stood just slightly from my body while gripping my hand in the air. He began to dance, leading me in a waltz. I wasn't surprised, since I knew of his childhood lessons, but I was thrown by how confidently he led me. I moved easily with him, unable to hold back a big smile.

We glided across the floor, darting through some couples while the less experienced ones moved aside to watch. He danced in sync with the tempo, and I let myself get carried away, spinning faster and faster as the music hit its stride. His posture lengthened with the acceleration, and soon all I could see was the flurry of my skirt, and all I could hear was the violin. Just as the music hit its apex and Bill whirled me, chestnut brown eyes hit me like a wall. At David's masked glare from across the room, I lost my step, and Bill broke just in time to catch me. My smile fell instantly at the piercing fury radiating from David, despite the distance between us. Bill whisked me around again, and David was gone. I finished out the dance, not wanting to ruin Bill's moment, but dread built inside me.

Lucy and Andrew rushed over before I excused myself to the bathroom. Bill gave me a hurried kiss on the cheek, laughing as he explained to them how his parents had forced him into classes as a teenager.

I exited through the doorway where I'd seen David. A quick scan of the foyer gave me nothing. My next stop was valet in case he meant to leave. It was then that I saw him, pacing off to the side of the house, dark and portentous like a brewing storm. I picked up my skirts and ran over to him, not knowing what I would say but just that I had to know what that look was for.

"David," I hissed, and his head jerked up.

"What?" He resumed his march.

"I thought you were in New York."

"I was," he snapped. "I got back last night."

"You're mad," I said, moving my mask to my forehead.

"I can't even look at you right now."

"Me? What did I do?"

He stopped pacing in front of me and ran a hand through hair as black as his tuxedo. His grip tightened on the silver mask in his hand when he asked, "Are you happy with him?"

"David," I said, my eyes darting around. "We can't do this here."

"Answer me, damn it! Are you happy?"

I glared at him a moment before walking further around the house. I heard him tramping behind me as I led us to the first concealed spot I could find – a small, intimate garden.

I jumped when he threw his fist into a tree. "I can't do this anymore!" he yelled. "To see his hands on you! It's too fucking much!"

I blanched for a moment, unprepared for the assault. He fisted the mask so tightly in his other hand that it cracked in half.

"Please, calm down," I pleaded when he started pacing again. "Let's talk about this rationally."

"I should be the one touching you like that, not him. It should be me."

I drew a sharp breath. "David, we need to – to talk," I said. My heart jumpstarted as though it were on the verge of exploding. I readied the words in my head, fighting back hot tears. *We're through. You have to go away. I have to push you away even though what I want is to run to you, to drown in you . . . .*

He shook his head hard. "I can't. I can't share you like this. It makes me want to just . . ." His gestures were wild and desperate as he spoke. I gasped when I noticed his bloody knuckles, but he pulled back when I reached out. "He has you, and it drives me fucking crazy. It's all I can think about and then to see you in there dancing with him . . ."

"He's my husband," I said in a small voice.

"No fucking shit. I can't believe I let myself get so involved with this."

I attempted to swallow the lump rising in my throat. "I don't know what to say. You knew what we were getting into."

"So it's my fault, I guess."

"*We* did this to ourselves."

"You have to tell me what you want. I can't do this anymore."

I gritted my teeth, fighting back unwelcome tears. "I – he's my husband."

"So that's it? You're not even going to consider . . . ?"

"What, David? I don't know what you want from me."

"If I tell you what I want, then this is it. You have to decide."

"Decide what?" I screamed, surprising us both. "I already told you. My decisions are made. There are no options."

"Well, then what the fuck am I even doing here? Go on and be happy with him, your *fucking* husband."

"Me? What about you?" I shot back, suddenly incensed. "Why are *you* here tonight? Did you come with Dani?"

"I told you, it's over."

"Then why are you here?" I demanded.

He was quiet as he paced, shaking his head from side to side. Pieces of his hair had broken from their marble wave, and it was the most disheveled I'd ever seen him.

I nodded and crossed my arms. "That's what I thought."

"She begged me – "

"You claim you want more, but you can't even give up *one* of your girls. How many others are there? Are you still with Maria?" I stepped in his path, and he stopped short. "Answer me! When was the last time you fucked Maria?"

"Olivia," he pleaded.

"You can't even give one of them up for me."

"For you?" he growled with menacing heat. His expression shifted into something that had me cowering back. "For you I would give up anything!" he raged. "It's all for you, everything I do! Can't you see that? Everything I've worked for, everything I've ever built is for you!"

His words sliced through to my heart. I backed away and shook my head. "You don't . . . Stop."

"You asked what I want, Olivia, I want *you*. I need – "

"Stop!" I cried. "It can't be, please just stop. It can't be."

"I need you," he said, lunging forward and grasping my shoulders with his hands.

"Don't *touch* me. Stop!"

I turned to leave, but he caught my waist and yanked me against his concrete body.

"Stop!" I yelled, pushing his chest as he backed me into the tree. "We're done! We can't do this anymore!"

He suppressed my words with a hard kiss. His pelvis pinned mine to the trunk, stilling me while his hands feverishly gathered up my dress. His hand ran up my clenched thighs, and when he released an animal growl into my mouth, I responded with a traitorous moan. I shoved him again, knowing I wouldn't be able to resist if his hands lingered any longer, but not even our lips separated. A fiery need tore through my body as he found my panties and effortlessly ripped them away.

He bit my lip as he slipped a finger inside me, and I whimpered into the kiss. He had yanked my mask around my neck and feathers tickled my jaw. The hiss of his zipper spiraled me into a frenzy. He would be inside of me any moment, quenching my need and filling me in the way only he could. I fisted the lapels of his tuxedo and yanked him closer, kissing him back heatedly.

He opened me urgently with his fingers. I instinctively wrapped a leg around him, and we moaned together as he thrust into me. He drew back and drove into me, bouncing me against the tree. His drives grew quickly frantic, and as out of control as the look in his eyes. Harsh punishments tore across my back from the bark, but I barely noticed. I bit down on my lip to keep from screaming my pleasure.

"Christ – yes, Olivia," he hissed into my ear.

At the sound of my name, I cried out, and he clamped his hand over my mouth. "Yes," I yelled into it.

His eyes squeezed shut, and he pumped as fast as our position would allow. With another throaty growl, he seized my other leg, fastening me to the tree. I accidentally bit down on his hand and he snarled, tightening his grip on my face. When I thought I couldn't take anymore, he took both hips in his hands and hammered me so wildly, that I had to grip his shoulders so I wouldn't fall off the trunk.

"Yes," I breathed, "don't stop, don't stop, David, fuck me." He didn't stop, and within seconds, I was coming around him, tormented by the feathers at my neck and grasping for his body while I was hit with waves so extreme that they bordered on painful.

"Shit," he breathed. "I'm gonna come."

"Come, baby," I urged.

With a guttural groan he withdrew and, supporting me with one hand, came feverishly on the inside of my dress. My labored breathing hitched in my throat as I looked down between us. He set me harshly on the ground, and my cum-soaked skirts fell around me.

"What was that?" I cried.

He zipped his pants up and leaned over, placing his hands on his knees to catch his breath.

"Did you just come on my dress?"

"I told you, Olivia," he said, snapping upright. "I won't come in someone who doesn't belong to me, and *you do not*."

I gaped at this man I didn't know. His demeanor was cold; a stark contrast to our last clandestine meeting. He cursed and turned his back to me, kicking a concrete bench in the process.

"I – I . . ." I stood there in shock, trying to wrap my head around everything that had just happened; the words, the actions . . . the implications. "I have to get back."

"Go, then," he bit out. "Just fucking go."

My hand flew to my mouth as I stifled a sob. It wasn't just the daggered words that hurt but the dismissal. This was the David I'd been expecting, the one I always knew would appear.

I stumbled backward before turning to run up to the house. I wanted to run *to* him, not away – to comfort him, find comfort *in* him, let the world fall away in his arms . . . . The pain was physical, almost too much to bear; it was the reason I never let anyone get too close, even Bill.

CHAPTER 19

I NEARLY COLLIDED WITH BILL in the foyer. "I was just coming to look for you," he said.

I fought for a deep breath, suffocating in his proximity. "I – I just have to run to the bathroom," I said, backing away.

"Didn't you already go?"

"There was a line."

"What are you talking about? I was just over there. No line."

I could feel David, sticky against my thigh, fingers digging into my face, and I needed to get far away from Bill. My heart stopped when I noticed he was peering at my dress. He reached out, but I jumped back.

"Is that blood?" he asked.

"No," I hissed as I blew past him toward the staircase. I cursed as I hastened up it to find somewhere private. As soon as I locked the bathroom door, there was a knock and the knob jiggled. "Hey? Did you hurt yourself?"

I went to whip the door open, but stopped myself. I loosened my shoulders and eased it ajar. "I'm fine," I said calmly.

"You don't seem fine."

"Well, I am. I don't know what that is," I said, motioning at the stain, "but I'll be sure to complain about it when I return the dress."

His expression was accusing and taunting, except that it wasn't. He really only looked confused.

"What?" I asked defensively. "Why are looking at me

like that?"

"You're acting weird," he said.

"I just need to use the restroom."

"You're turning on me again."

"What?"

"You're turning – "

"Can this wait until we get home?" I clipped. With a look that told him the discussion was over, I closed the door.

Once alone, I gathered up the dress and splashed water on my naked lower half. With a decorative, perfumed hand towel, I tenderly wiped myself of cum and the blood from David's hand. I was soiled. *Used. Degraded.*

With shaky hands, I repaired my hair. Red scratches smarted from the bark and soreness crept into my spine. I gave myself one moment to crouch down and put my head in my hands. I breathed through the urge to break down there on the bathroom floor. *Oh, David. How could you? How could I? What the fuck am I doing? I've* completely *lost control.*

Downstairs, I weaved through the ballroom and spotted Bill seated at our table. "I'm sorry," I told him. "I shouldn't have snapped at you." And I was sorry. Terribly, terribly sorry; so sorry, that I was tempted to tell him everything right then and there. The lies were rotting my insides, and they might very will end up poisoning me.

He took my hand, and I sat down next to him. "I thought things would improve after talking to Mack," he said. "They haven't," he added dumbly.

I plucked my hand from his and crossed my arms. He sat back in his chair, waiting for an answer.

"Well, that's because there's something else going on," I said.

He looked uncomfortable. "Um, what?"

"It's – I've been . . ." I looked around, unable to believe that this was tumbling out of my mouth now, here, in the middle of a fundraiser. "I've been having doubts. The house, for instance. In Oak Park. All those things you described – birthdays, holidays, kids in the yard – I just can't see it like you can, and that scares me. I think about it – a lot, and it gets in my head."

His eyebrows folded. "I've told you before, once everything starts to happen, it will all fall into place. You have to trust me, babe."

"No," I said, wringing my fingers in my lap. "I really don't see it. Especially the kids. I don't know if that's – that's what I want."

A shriek of laughter across the room caused us both to flinch. Bill's eyes drilled into me, searching for something. "How can you even say that to me? And here . . . ?"

"I'm sorry," was all I could think to say.

He set his elbows on the table and put his face in his hands for a long moment. When he looked up, he seemed calm. "This is why people fall in love and get married. To have a family. That shouldn't be news to you. I'm not giving up on my dream because you don't feel like it. You've gotta get on board. And I don't want any more sulking, k? It's enough, for Christ's sake."

"I'm not sulking. I'm really confused."

"That's enough. You had better snap out of this, and soon or – or I'm gone."

"You'd leave me here?" I asked, taken aback.

"I mean I'm done," he snapped.

A woman took the stage. The sound of her finger tapping the microphone scraped over me.

"You're done?" I repeated. "With me?"

"Sorry to interrupt your meals everyone, I just have a quick announcement."

"You're being unfair, and – "

"Earlier this evening we received a very generous donation . . . "

" . . . quite frankly, really selfish. You're not acting like the woman I married, and you haven't been for a while."

". . . fifty thousand dollars . . . "

I gasped. *Fifty . . . thousand? Done? Leaving?*

" . . . an anonymous attendee."

The room erupted into applause, but I sat gaping as Bill plastered a smile on his face and stood. *He* was threatening to leave *me*?

I knew without looking of David's position in the room; I couldn't help that. It were as if I had a sixth sense that felt only him. I turned to him without thinking. He sat rigidly still and motionless as he watched the stage. He was the donor.

My gaze returned to Bill as the ovation concluded. "What are you saying?" I asked under my breath.

"Never mind."

"No," I prompted quietly. "Are you threatening to leave me?"

"No, I just – "

"It sure sounded like – "

"What I meant was – "

"You would leave just like that?"

"No, damn it!" he yelled, pounding his fist on the table. I felt a roomful of eyes turn to us. He was quiet as he stared down and seemingly tried to regulate his breathing. He lowered his voice so only I could hear. "Never mind what I said, but put yourself in my shoes. You've been nothing but nasty to me for months, and I've had it." His voice raised an octave as he sliced his hand through the air. "I've had it up to here with this, and you need to get it under control."

From under my lashes, I glanced around the room. Everyone had looked away – everyone but David. My eyes darted back to my husband. "Bill – "

"Don't. This is embarrassing. We can discuss it later."

It was then that I realized his patience was approaching its limits. Bill, unperturbed as he was, rarely got riled. But when he did, it was a combustion – an explosion of all the things he tucked away.

In that way, we were similar. I'd learned to shut off my emotions early on, and Bill's parents had covered his up by keeping him busy. They'd instilled in him that feelings were frivolous, and it was more worthwhile to focus on tangible things like work and money.

It occurred to me for the first time that maybe Bill and I had chosen each other for the same reason. For me, Bill was a practical choice who never tried for more than what I gave. In turn, he never had to dig too deeply. Because maybe he knew that if he did, if I did, we would both uncover things that would change everything. And for him, things were fine as they were. They had been for me too. But I wasn't so sure anymore.

I had drawn my lips into a tight line and was slumped in my chair like a scolded child.

"Eat," he said, motioning at my plate. I pushed it away. "Eat," he coaxed gently as if he hadn't just threatened to leave me and then taken it back. "I'm starting to wonder about your diet."

I picked up a fork and took a bite of grilled chicken to appease him, my jaw tingling as I chewed.

"Thank you," he said.

I felt David watching me, and I wanted to scream at him to stop. I couldn't focus with his gaze glued to me, reminding me relentlessly that he was there – just so *there*.

Tears sat heavy behind my eyes, but I lifted my chin and smiled through the rest of the evening. I could not go moments without remembering what I had just done behind Bill's back, but I swallowed it until we were home in bed.

Once Bill was asleep, I climbed from between the sheets and onto the floor. My chest stuttered fiercely as I crawled to the bathroom. When I hit the cold tile, I slipped the door shut behind me and doubled over my knees. I unleashed a violent

storm of scalding, shame-laden tears. My hands dragged
through my hair, snagging on tangles. I gagged through my
sobs, heaving against the hollowness.

I'd never done anything so appalling, so hurtful in my
life. Bill trusted me, and I had pissed on that. I deserved every
one of David's harsh words. I wanted to wish it all away, turn
back time and start over. But I couldn't bring myself to wish
that. As awful as everything had been, there had also been
David.

~

Bill was already out of bed when I awoke, and a mouth-
watering aroma floated into the room. I put on a robe and
sleepily padded into the kitchen.

"Hey," he said, excavating bread from the toaster.
"Hungry?"

I nodded and sat down cautiously.

He casually buttered the toast before setting it in front of
me. He passed me a mug of coffee.

"I know I've been a mess," I rasped. "And I'm sorry."

"I'm sorry, too," he said without looking at me.
"Obviously I didn't mean what I said. I was just angry."

"You're not thinking of leaving me?"

He looked up and laughed. "Babe, really? No. Of course
not."

"But you said . . ."

"I've been stressed out too, about the house, about work.
Hell, I've been stressed about you, but that doesn't excuse
what I said." He studied me, peering at my face.

My swollen eyes were red and puffy, I knew without
even having seen myself. I started to explain, but he
continued.

"Besides, you know how I feel about that. People who
separate or divorce have all sorts of problems. Things that run

much deeper than what we're dealing with. That's not, and will never be, us."

I stared at him blankly. Could he not tell that I had been up all night crying, or did he not care? Anger crept into my heart for the way he ignored it.

I remembered my eye-opening thoughts from the night before. True, I had kept him at a distance since the day I'd met him, but wasn't he partly to blame? He never tried to break through, never asked questions he didn't want to hear the answers to.

I sighed and rubbed my eyes. "About the house and all that – "

"It's okay," he cut me off, raising his hand.

"It is?" Overwhelming relief flooded me at the thought that he might agree to slow things down.

"Yes. I know you're stressed too. And I think I know what this is really about."

I inhaled as panic bubbled to the surface. "What?"

"You're afraid. I know you've never had a good relationship with Leanore. But you aren't your mother. *You* are going to be a great mom."

"Bill," I started, shaking my head sadly. "I really don't think it's about that."

"But it is, sweetie. You're afraid, and I don't blame you. Your mom's been tough on you. But you're not her, you've got to let go of that." He paused to take a sip of his coffee. "In any case, this is not something I will ever change my mind about. I want a child – children. So you'll have to, I don't know . . . figure this out. Because I know, deep down, you want this too. If I believed you didn't, we'd be having a different conversation."

My heart fell as he spoke. He was so convinced that this was right for us. He was asking me to trust him because he didn't have any doubts. And then it hit me. I wondered if maybe, just maybe . . . he was right.

CHAPTER 20

WE'D GIVEN UP our respective Sunday plans to spend the day together, silently apologizing outdoors on an autumn day. We explored the neighborhood, drank beer in the afternoon and took a long late-afternoon walk to admire the way the leaves were changing.

I had promised to try harder, and though it took every ounce of my energy, I put my sorrows over David aside and made myself affable for Bill. We made plans to visit his sister and her four kids the following weekend so I could see how alive a house full of children was. And finally, at his firm request, I agreed that I would stop taking birth control.

He seemed vastly pleased in turn. It was only once Bill fell asleep that I fretted, and as a result, I had barely slept. There was no more time. Bill had hit the end of his patience. It was time to grow up, forget David and make the right decisions with Bill. I owed him so much more than I gave him and now, I would make it up to him by trusting in his version of us.

But there was something else to deal with first. Now, days after my confrontation with David, I sat staring at an e-mail that knotted my stomach.

From: David Dylan
Sent: Wed, October 03, 2012 02:26 PM CST
To: Olivia Germaine
Subject: Important

Olivia,

We need to talk. This isn't over, and you know it. Come by
my office when you get off today.

DAVID DYLAN
SENIOR ARCHITECT,
PIERSON/GREER

On the heels of his e-mail was a message from Bill,
informing me that he would be by at five o'clock to pick me
up from work. I sighed. I had things to do that would keep me
well past five, but they would have to wait.

I began crafting a response to David when Serena
popped her head in my office. "Hey, boss. Beman wants to see
you."

I ran my hand over my face in frustration.

"Are you okay?" she asked.

"Fine," I chirped. "Just fine."

When Beman had finished upbraiding me for one of
Lisa's errors, I stormed back to my office and shot off an e-
mail to David.

From: Olivia Germaine
Sent: Wed, October 03, 2012 02:58 PM CST
To: David Dylan
Subject: Re: Important

David—

I can't.

Olivia Germaine
Senior Editor,
Chicago Metropolitan Magazine
ChicagoMMag.com

His commanding tone both irked and flustered me, even over e-mail. I quickly scanned another e-mail from Bill, which ended by asking what I was making for dinner. I groaned, surrendering to the fact that there would be no peace today.

And about that, I was right. Hearing from David stuck with me all afternoon and hurtled me into an open state of brooding. I played Saturday night over and over until my hands shook as I edited copy. My mind wouldn't let it rest. He wanted to talk. What was there to say? He said it wasn't over – but didn't he know that it was over before it had even begun?

I dreamed violently that night. Bill, David and Mark Alvarez each angrily demanded something from me. I had lied to them, they told me. I had made fools of them. I was the cancer in their lives. When Mark called me names, David and Bill somberly nodded their agreement.

I woke heavily at the edge of dawn, wishing I could sleep for days upon days. Grey clouds mirrored my unrest. I crawled out of the warm bed and slogged into the kitchen for coffee. I didn't want to upset Bill again, so I decided to cover my foul mood with pancakes, prepared with equal parts guilt and love.

As planned, the pancakes diverted his attention. "This is a surprise," he said excitedly. He sucked his teeth and rubbed his stomach. "This is exactly what I wanted, and I didn't even know it. Such a good wife."

I let him kiss me on the cheek as I stared at the griddle with my spatula cocked.

"Looks like rain," he commented after retrieving the newspaper from the doorstep.

"Great," I muttered and flipped one pancake after another. *Flip, splat. Flip, splat. Flip, splat.*

"Hopefully it won't go through the weekend. I made an appointment with Jeanine on Saturday."

I pushed a stray hair from my face with my forearm and turned to him. "What?"

"She has three different places to show us. Sounds optimistic, too."

"Aren't we supposed to see your sister?"

"On Sunday. It'll be a productive weekend."

"I wish you'd checked with me. I have plans with Lucy."

"Priorities, honey. We've already rescheduled once, remember? If we're going to start *trying*, we need to get going on the house. At this point, time is not on our side."

I gulped audibly, and my shoulders sagged with the weight of the news. Had he not heard anything I'd said over the weekend? Couldn't he see that I was already making my sacrifice by going off birth control? I needed time, not another excruciating car ride with Jeanine. "About that . . ."

"About what?" he challenged.

"Maybe it would be a good idea to get settled in a house before we start thinking about a baby."

He resumed scanning the front page of the paper. "It takes some women months for birth control to wear off," he muttered. "By that time, we could potentially be in a new place."

I felt my throat closing. *Months?* "No," I said. I struggled to get the words out. "No baby until we've found a home."

He glanced up at me. I waited for him to react, uncertain of which way he would go, but he only gestured behind me. "Liv, the pancakes."

Liv, the pancakes? LIV, THE PANCAKES? Are you completely fucking oblivious, Bill? He turned back to the *Tribune*. After a moment, he chuckled at the newspaper.

"I am not going off birth control."

He licked his finger and flipped the page. "Hmm?"

"And I cheated on you."

It took a moment until his head shot up. "What did you just say?"

I actually felt my muscles liquefying as panic flooded my body. My eyes lowered and darted over the linoleum floor. The spontaneous confession hung in the air, thick and palpable between us.

"Hey," he called. "What did you say?"

I looked up and shook my head, a silent beg that he wouldn't make me repeat it. *It was a mistake. I shouldn't have said it. I'm not ready.* But he waited until I couldn't stand the silence another second. "I – I slept with someone else."

"When?" he cried, standing. "Who?"

"It's not important," I mumbled. "I did it, and that's it." The smell of burning batter filled the kitchen, but I couldn't tear my gaze from him.

He fell back into his chair blindly. "This is some twisted way of trying to get out of the birth control thing."

If only. I shook my head at the floor, shrugging my shoulders helplessly.

"Isn't it?" His voice shifted from desperate to soft and despondent. "How? Who?"

I continued to shake my head. Did it matter? Why make things worse with details?

"When?" he asked.

"About five months ago."

He laughed in a burst of dead air before dropping his forehead in his palm. "All this time, I thought . . ."

My hands flew to my face, an attempt to hold in the tears. We sat that way for a long moment, not speaking.

"Who?" he asked again. "Who was it?"

I kept my face buried. "You don't know him."

He snorted. When I looked up again, his elbows were on the table, his face in his hands. "I'm such a fool," he said. "I feel so . . . stupid. Is this what you wanted? To make me look stupid?"

"Of course not," I said, furrowing my eyebrows. "It just . . . happened."

"Once?"

I cleared my throat and looked away. "Twice," I lied. I knew I could never bring myself to tell him the truth about the masquerade ball.

"After everything that I've done for you." His voice pitched. "How could you do this? And why are you telling me now?"

"I'm so sorry. You deserve better." I approached the table cautiously. My heart pounded as I eased into a chair. "What can I do? To make it better?"

"Seriously? What kind of question is that?"

"I'm sorry. I don't know what to say."

He shot up and overturned the chair. As he bent to pick it up, he said, "I have to get to work."

"Now?" I exclaimed. "We need to discuss this."

"I should take the day off because you picked now to tell me?" he snarled. "Hell of a time, really, Liv. Now I have to sit through work thinking about it all day."

I looked at him pleadingly, even though his eyes were fixed on the floor. "Don't go. I'll tell you anything, just stay."

"Yes, you will tell me everything. Later. Right now, I have to go to work."

"Call in sick," I implored. "We have to talk about this now. Do it for us. Let's fix this right now, today."

He gave me a lingering look. "I just really can't deal with this right now, on top of work? Shit." He rubbed his temples and muttered, "Why now?"

"Are you going to leave me?" I whispered.

He looked over my head and squinted. His chin trembled slightly. "No. I don't know. Maybe." He turned away and snatched his blazer from the couch. "And I want the truth tonight. No more secrets." Not long after, the front door slammed.

I straightened up and took an unsteady breath. I unplugged the grill and overturned the burnt pancakes into the sink. It was done. I sought relief, but I only felt ill to my core.

I grabbed my coat and left for the office, replaying the morning over and over on the way until I thought I might vomit. Not until I was behind my locked door did I sink into my shame with the onset of rain. I had done to Bill what I'd shielded myself from all these years: I'd ripped the carpet out from under him; I'd shattered his trust. This would destroy him.

I agonized over what would come next. Would he leave me? And what would I do? Where would I go? I tried to understand what I was feeling. At the thought of him leaving, I was sad and scared but not surprised. I almost felt relieved that the day had finally come that my marriage would end the same way as my parents'. As if I had known all along that I was cursed.

But Bill's belief in the bond of marriage was stronger than that. He might take this out on me forever, but he wouldn't leave. It wasn't him. It was part of the reason I'd agreed to marry him in the first place; he was constant and reliable.

I couldn't blame my infidelity on a bad marriage. What had happened between David and me was unable to be contained. Before I'd met him, I wouldn't have classified Bill's and my relationship as anything but stable. But if Bill didn't feel like home, didn't that mean something? I wondered shamefully if being with Bill was still what I wanted.

And then I thought of David. Now that Bill knew, it was more than over. I had tried to forget him, but it was impossible. Nobody made me feel the way he did. He had awoken something, and I would never be the same for it.

Despite the way he had crushed me on Saturday, I didn't want him any less. If anything, our magnetic pull intensified with every minute that passed, regardless of whether we were together or apart. I still wanted him. And I wanted him all to myself. No Maria, no Dani, no Bill.

I was an hour through revising an editorial that should have taken me thirty minutes to complete. I'd been stuck on the same sentence for five minutes when I stopped and took out my phone.

I swallowed hard as I stared at it. I didn't want to do it. But it was no longer about what I wanted. It was about making things right – no matter how painful that might be. Because Bill and I could not move forward this way.

Maybe in some other life, we were meant to be. Soul mates, even. I allowed myself a small smile for how he'd turned me into a believer.

I didn't know how I would end it once and for all, but it had to be done. David's e-mail told me that it wasn't over. If there was any doubt between us, I had to put it to rest. David and Bill both deserved the truth.

With unsteady fingers, I crafted my message.

> *Oct 4, 2012 4:06 PM*
> *Meet me at your office in 20*
> *minutes.*

CHAPTER 21

WHEN I ARRIVED at Pierson/Greer, David's whole floor was empty. I peeked into his office but remained in the doorway to wait. My heart leaped when the door across the way opened. Arnaud Mallory, David's unnerving colleague with a tendency for leering, stuck his head out. I squeezed my eyes shut, hoping he wouldn't see me.

"Bonjour, Olivia."

"Mr. Mallory."

"Call me Arnaud. Expecting Dylan?"

I nodded.

"Such a shame. I would never leave a pretty girl like you waiting." I shuddered slightly as his voice crept over me. "Come in, have a drink."

"No, I think I'll just wait for – for Mr. Dylan here."

"But no, I won't have it. Come, come."

David strode into the office then, and I was almost relieved. But seeing him again aroused a host of other emotions. Aside from the inexorable need I had to run to him, shame washed over me with the memory of the coarse tree and even coarser dismissal.

"I got your text," he said, stopping abruptly in front of me. "What is it?"

"We need to talk."

He gestured behind me. "In my office." In Arnaud's direction, he asked, "Where the hell is Clare? Find her. She's not supposed to leave this desk."

As he shut the door, I dizzily inhaled the intoxicating scent of his office; spicy, natural but refined. Him, but stronger. I remembered our moment in the crowded elevator. I remembered him at the edge of the roof in the dark as I pressed my cheek against his back. I remembered the first time I was alone with him, at Lucy's engagement party. I remembered, I remembered, I remembered. "I can't do this," I uttered to myself, vibrating with fear and nerves. *Just say it. We're done. Bill knows, and we . . . are . . . done.*

He stalked in my direction, relief written on his face. "I'm glad you came. We need to talk about Saturday night. There's no excuse – Jesus Christ, you're shaking," he said, stepping closer. "What's wrong?"

"I can't do this," I said, moving toward the door.

"Whoa, whoa, whoa." He jumped in front of me. "What's going on?"

I crossed my arms into myself. "I shouldn't have come here. I thought I could do this, but I can't."

"Olivia," he said softly, but with authority. "Say what you came here to say." The hopefulness in his voice pulled at my heart. "Don't shut me out. Tell me why you're here."

I wanted to tell him. I wanted to tell him that I'd told Bill and that I could never see him again. I wanted to say that he'd hurt me on Saturday night. That I felt used and disgusting. I wanted to tell him that since I'd met him, life meant something different.

My stomach heaved, and I felt suddenly hot and clammy. "I don't think I can do this right now." I ran the back of my hand over my slick forehead. Nausea struck my gut. "Everything is going to be fine," I told myself.

"Fine?" he repeated, his voice rising. "You're going to pull that shit with me?"

I blinked at him for a long moment. My knees may as well have been knocking together. *Oh, God, this is it. This is it.*

"You don't look well. Do you need – "

"He knows!" I cried.

"What?"

"He . . . knows." I wrung my fingers. "It's over. This," I clarified, motioning between us, "is so over."

"You told him?"

"I don't want to lose you," I said, sniffling back tears. My breaths were short and shallow as I continued. "But that doesn't matter. I can't, do, this, anymore."

"No." He shook his head. "If Saturday night proved anything, it's that this needed to end."

A knife in my heart, even though he was right.

"Not – I only meant that we couldn't keep going like this," he explained.

I nodded and wiped away an invisible tear. "Like I said, it doesn't matter anyway. I just thought you should know right away."

"You look scared shitless. Did he hurt you?"

"He would never," I said.

"Tell me what happened. You should have come to me first. I would have told you with him so he could take it out on me."

"There's nothing to tell yet. I told him right before he left for work."

"He went to work?" David asked, incredulous.

"He said we'd discuss it tonight."

He rubbed his hand over his forehead, muttering something about Bill being a fool. "Fuck. He might ask for a divorce. Is that what you want?"

"His family is strictly against it, as is he. He won't."

"But what do *you* want, Olivia?"

"I don't know," I said with blurry eyes. "I came here to tell you that you and I are done."

After a brief silence, he asked, "Don't you want to know what I want?"

"No," I lied.

"Things can't just end this way. There's too much here."

I closed my eyes and whispered, "Please don't make this any harder."

"So that's it?" he asked, his voice simultaneously rising and deepening. "Did you think you would just come here and tell me it's over?"

I nodded. "What else is there to say?"

"Everything." He came to me slowly and gently cupped my face. I felt myself melting under his loving gaze. "This was never a fling for me, baby. You mean so much more to me than that." He swallowed audibly. "I'm not ready to let you go."

It he hadn't been holding my jaw, it would have dropped. "What are you saying?"

"I'm saying what I've always said. I want more. We can do this – "

There was a knock at the door. "Mr. Dylan?"

"Not now, Clare," he called irritably over his shoulder. He looked back at me. "I want – "

"Mr. Dylan," the voice came again. He groaned and dropped his hands. "There's a very important client on line two."

I watched as he stalked away, pinching his nose. I waited with bated breath. What did he want? What would he say? Did I want to hear it? I didn't only want to; I was aching to hear it.

He wrenched the door open. "Where have you been?" he yelled at her. "Reception was empty for over twenty minutes."

"I'm sorry, I had to make a quick call," Clare said. "But there's – "

"You're fired."

My mouth fell open.

"What?" she asked. "No, it was an emergency! I'm sorry!"

"Do you have emergencies every few hours? I've told you before, no personal calls in the office. Pack up your shit. You're fired."

As I watched her through the sliver of doorway, I had to look away from her shocked expression. I considered interjecting when something on his desk caught my eye.

"It won't happen again," she pleaded.

"If you're not gone by the time I finish here, I will escort you myself."

Their voices faded into the background. I leaned over and slid a stack of papers closer. My heart began to thump as I stared at the address on the sales contract in front of me. *No. It can't be . . . . It can't . . . .* I flipped the page to see the signature: *Lucas David Dylan.*

He slammed the door and turned back to me. "I'm sorry," he said. "As I was saying . . ." I made a sound as I scanned the document, but it was getting harder to read with the tears that were pooling in my eyes. "This is our chance – "

"What is this?" I whispered, turning to face him. I held up the contract. "What is this, David?"

He stilled. His face became anxious as he stared at me, unmoving. "You weren't supposed to see that," he mumbled.

"You *bought* the Oak Park house?"

He sighed deeply and swiped a hand over his face. "Yes."

A vicious tremble overtook my body, and the papers rustled audibly in my hand. "You asshole," I fumed.

"Let me explain," he started.

"You lied to me?"

"I didn't lie, I was going to tell you."

"That's bullshit, and you know it! How could you do this to me? You know how I loved that house!"

"Hang on, let me – "

"Was this just a game for you? Did you get some sort of sick pleasure from destroying my marriage?"

"Of course not, Olivia, if you'll just be quiet – "

"How could you?"

"That's enough!" he boomed.

"It doesn't matter," I said quickly. "None of this matters. You've made yourself very clear." I waved the papers at him and threw them on the desk. "Thank you for making this easy."

"Goddamn it," he thundered, as I started across the office. "Stop running away. For once, stay and face the truth."

I whirled toward him. "Why'd you do it?"

"Sit, and I will explain everything. I'm not going to tell you through a screaming fit like a couple of teenage girls."

"And give you the chance to think up an excuse?" I shot back. "I'm not stupid." I picked up my trek, but he stepped to block me from the door as I reached it. "Don't you dare come near me," I said with as much venom as I could muster. "This time I mean it."

"You listen to me," he snarled, pointing at the exit. "Walk out that door, and that's it. I'm not coming after you anymore. Everything I've put up with – you owe me the chance to explain. So sit down."

I was frozen to the spot by his forceful tone, but no less infuriated.

His hand jerked back toward his desk. "I said sit the fuck down. I will explain everything, I will *give* you everything, but I'm no fool. I will *not* chase you anymore."

There was no doubt in my mind; what he'd done couldn't be explained away. It was unforgivable. I gave him a pointed look before whipping open the door and slamming it behind me. Clare looked at me with huge eyes and started throwing her things together faster.

Alone in the elevator, I ordered myself to curb the tears. It wasn't worth it. I didn't know what perverted satisfaction he got from buying the house out from under us, and I didn't want to know. *Do not cry*, I instructed myself. *It's not worth it.* But it didn't work that way. By the time the elevator hit the ground floor, big, dense tears were leaking from my eyes. I was drowning quickly, and there was only one person I could call.

~

"Hey, girl!"

"Hi," I said through a clogged throat. I held the cellphone away from my cheek as I waited out the urge to bawl. "I need to talk."

There was a moment of silence before Gretchen spoke. "Okay, yes, let's talk. Now?" Her voice was excited.

"Now. Can I come over?"

"I'm just leaving work. Meet you there."

I wondered if she'd still have ice cream from when Lucy and I had been there, but the thought of eating made my stomach lurch.

When she opened the door to her apartment, I jumped into her arms and hugged her tightly.

"Oh my God, what?" she asked frantically, peeling me off by my shoulders. "What is it?"

"I did it," I said. "David Dylan."

Her face fell visibly. "Oh, Liv. No. You didn't."

I only nodded.

"Come inside," she said, coaxing me over to the couch.

And on the couch, I told her everything from the beginning. I told her about the first night at David's apartment – how I'd lied about going home sick and the months of rock-bottom despair that followed. My hand clawed into a decorative pillow when I told her how being with him in his hotel room had changed everything. Our connection had solidified and powered through me like a tornado. My feelings were strong and deep-rooted, I said, and I didn't know how to handle them. Everything was out of control. I hung my head as

I recounted the ball; how we'd had sex against a tree, and he wouldn't even look at me afterward.

"And that's how it ended?" she asked after a long silence.

"No," I stated, raising my eyes to hers.

She blinked at me. "There's more?"

"This morning, I told him."

"Told who?" she asked eagerly. "Told who what?"

"Bill."

She gasped and covered her mouth. "Holy shit," she muffled. "How did he react?"

"He wanted details."

"Did you tell him it was David?"

"No. I don't know how much I should tell him."

"Everything. Wouldn't you want to know?"

"I guess. I don't know. Maybe not." I shuddered, and she took my hand.

"Oh, honey. He won't leave you. It's not like him. Don't worry. It'll be hard, but you guys will make it through this."

I cocked my head at her. "I hurt him so much. But it was as if I couldn't help myself. David has this power over me. When I'm with him, nothing else matters. And now I just forget him? Yes, I hurt Bill, but that's not what is breaking me."

"Shit," she said, massaging between her brows. "It's not Bill you're upset over."

I shook my head hard. "I really am so distraught over what I did. Of course I feel awful. You have to believe me. But losing David feels . . . physical. It's like somebody is squeezing my insides."

"This is bad," she whispered. "Are you thinking about leaving Bill for David?"

My chin quivered, and I waited to continue.

"Honey," Gretchen said, "if you need to cry – "

"David and I had a fight," I interrupted. "He did something . . . vile."

"More vile than the ball?"

I nodded and took a deep breath. "He bought the Oak Park house."

Her head tilted to the side, and I waited until understanding dawned on her face. "The house you and Bill tried to buy? *David* bought it?"

I confirmed with a short nod.

"Why would he do that?"

"I don't know. It was a good deal, he told me himself. I guess he intends to flip it for a profit."

"That can't be all."

"I agree. There has to be something else. A sick fascination with slowly picking my marriage apart, I don't know."

"Wow. Well what did he say was the reason?"

"I ran away before he could explain. I was shocked. And heart – " My voice hitched, so I paused for a breath. "Heartbroken."

"Oh my God. I am so sorry."

"You told me so, right?"

She just shook her head. "I had no idea. I believe you if you say it's more than just sex."

"It was," I whispered. "I shared things with him I've never even told Bill." Shame, regret, sadness washed over me when I said, "I opened up to him."

Her mouth parted. "You're kidding."

"Things with him are . . . different."

"That's shocking. And exciting. I've never heard you talk like this about Bill."

"Bill has still never asked me about my scar. He doesn't know about the hospital or what my mom did."

"You'd think as a lawyer he would pay more attention to the details," she said with a small smile.

226

"He knows it's there. It's small, but it's not invisible. He just doesn't know how to talk about it. It means opening up a whole Pandora's box of complicated things."

"But that's what you do in a marriage. You let him help."

"I don't know that deep down he really wants to help." I sighed and looked away. "The way he grew up, they didn't talk about feelings. He's used to trivializing them away. But it's all coming out now."

"He's really gotten to you, hasn't he? David?" she asked after some time.

"You have no idea."

"What happens now? Do you need a place to stay?"

"I don't know. Bill and I have a lot to talk about when I get home. Thank you for listening, it's a huge load off my shoulders."

"I can't believe you've been going through all this by yourself. It means a lot that you told me."

"I know," I said with a smile that could only be described as weak.

"Now that it's over with David, does this mean you're going to turn into a mega-bitch again?"

My laugh ended in a frown. "I don't know. At least now I don't have to keep it inside. But how do I move forward with Bill after what I experienced with David?"

She hesitated and lowered her voice as if someone might be listening. "You don't want to hear David out?"

"What could he possibly say?"

"This is just seriously blowing my mind, Liv. It's been so long since I've seen you this passionate, putting everything on the line for someone."

"It's best that we don't see each other again," I said. "And after this thing with the house . . . maybe things weren't what I thought."

"Do you really feel that way?"

"No," I sighed. "But it doesn't matter. It's done."

Gretchen bit her lip and nodded. "Okay," she said quietly. "I'll support you no matter what."

"No matter what?"

"Of course."

"When Bill and I went to see Oak Park . . . I loved the house so much and yet, when I tried to see myself there with him and a family . . . Nothing."

"Maybe it wasn't the right house."

I nodded, but was flooded with the visions of David: he and I making love on the floor in front of the fire, baking in the kitchen, covered in flour as we laughed . . . I shook my head quickly.

"Is Bill still pressuring you about kids?"

"He thinks we're ready. I'm supposed to stop birth control."

She jerked her head at me. "What? I'm sorry, but is that really a good idea, considering . . . ?"

"He refuses to wait any longer. Although, after this, who knows?"

"That's seriously fucked."

"Maybe he's right, though. It will take a while for it to wear off, and maybe by then . . ."

She bit her thumbnail as she looked around the room. "Why did you say yes when Bill proposed?"

"Just wait until someone proposes to you," I joked. "And he's waiting there on his knee, and everyone is staring at you. It's harrowing." I laughed, but she just pressed her lips together. "I'm teasing. I said yes because I loved him, and I had no doubt that he loved me."

She exhaled loudly. "I think you owe it to yourself to give this some serious thought. Especially now that the clock is ticking. Even if you take David out of the equation, it sounds like you are having doubts about Bill."

I am, I thought, but I couldn't say it.

"I will support whatever you decide," she said. "You are my oldest friend, and I love you."

We hugged, and I told her I loved her too. "I should get back. Bill is probably waiting to talk."

She nodded. "Good luck."

"Thanks," I mumbled.

I decided to spring for a cab home. Having broken down barriers with Mack and Gretchen, I was beginning to feel more like my normal self again. David was done. Bill knew the truth. We could all finally move forward. The problem was, none of that made me feel better.

CHAPTER 22

THE APARTMENT WAS DARK when I got home. I switched on the kitchen light and started. Bill was leaning against a counter littered with empty beer bottles. "Bill?"

"Yeah."

I set my purse down and removed my coat, staring at him as I tried to gauge his mood. I waited for him to speak.

"Where've you been?" he asked without looking at me.

"At Gretchen's."

"How do I know that?"

I sighed. "I don't know. I guess you have to believe me."

He laughed softly and held out his hand. His eyes were red-rimmed. "Give me your phone."

"What? Bill – "

"Give it to me."

I dug into my purse and handed it over. I watched as he scrolled through it. "If you were with Gretchen, why did you call her half an hour ago?" he asked, holding up the screen to show me the call history.

"She thought she left her phone at work, so I called it. Ask her if you like."

He set the phone down. "Who was it?"

I swallowed dryly and stared at my hands.

"Who?" he yelled, and I jumped.

I looked up. "David Dylan."

He snapped his gaze to mine. "David . . . who? Andrew's friend? The architect?"

"Yes," I said, dropping my eyes back down.

"That could have been our future home," he whispered.

"What?"

"Oak Park. What if we had bought it? He would have been in our home, where our children live, where we have dinner every night. Where we make love," he said through gritted teeth. "For God's sake, what the hell were you thinking?"

"You're right. You are absolutely right."

"So everyone knows then?"

"No," I insisted. "Lucy and Andrew knew nothing about this."

"But Gretchen does." He shook his head in reproach. "I always knew she was a bad influence on you. I should have put a stop to that."

"She's my best friend."

"The night he helped you with Alvarez. Was that a cover-up?"

"Nothing happened that night."

"I'm supposed to believe that?"

"It was the next night."

His face went blank. "Isn't that the day Davena died?"

My voice broke. "Yes."

"Huh. All this time I thought you were mourning. Unbelievable."

"Of course I was mourning Davena. You know how close we were."

"You let me believe," he said over me, "for almost five months, that this was because of her death. You're in the wrong profession, baby. You should be an actress."

"This hasn't been easy, trust me."

"Look, I knew when I married you that you were still dealing with shit from your childhood, even though," he paused, holding up his palms, "it's been *years*. I knew that you had . . . issues that run deep. But I'm only beginning to realize just exactly how cold you are."

I had a horrified feeling in my chest. There it was, my pedestal: teetering underneath me, tipping . . . and falling, crashing to the ground and smashing into a million pieces.

He shook his head at the floor. "What did I do to deserve this? Haven't I been good to you?"

His words delivered a sharp chill to my spine. "You do not deserve any of this. I am so sorry. I made a terrible decision."

"Decisions," he corrected. "When was the second time?"

I felt my jaw working side to side nervously.

"You said it happened twice. When was the second time?"

"When you went fishing with Hugh."

"That was two weeks ago."

I nodded.

"I'm assuming that was also the architect."

My mouth dropped open. "Of course. I'm not running around town with anyone I can find."

"Why him? Why did it have to be him?"

"It didn't have to be anyone. It just – happened."

"Who initiated it?"

I made a soft noise as I stalled, racking my brain for a response. "I guess he was the first to vocalize it."

"I don't even know what that means."

"He initiated it, but it was my choice in the end."

"Did he know you were married?"

"Yes."

"A real class act. I guess when you have money and looks, you think you can do whatever the hell you want."

Despite the blatant slap in the face that David had delivered only hours earlier, my instinct was to defend him. I bit my cheek and nodded instead.

"I'm going to make sure he knows that isn't the case," Bill said. "I could sue him for this, you know."

"Bill, please. I'm here, ready to take the blame. It's not

worth involving David; he knows what he did was wrong."

"You talk to him?"

"I just meant that – "

"When was the last time you talked to him?"

"He knows that you know. Because I told him."

"Today."

My heart squeezed. This would never work if I wasn't honest. "Yes. After work, before Gretchen's, I stopped by his office to tell him."

"Did you fuck?"

"No!" I cried. "I just told him it was – I thought he should know."

He turned away to lean his elbows on the counter and massage his face.

I edged closer to him and put my hand on his back. "It didn't – " I paused. When was the time to be honest, and when was the time to lie? I struggled with myself for a moment as I stared at his back. "It didn't mean anything, Bill. You and I can start fresh from here."

"I don't know what to do," he said into his hands. "How am I supposed to move on from this?"

"I don't know. I wish I did. It's something we have to do together."

"I think you should sleep on the couch tonight," he said without looking at me.

"That's fine," I agreed softly.

He pushed off the counter and left the kitchen.

Later, I pulled linens down from the hall closet. When I passed by the bedroom, I heard him crying. I flattened one hand against the door and the other over my heart.

I flipped against the abrasive couch. I wondered how long it would take us to move on from the affair – until I realized that we might not ever. It would always remain there between us, no matter how much time passed; a permanent mark on our life together. I had never truly grasped the irrevocability of my betrayal until now. This would never go away.

I wanted to regret those moments with David, but I couldn't bring myself to. During the months after our night in his apartment, I had chased every detail away when it threatened. Remembering was torture.

Now, alone in the dark, I fought to remember. Suddenly, forgetting the details scared me. I clung to them like pieces of shattered glass so I could glue them back together. Like the way adoration filled his eyes when he looked at me. Chills lit over my body as I remembered the way that look would melt into lust. I let that look warm me on the cold brown couch.

~

"Why?" Bill asked the next night.

He'd insisted on picking me up from work, but hadn't spoken to me until now. I didn't know what time it was as he perched on the edge of the couch, rousing me with his one-word question. *Why?*

I rubbed my eyes and examined his silhouette in the dark. I sniffed the air. "Have you been smoking?" I asked, the words grating from my throat.

He shifted. "Just answer the question."

"Why . . ." I repeated. I didn't think I could ever explain it. Even if I was courageous enough to try, it would never make sense to him. "I was attracted to him. When Davena died, I felt . . . threatened. Scared. Life is so momentary. I didn't know it at the time, but I panicked. I was attracted to him," I said again. "That night, he was there."

"And I wasn't."

I wanted to reassure him that if he had been, things might have been different, but it would be a lie. The events leading up to that first night had made me reckless. But it would have happened anyway, I knew. The proof was there every time I was near David.

"Things were perfect before," he said into the darkness. "This will change everything."

"Bill," I said, hedging. "Things were not perfect."

"We're happy, though. I don't hit you, I don't call you names. We eat together almost every night, we have good friends, we don't fight. When was the last time we fought?"

"I know that to you, it doesn't make sense. But there are," I proceeded carefully, "other things that played a part in all of this. You put so much pressure on me about the future."

"But you knew this was coming. The house, a baby – you knew."

"And because I knew, I feel guilty that I'm not ready."

"I can't believe we're discussing this once again."

I sat up against the arm of the couch and flipped on the bedside lamp. "Don't dismiss my feelings."

"What am I supposed to do? Tell you that it's *okay* you don't want kids? That it's *okay* to continue living like college students in this shoebox? Sure, honey, let's wait until we're forty to decide. No, Liv. It's unacceptable. It's impossible. *You* don't know what you want."

"I'm not saying I'll never want those things, but I don't feel that way now. And when you tell me what I want and ignore my concerns, I shut down."

His voice sounded far away when he responded slowly. "I hope you aren't trying to turn this on me."

"I'm not, but you asked why I did this. I'm telling you that sometimes, I don't feel that I have your support."

"How can you say that to me? I've always supported you. You're the one who is emotionally unavailable."

I cocked my head. "And you love that. It means not having to deal with the real issues."

"I love that? Don't be ridiculous."

"Yes, you do," I said boldly. "The truth is, you see what you want to see. It's easier to ignore the problems."

"What *problems*?"

"Problems between us. My issues growing up. My fear to open up, to move forward in this marriage."

"Hang on a sec. You've told me several times that you hate when I ask questions. You hate talking about your parents' divorce."

"Then make me tell you!" I pleaded. "God, Bill, all those times I brushed you off, you never cared enough to try harder. Things are always enough for you, and they aren't for me."

"This doesn't make any fucking sense. *You* don't make any sense. Give me one example."

"I'm not playing games – "

"Tell me!" He pounded his fist on the coffee table, his words tearing through the silent night. "You want me to ask questions, well, I'm asking. Tell me!"

"My scar!" I screamed. "How could you have never asked about my scar?"

He sat in silence, watching me with wary eyes. When he spoke again, his voice was low and uneven. "I knew it had to do with the divorce, and you never want to discuss the divorce."

"You never wanted to know where it came from? Your own wife? It never occurred to you that it was a source of pain and sadness and regret? You never wanted to know what it represented? To make me tell you, no matter how much it hurt me?"

"Of course I wanted to know, but whenever I bring up the divorce you turn frigid on me."

"It scares me to think," I said quietly, "that you might've taken her side anyway."

"She didn't mean to hurt you."

My eyes crept up to his. "You knew?"

"Your mom told me once. She and your father had an argument, you jumped in the middle and she stabbed you by accident. And that's what prompted the divorce. You can't

236

blame her for assuming that you'd already told me."

"I don't even know what to say."

"And I don't get how this relates to sleeping with another man. Are you trying to tell me that – " He glanced down at my side, staring daggers at the scar just underneath my t-shirt. "That he asked? And you *told* him?"

"He wouldn't take no for an answer. He knew it was painful, but he wanted to take some of that pain away."

"Well, this just keeps getting better. Are you – this guy, David, do you have . . . ?"

My breath caught as I waited for his question. I didn't know how I would tell him the truth, but if he asked, I would do it. I would find the strength to tell him that what David and I had had wasn't just physical.

But instead he shook his head and looked away. "Never mind."

"Never mind?" I asked.

"It hurts that you would share something like that with him, but you didn't with me."

"I know. And I am so, so sorry."

"You say there were problems between us, but I didn't see them. I thought, like a fool, that we were happy."

"We are happy. But it doesn't change the fact that everything is moving too fast for me, and I want to slow down."

"Well, this is certainly one way to slow things down."

I tried to hide the relief in my sigh. "So can we? At least until we sort all of this out?"

He was quiet for a long time. "It's like you've put this . . . void in my chest. As if something's gone missing, something that's supposed to go right here." His hand clapped over his heart. My breath caught audibly, and he turned his head to me. "Emptiness. Blackness. That's how this feels."

Tears burned in my eyes, but I blinked them back. "I understand," I whispered.

"How could you understand?" he asked simply.

Because I, too, had lost something. And sometimes I thought my hollow chest might collapse from the weight of my grief.

He looked away again. "None of this is fair. I don't know what I did wrong, that you're saying and doing these things to me."

~

Our conversations continued that way throughout the weekend. I thought I might suffocate from the apartment's stale air, but consistent rain kept us indoors. Hours passed as I stared out the grey window, waiting for the next stream of questions. We were in his courtroom now, and I was on the stand.

He wanted to know how David and I had ended up in a hotel room the second time. And whether or not I had spent the night afterward. Reliving the details cheapened the experience. It made everything seem so dirty, when it had actually been its own kind of beautiful.

He continued to remind me that it wasn't fair, that he didn't deserve it, that he hadn't done anything wrong. All things I accepted with an apology. He threatened to go see David.

It was easy for us to forget during working hours; we had no choice. But as soon as he picked me up, our masks came off. After the first couple nights, I didn't think things could get worse, but as his shock wore off, he became more upset. I did my best to make things right by answering his every question and playing the role of honest and transparent wife.

He invited me back to bed on Tuesday. It was what I had wanted until he said the words aloud. I wasn't ready, so I told him so. '*How are* you *not ready?*' he had asked.

As weeks went by, his questions became more creative,

more intrusive. But I felt that I owed him the truth, no matter how hard it was for both of us. I wasn't sure what I feared more: that he might ask about my feelings for David, or that he might not. The question never came. I didn't know if it was because it never occurred to him – or because he was afraid of the answer.

CHAPTER 23

ONE SOGGY, WINTRY MORNING in November, Bill came to the couch not long after sunrise. Deep sleep had eluded me lately, so I woke easily when the cushion dipped under his weight. He looked as puffy and tired as I felt, but his eyes narrowed on me. He stuck his hand between my legs.

I flinched and began to protest. His gaze was unnervingly fastened on me as he tugged gently on my underwear. "If you can do it with him," he said quietly, "you can do it with me."

I didn't know what he meant by that. I thought about his words as I searched his face. It wasn't until he stripped and climbed on top of me that I realized what he was after.

I swallowed. "He didn't."

He exhaled with closed eyes. He was positioned over me, but somehow not touching me. "I need this. I think. I'm revolted, but I also want you. Bad." He dropped his head into my shoulder. "I want you," he repeated, kissing my neck.

"We're not in the right place."

He dropped his weight on me, and I thought I felt his shoulders heave. "I want to come inside you," he said in a watery voice.

"Not this way," I said. "What if I was to get pregnant?"

He drew back and looked at me with red eyes. "And that would be so bad," he whispered.

"I don't want to bring a child into the world like this. I know you don't either."

"Please," he said, kissing my cheek and putting his hand

back between my legs.

I grabbed it. "I'm not ready."

I could see him thinking, fighting his need. He sat back on his calves, still hard, and pushed the heels of his hands into his eyes. "Am I crazy to want you? I fantasize about it, but I don't want to want you."

"It's normal to feel confused."

"You told me you screwed him without a condom."

"I did, but . . . he pulled out."

"It took me years to get you to do that with me."

"I'm sorry."

"Sorry that you did it, or sorry that you told me?"

I looked away, seeing no way that answering the question would help anything.

"It's lucky you didn't catch something," he continued, "knowing that filthy piece of shit."

I nodded, remembering the embarrassing ordeal of Bill marching me to the gynecologist to get tested. But deep down I knew that David wouldn't put himself or me in that position. It had never occurred to me that he might, because I trusted him.

"Is this because of him?" Bill was asking. "Is that why you won't have sex with me?"

"No," I said, taken aback.

"But you're still there. What do you need to get over him?"

"Nothing," I said emphatically. "It's over."

"I just don't think I believe that."

My nostrils flared. "I've been completely open with you. I let you read my e-mails, my text messages. I tell you where I am all the time. This will never work if you don't even try to trust me."

"It's going to be a *long* time before we get back there." He went to the bedroom and shut the door. I knew he wasn't coming back, so I turned on my side and closed my eyes until it was time to get up for work.

~

There was ringing. I blinked. How long had my desk phone been ringing? Bill was the only person Jenny would patch through without notification. I wasn't surprised; he called frequently these days. Still, I braced myself. He had only dropped me at work an hour earlier.

"It's me," he said before I even spoke. The two somber words were enough to remind me that I was the source of his constant pain. "They're sending me to take depositions in St. Louis for the rest of the week."

"No," I objected. "I don't want you to go."

"Well, you don't really get a say in what I do right now."

"I'm serious. I'm putting my foot down. You can tell the Specters that I won't let you. We need to spend this time together."

"It's been over a month, and you won't even sleep next to me."

"That doesn't mean anything. We can't be apart right now."

"What, are you worried I'll revenge fuck someone else?"

The receiver slipped from my hand, but I caught it before it hit the ground. My mouth, however, hung open through the silence that followed.

"I'm sorry," he said after a minute. "I didn't mean that. I would never . . ."

"I just think you should stay," I said gently. "You have to stay."

"Honestly, I could use some time alone."

"Then I'll go to Gretchen's for a few nights. You can have the place to yourself."

"I can't say no, you know that. I leave tonight." There was a hesitation on the line. "Look, I meant what I said before.

I don't think we can move forward if you're still talking to him."

"I'm not, you have to believe me."

"Unfortunately, I can't. What do you need to end this? Closure?"

"Don't be ridiculous. There's nothing to end."

He sighed. "Liv, please. Your demeanor hasn't changed, which leads me to believe there's still something going on."

"I don't understand what you want me to do," I said, although I feared that I did.

"While I'm gone, end this for good. I don't care how. If you e-mail him, CC me. If you go see him, take Gretchen with you. It's not an excuse for a last hook up."

"I refuse to play this game."

"It's no game," he said calmly. "I have to know that this won't happen again. You still haven't said anything to Lucy, have you?"

"No, but at some point we have to – "

"I won't be made a fool in front of my friends – or my family for that matter. Nobody else needs to know about what you did, end of story."

"Okay," I relented.

"I have to go. I'll call you from the airport."

I was still staring at the phone long after he hung up. There wasn't anything going on. But he was right not to trust me. Late nights were my time with David. As I fell asleep and as I dreamed, he was there. I swam in his brown eyes, pressed my cheek against his stubble or touched his hair. His hair – I could not forget the way his hair felt in my hands; so shiny and smooth like the obsidian rock it resembled. The pain was still acute, like a knife wound, but at night it was soothed by the memories.

~

The empty apartment I came home to wasn't much different than it had been the past month. There had been an emptiness there since the morning of my confession.

I flipped on all the lights, suddenly not wanting to be alone. I turned the television on. It was always on ESPN, the only channel Bill watched, and the barking sounds of some sporting event were comforting.

I sat in front of it with a bowl of Cheerios, scooping them onto my spoon and then watching them slide off the tip, back into the milk. I looked at the call history of my cell phone. Several missed calls from Lucy, unreturned. One from my mother – a conversation so heinous to even think of that I hid the phone under the nearest pillow.

But even from under there, she judged me. Her insecurity was almost something I could touch as a child. She was so convinced that my father was cheating on her that he might as well have been. It ate away at her. If she ever found out what I'd done, she would surely disown me. So be it, I thought. I wouldn't take it back for all the love she'd always denied me.

I took a bite of cereal and swallowed. I grabbed the remote and turned the volume of the game up to a deafening level. The ceiling shook as the upstairs neighbors banged on their floor. My jaw clenched; my nostrils flared. I launched the bowl across the room, finding comfort in the way it shattered against the wall, splattering it with milk. "How could you, David?" I screamed into the apartment. Hot tears spilled over my cheeks. But, God, how I fucking missed him.

I planted myself face down on the couch and cried into a pillow. I didn't even care about the Oak Park house or why he'd done it. I just wanted more, more anything. More of his touch, more of his eyes on me, more rides in his car, more fucking, more walks, more reflections.

I didn't know how to go on without him. I compressed the pillow in my grip and cried harder. Did he ever care or was it all just a game? Even through my anger, I knew the answer:

there was no faking what we'd had. The force we'd given in to was one thing. But he'd purposely driven a knife through my marriage by buying that house. That was a side of David I didn't know. It was the same David from the masquerade ball. The type of man who slept with women for sport, stringing them along until he didn't need them anymore.

"It's too much," I insisted, biting into the pillow. Bill had my love and respect, but he no longer had my heart. I'd left it in David's office, at his feet, and I didn't care if I ever saw it again. I didn't deserve it. I deserved to cry, deserved to *die* right here in this black hole, on this horrible, shit-colored couch, because of what I'd done. And because I would do it again. I had fallen from a strong, capable woman into a weak, piddling mess, and I hated myself.

"David," I begged. "David, David." *How could I have risked everything for you? How could I have ruined a life for you? And how can Bill and I ever be happy again in my black hole?*

Clenched into a ball on the couch, I admitted that it was because I needed David. That there was something stronger than the two of us forcing us together. We'd made mistakes, we'd made decisions that could never be changed – but we belonged together. And now I would have to live the rest of my life knowing that I was separated from the person I was supposed to be with. And knowing that as much as he had pushed me away the night of the ball, I had pushed him back.

It wasn't something that could be remedied – the damage was done. People didn't just leave their husbands on a hunch that they'd met their soul mate. I realized that that was never an option, no matter what David had thought. He and I were destined to be together, but destiny had torn us apart.

~

When my phone rang from under the now damp pillow, I

almost sent it in the direction of the cereal bowl to shut it up. But instead, I extracted it and, sniffling, answered. "Now is not a good time," I told Gretchen.

"Bill called me."

"What? What did he say?"

"He asked me, in a very clipped tone, to keep an eye on you while he's gone."

"I'm sorry," I said. "He shouldn't be involving you. You're the only person who knows though. What did you say?"

"I told him to fuck off."

I smiled barely. "No you didn't."

"No, I didn't, but only because you need me around right now. What the hell is he thinking? Are you really going to see David?"

"Of course not. You know it's really over. But I can't tell Bill about the house. He would flip."

Her tone changed. "Maybe you *should* go see David."

I sighed. "No. I just can't."

"Are you all right, really? I can tell that you're crying."

"I'm – " I stopped before the word 'fine' left my mouth. I wasn't fine, not in the least. "No. I'm dying, Gretchen. It just keeps getting worse and worse. I've never felt anything like this in my life." There was dead silence on the line, and eventually, I continued. "I'm so hurt and angry. At David, at myself. At Bill."

"Bill?"

"I need him now, and he needs me. But he left. Without him here, all I can think about is David. I feel," I paused when my voice cracked, "like I'm slipping, and there's nothing to grab onto."

"I'm worried about you," she said fervently. "I'm coming over."

"No," I insisted. "You don't have to."

"I will be there in twenty minutes," she said and hung up.

I fell immediately back into my couch. When she arrived, she let herself in, looking concerned as she peeled her trench coat away. She ran a hand over my hair with sadness in her eyes. She wiped the spoiled milk from the floor and the walls. She turned off the television and helped me into my pajamas. I wanted to stay on the couch, but she forced me into the bed I'd come to fear. She held me as I cried myself to sleep, shaking for David like an addict.

~

It's only a shadow, but it is as real as the bones in my body. If I stop moving – if I look behind me – it will consume me. But it's already here, inside me, waiting. It's been waiting; waiting to pounce, waiting for the end.

"It's okay," I hear. "You're safe now. I'm here, and nothing can touch you." I breathe a sigh of relief. Finally, I am safe in his arms. David strokes my hair and tells me it's okay to cry. My chin quivers. My eyes water. It was just so sad. So profoundly sad. My grief was bottomless, but it's over now.

I opened my eyes to the same blackness of my dream. Everything was still at that lifeless hour. The shadow from my dream was there with me, because it was part of me. Underneath my head, the pillow was a cloud; beside me, Gretchen was warm. But it felt like the end. And that night, a piece of me died.

CHAPTER 24

THUNDER SOUNDED SUDDENLY, ripping me from my trance. Looking around the bedroom, I saw our life together – a framed wedding photo on the bookshelf, Bill's dirty socks just inches from the hamper, a coffee table book about the Chicago Bulls I'd given him for our first anniversary.

I didn't know when the sun had set, or how long I'd been standing in the doorway. The day was a haze of crying and vomiting and fits of broken sleep. After calling Beman to say I was sick, Gretchen had insisted on staying with me. I'd sent her away. I'd caused enough hurt to everyone already, and I'd needed to be alone with my thoughts – to live alone through the mess I'd made.

Everything was dark grey, and fog veiled the city. Clouds weighty with rain crept languorously across the sky, settling overhead like an old man in his favorite chair. My mood was as heavy as the atmosphere, and I let the gloom wrap itself around me like a cloak. The air was thick, and the rain started abruptly and severely, suggesting a violent storm.

The faintest glow came through the window as the day ended, casting darkness everywhere it didn't touch. The light switch flipped with an empty thud. I felt my way to the hallway closet, where we kept candles for the times when the electricity cut out. I lit each one in the bedroom along with the decorative ones that were already out. Little tea candles glowed, and the room filled with scents of cinnamon and vanilla.

I sat alone in the silence, on the edge of my plush white comforter, unsure of what to do with myself. Everything was eerily still, and all I heard was the increasing violence of the falling rain. Lightning lit up the room. As when I was a child, I counted – one one-thousand, two one-thousand, three one-thousand – until I heard thunder cackle somewhere in the distance. I thought of David and our last words to each other.

There came a slow but deliberate rap against the apartment door – *knock, knock, knock.* I passed the bedroom mirror. By habit, I glanced at my reflection. I could only see the faint glow of my pale skin against Bill's navy crewneck sweater. It hung from my shoulders down to my mid-thighs and over ratty jeans. My hand went instinctively to the hair knotted at the top of my head, and I tucked some renegade pieces behind my ear. I was thankful that it was likely only Gretchen, back to check on me.

I put my cheek to the door. "Who is it?"

"Open the door, Olivia." *David.*

The wood burned against my cheek, and I suddenly felt hot in Bill's sweater. Life seeped out of my muscles, leaving them fatigued. I didn't say anything, but fitted myself against the door.

"Olivia."

"What are you doing here?" I asked so softly that I doubted he had even heard. "What are you *thinking*?"

"Do you want me to tell the whole hallway why I'm here?" he countered in a voice equally as low. I unlatched the door and looked at him with hard eyes. He pushed his way in, slamming the door behind him. He followed me into the bedroom where the lighting was slightly more affable than the dank kitchen.

"What are you doing here?" I demanded. "You can't come here. Ever." I knew by the look on his face that he heard the wavering in my voice. Sweat trickled down my stomach, and my jeans stuck to my legs, stifling me.

He surprised me with his next words. "I didn't want to come. I meant what I said in my office, and I'm furious that you didn't give me the chance to explain. I deserved that chance."

I widened my eyes at him. "*You're* furious? How dare you?"

He held up his hand. "Do not interrupt me."

I recoiled as though he'd slapped me.

"Gretchen called me," he deadpanned.

My jaw dropped. "She what?"

"She told me that Bill's out of town and that I should come immediately."

That was when I noticed the dark scruff on his face. His wild black hair, damp from the rain. Chestnut eyes, angry but glowing in the candlelight. His impeccable posture remained, but he was a different man, his composure cracked.

"Why did you come?" I pleaded. "You promised you wouldn't chase me." My chin trembled. "You're making this too hard. You can't *be* here in my *husband's* home."

"And where *is* your husband? Where is he ever?" he asked angrily. He grasped my chin between two fingers, inspecting my tear-streaked face until I jerked away. "How could he leave you like this?"

Though his eyes were tired, there was determination there. I crossed my arms into my body, depressed my welling chest and braced myself for the conversation I thought would never happen. "You lied to me," I said. "And you hurt me that night at the ball."

"I know that I hurt you, and I've spent weeks regretting that night. But the idea of him touching you – holding you, dancing with you, when it should have been me . . . The hardest part was that you looked so goddamn happy. It ripped my heart out."

"You made me feel like trash."

"I lost control," he uttered, swallowing audibly. "I saw

red, and I should have left the party immediately. I never meant to make you feel that way." His bearing was stiff, almost cold, but he flinched when he said, "For that, I'm sorry."

"None of this matters, David. Just say what you have to say, and get out."

He scrubbed his face a moment and sighed. His jaw worked from side to side. "There's no excuse for buying the house. But here's the truth. Everything. I don't care anymore if you're ready to hear it. But you have to know that this is the truth, because I'm not going to repeat myself."

I didn't respond, but crossed my arms tighter.

"When you told me that Bill had made an offer, I panicked. I'd never been as scared as I was in that moment. I could not – would not – let him buy that house. I instructed my realtor to make the owners an offer they couldn't refuse."

I closed my eyes and took a shaky breath. "Because of a measly profit? I thought you were – "

"Because I wanted it to be me."

I blinked my eyes open.

"Because *I* wanted to be the one buying you your dream home and fixing it up for you. I wanted *us* to be the ones to grow old in it."

The memory of David in the house flooded over me, and I gripped the ends of my sleeves. It was so real; I had seen him there. *Did he see us there too?*

He looked so painfully beautiful in the candlelight. His shadowed face was raw with emotion, and I wanted to pull him to me. I had spent months fantasizing about pulling him to me and never letting him go. "That's what you want?" I asked. "That home?"

"I want it with you. Only you. Because we belong there."

I inhaled deeply, absorbing the meaning of his gesture. A future – with me. He'd had enough faith in our connection that he'd bought a house, even knowing it might drive me away.

And I – oh, *I could see it*. I wanted those things too. It was a future that sounded right, that didn't scare me. But none of that changed the facts. It didn't change the past or the present.

Silence crept into the space between us, save the pounding of the rain outside. Flames danced in the darkness. He stepped towards me slowly, as if testing the water.

"No," I said firmly and held up my hands. My voice broke. "You have to go."

"I love you."

I gaped at him. *Love?* When had love come into this? But hadn't I known it all along? And didn't I love him too?

But I shook my head. "No, David, no. I can't . . . *We* can't." I felt the threat of fresh tears. "You don't love me."

"*I love you*." He stepped closer and pulled me into his arms, but I pushed against his chest violently.

"No," I said loudly, and he took a step back.

"I loved you from the start, don't you know that? I never stood a chance."

Lightning illuminated his face, and an unsteady future flashed before my eyes. Thunder rumbled low above us before cracking like a whip. I burned, like my vanilla candle, and yearned, my fingertips tingling with impatience to feel him.

Instead, I looked down. The carpet sprouted between my toes, and I wished I could crawl into the floor to hide in its welcoming softness. Because I knew what would happen next. I felt like crying, like running into the rain and letting it merge with my tears. The pendulum of emotion inside me swung high and fierce.

When I looked back at him, he basked in the soft yellow glow. My pulse quickened in seconds. He didn't even need to touch me.

He fell to his knees in front of me, pulled up my sweater and kissed the skin underneath. Slowly, he unbuttoned my jeans and pulled them down before running his hands over my legs.

His lips explored me, kissing the backs of my sweat-dampened knees, the insides of my thighs, then my pubic bone through my panties. My legs trembled as I stepped out of my pants, away from him. He cast them aside and pulled me forward by my sweater. He rocked back off his knees and leaned forward to put his mouth on my parted lips but stopped inches away. He remained there as though he were sucking my spirit out through my mouth, and not only my spirit but *my heart*, which beat faster and faster because *I'm afraid, David, so afraid.*

His body heat radiated and mingled with mine; I wondered when he had removed our clothing. Despite my nakedness, I was flushed. My eyes searched his face. I almost couldn't decipher the words when he breathed, "I love you."

I shook my head, blinking back tears. One escaped and drifted down the side of my cheek, over my cheekbones, falling to our feet. "No," I said. "This is something more."

I threw my arms around his neck, and our shaking bodies absorbed one another in an urgent kiss. His hands ran along the sides of my breasts and then down to encircle my waist, clutching me against his hard body. Every touch was real, every touch sent chills over my skin.

We fell back into the carpet that had promised refuge only moments before. My legs steepled, and he drove all the way into me. My hands raked through his hair, his cheek scraped against my neck, and he began to fuck me. When I clenched him inside me, he released a shuddering cry against my skin. His pace hurried, and his thrusts became so powerful that soon our bodies dripped with sweat.

"Look at you," he rumbled in my ear, "so fucking sexy, so tight."

My hips eagerly met the force of each delicious plunge. "I want to make you come," I rasped, "harder than you ever have."

"For you, baby, yeah," he growled as thunder vibrated

253

the room. He bucked harder, *deeper*, a drop of sweat trickling from his body onto mine. I craned my neck to watch as his abs flexed with each drive, and I swallowed up the thick base of his cock.

As I approached the edge, there was only him to cling to. My vision speckled with white flashes as my body responded, constricting around him and trembling under his hulking body.

"Never letting you go," he uttered hoarsely. "You feel so fucking amazing."

"Come," I begged. I grasped urgently at his hair and pulled him down so our foreheads met. "I need you, David," I begged into his mouth. "I need you, all of you."

"No," he hissed. "Not . . . until – "

"I'm yours," I cried. "I'm yours, David, I'm yours, I'm yours."

"Olivia," he moaned. His muscles tensed and released, his body convulsed, and he finished me off with unwavering focus. I gasped, arching from the floor as my nerves shattered into a million divine pieces. I writhed into his punishing final thrust, and with a deep grunt, he erupted inside me.

He collapsed, pinning me to the floor with his solid, sweaty body. Heat radiated from us, engulfed us. My hands touched his shoulders, his back and his face, pushing the matted hair from his forehead. He drew back and ensnared me in a frantic kiss. His hand tangled in my knotted hair and pulled so he could fall breathlessly back into the curve of my neck. In that moment, nothing mattered more to me than the feeling of him, real and secure on top of me.

~

I struck a match and lit one candle on the kitchen table. We had dressed quickly in the dark and hurried from the bedroom, though I knew well enough that his spell could not be confined to any particular space. I moved to sit across from him, but he pulled me down, and I fell into this lap. He sat back and rested me against his arm, giving me a quick but sensual kiss.

"Did you hurt yourself?" I asked, capturing his hand in mine. "When you hit the tree?"

"No," he said.

"I'm sorry."

"So am I."

I hesitated and clutched his t-shirt as though he might disappear suddenly. "Did you . . ."

"What?" he asked, tugging on my bun so I had to look up. I could feel his heart pounding, but his expression was soft.

"Did you mean it?"

His face creased. "Do you think I would say it and not mean it?"

"I don't know."

"I'm in love with you. I've known for so long, but I also knew it would scare you away. You gave me no choice though."

Silence fell between us. With David's past and my present, I couldn't tell him that I loved him too. I looked away and rested my cheek against his chest.

He ran a hand over my hair. "Olivia."

"David," I replied, squeezing my eyes shut and tensing in his embrace.

"I want more," he whispered in my ear. "I want you."

"It can't be."

"Why not?"

I shook my head. "This is wrong. It's the last time. Bill knows, and you and I are done."

"There are other options."

I climbed off of his lap, tension settling again in my neck. As the glow wore off, everything I'd been shouldering seeped back into my thoughts, wakening my conscience. "He's not going to leave. He doesn't want a divorce."

He bolted upright. "That's not what I mean. This can work," he said with blazing eyes. "If you want it to," he added.

"H-how?" I stammered, taken aback by the intensity of his glare.

He lifted a hand and ran his knuckles over my cheek before taking my jaw. When he spoke, his voice was urgent and grave. "You leave him."

CHAPTER 25

DAVID'S WORDS SANK AND SANK until they settled heavily in my consciousness. I had no idea how long I'd stood there gaping at him before breath rushed back into my lungs. "What?"

"You leave him."

I pulled my chin from his grasp. "Think about what you're saying," I implored, stepping back. "You want me to leave my husband for you? Do you have any idea what that would involve?"

"We can handle it. Together."

"David," I said with an unsteady breath. "What I've been through since . . . There was a moment when . . ." I let the sentence trail off. Saying these things aloud were different than thinking them. I'd opened up to him, but not like this. The thought terrified me, but I looked him straight in the face. "There was a moment when I thought I might die without you. But you – you don't know what you're asking. I can't just leave. And you aren't ready for that commitment. I've already ruined so much," I said, pressing my fingertips to the corners of my eyes. "I have to make things right."

His voice was stern. "When I said that everything was for you, I meant it. My whole life I've been building and saving and preparing for the woman I knew would come along. I had to believe you were out there, because if I didn't, I would have nothing." His big shoulders heaved as he took a breath. "I'm not a religious or spiritual man. I am guided solely by my instincts, my gut. And they have led me to you. Without you, I have nothing to believe in."

I blinked, shocked into silence. His words were needy, romantic, loving – misaligned with the man I had originally suspected him to be. Even though his bearing was stiff, tense even, I could see that there was only truth in his eyes. "I – I don't know what to say, David." I did though – I wanted to say that it was beautiful. That no one had ever said anything like that to me.

"It's just the truth, the plain fucking truth."

An awed smile touched my face. He was looking at me again the way he had that night at the hotel. *Love. Love is what I saw that night, and* that *is what scared me. I already knew on some level that you loved me, David Dylan.*

I inhaled. "You want me to leave my husband? Is that really what you're asking?"

"Divorce him, Olivia."

I shivered at the word. "I don't think I could do it," I said honestly.

"I would be there every step of the way."

"I can't even – have you even talked to Dani?"

"I tried to tell you. I ended things, but she begged me to take her to that one last event. I owed her that much."

"You owed her?"

"She's been patient and sweet, but I can't give her what she wants with you in the picture."

"And if I weren't?" I bristled.

"I don't even care enough to wonder. She said she had already paid for the tickets and that she was embarrassed to go alone. I'm only human."

I scoffed to myself. "That was a lie, they were Gretchen's tickets."

He pursed his lips. "Regardless. Do you trust me that nothing happened with her? She kissed me that night, but I stopped it. She was desperate."

I nodded and looked away. "What about Maria?" I asked into the dark kitchen.

He exhaled a short laugh. "Do you think I'm playing games, Olivia? I don't want Dani, I don't want Maria, I want *you*. I would never ask you to leave your husband if I wasn't ready for the commitment. Not just ready, but dying for it."

I shook my head in disbelief. "Why? I don't understand why."

"Why what?"

"Why me?" I whispered. "What makes me worthy? You could have anyone."

His face fell. He cupped his hands under my jaw and looked directly at me. "How can you say that?" he asked sadly. He sighed, looked around the room and then back at me. "I've never had trouble meeting women, that's true. But I knew as early as my first kiss that there was something missing. I never gave up hope that the right girl was out there. I knew you were it the moment our eyes met." He paused and ran his thumbs over my cheekbones. "I didn't need any other proof after our first night together. If you don't see it now, you will."

Tears were streaming down my face, not only at the grave sincerity of his words, but because of how they echoed my own thoughts. How long had I secretly wished that Bill would tear me open and teach me what it meant to love? I still naïvely believed that he might one day. Had he waited too long, though?

"You want me to leave him?" I asked again.

He brushed a piece of hair from my forehead. "With everything I am. But even more, I want you to *want* to leave him. I want you to realize that he's not right for you and that you deserve to be loved fiercely. And if I'm lucky, you'll choose me to do it. You said you were mine. And I know you meant it."

My face screwed up as more tears fell. Even if I left Bill,

could I let myself love David the way he needed? Did he deserve someone as cold as me? Would just loving me be enough for him? I searched his face. His eyes had always been my refuge; they seemed to know things that I didn't.

My heart jumped in my chest when I realized that I *could* love him the way he needed. Without boundaries. Without control. I wanted to tell him, but it scared me more than anything. It scared me even more than leaving my life behind. I could fall into those heavenly brown eyes and never find my way out.

He wiped my face of the tears before leaning in to kiss my closed lips. "Talk to me. This won't work if you're not honest."

I hated myself when I said, "I made a commitment to Bill."

He dropped his hands to his hips, and his eyes narrowed. "I realize that. Trust me, it's kept me up many nights. But this isn't something we can just walk away from."

"Don't you think I know that?" I cried. "Don't you know that I felt it from the beginning? What do you want to hear? That I'm yours? That you are the one who has my heart? You know you do! But what can I do? I made a commitment!"

"That's no way to go through life!" he roared. "It's not fair to either of you! This last month has been a glimpse of how life will be for all of us. Is that what you want?"

I shook my head hard.

"So then make the decision."

"Nobody would understand."

"Is that what this is about? Other people?"

"No." I sniffled. "And yes. I don't know. I don't know what's right anymore."

"I won't let anybody hurt you," he said. "You make this decision, and we're in it together. I will be your shield."

"David, I can't – how can I? How can I leave him after what I've done? And after he stood by me anyway?"

"What we have is stronger than all of it. Have you ever felt anything like this?"

It was always *all* of my strength to fight our magnetic pull to each other. I didn't know how David knew, but I had not ever had this with Bill, or with anyone else. "I need time," I squeaked.

"No. There's no more time."

My insides jolted, and I clasped an arm over my stomach. "What?"

"I said no. I cannot do this anymore. It's killing me. I love you, and you either love me or you don't. But please, put me out of my misery," he pleaded. His hands ran over his face and dove into his hair maniacally. "You have to decide."

"I – I can't," I stuttered. "Please don't make me."

"You have to decide!" The bass of his voice bounced off the walls. Veins pulsed from his neck, and his face flushed with rage. "Can't you see that this is it? It's me or him. End this, now."

"No, please, just give me some time – "

"I've given you enough time." He took an easy stride and grasped my face in his hands. "I love you," he said earnestly, "but this is destroying both of us. End this. If you don't, then I will. And once I walk out that door, it's truly over." I whimpered as he stared into my eyes. He kissed me gently. "My sweet," he murmured, between soft kisses. "Say the word, and I will give you everything."

My chin quivered viciously in his hands. My eyelids blinked fresh tears onto my cheeks. *Everything?* But there was only one thing I wanted. I wanted him, wholly and completely. Somehow, inexplicably – incomprehensibly – he was the only thing that had ever felt absolute in my life. "David," I whispered.

The corner of his mouth twitched. I loved the corner of that mouth. I loved the sexy crease in his chin. I loved the rawness of his almost-gold eyes. I loved him, and I wanted to spend forever proving it to him.

But the words wouldn't come; they stuck in my mouth, lodging in my throat. I swallowed them down, along with a hard, painful lump. It meant breaking a heart, a commitment, a *life*. I wasn't choosing between Bill and David. I was choosing between Bill and me.

David's eyes darted between mine, and I watched the hope drain from his features. "It's him?" he asked. He dropped his hands and stepped back. My knees gave, and I fell to the floor in a broken, sobbing heap. How could I have done this to everyone? How was I the source of so much despair?

He hesitated only a second before he strode away. He pulled open the door and without looking at me, turned his head over his shoulder. "You can have the house."

I choked back an aching sob. "No!" I screamed, but it was muted by the slam of the door.

The first time I saw David was electric. Our eyes had met across that shining lobby, and it was as if the heavens had smiled right on me. What was that feeling? Was it lust? Was it love? Was it nothing? Or everything?

As I broke apart on the kitchen floor, I realized that losing David meant losing myself. Life without him – the anguished months I'd spent spiraling downward – was no life at all.

And then I knew what the feeling was.

I scrambled to my feet and flung open the door. I ran into the rain after him, and with everything I had, I screamed, "It's you!"

He stopped. His shoulders tensed, but he remained frozen as the sky fell around us.

My voice cut clearly through the rain when I said, "Of course it's you. You are my home."

After what felt like an eternity, he turned slowly. Pain etched his face. For a heartbreaking moment, I thought I was too late. But then he stepped forward, and suddenly I was running. He opened his arms, and I jumped, and I was home.

COMING SOON

THE CITYSCAPE SERIES:
BOOK THREE

ABOUT THE AUTHOR

Jessica Hawkins grew up between the purple mountains and under the endless sun of Palm Springs, California. She studied international business at Arizona State University and has also lived in Costa Rica and New York City. Some of her favorite things include traveling, her dog Kimo, Scrabble, driving aimlessly and creating Top Five lists. She is the helpless victim of an overactive imagination that finds inspiration in music and tranquility in writing. Currently she resides wherever her head lands, which lately is the unexpected (but warm) keyboard of her trusty MacBook.

TO CONNECT WITH THE AUTHOR

http://www.jessicahawkins.net
http://www.twitter.com/jess_hawk
http://www.facebook.com/jessicahawkinsauthor
http://www.goodreads.com/jessicahawkins

Made in the USA
Lexington, KY
09 May 2014